Praise for the Eli Marks Mystery

THE MISER'S DREAM (#3)

"An intriguing cross between noir and cozy, with fascinating details about magic tricks and plenty of quirky characters. An easy, enjoyable read for mystery buffs seeking a bit of an escape from the usual crime fiction fare."

– *Library Journal*

"A finely-tuned, diabolical, sneaky, smart, stylish mix of magic and mayhem that plunges our hero Eli through a tangled web of danger and deceit that'll keep you guessing."

– Steve Spill, Magician and Author of *I Lie For Money*

"With twists and turns, flurries of romance, and a cast of characters that seem to be the unholy spawn of *The Maltese Falcon* and *The Third Man*, The Miser's Dream keeps the pages turning and the reader delighted from start to finish."

– Jeffrey Hatcher, Screenwriter, *Mr. Holmes*

"I loved this book. From beginning to end I was hooked. The story is fantastic and the cast leaves you wanting to know more. I can't wait to read the next book in the series."

– *Bookschellves*

THE BULLET CATCH (#2)

"This is an instant classic, in a league with Raymond Chandler, Dashiell Hammett and Arthur Conan Doyle."

– *Rosebud Book Reviews*

"Has many tricks up its sleeve as its likeable magician-hero. As the body count rises, so does the reading pleasure."

– Dennis Palumbo, Author of the Daniel Rinaldi Mystery Series

THE AMBITIOUS CARD (#1)

**The Eli Marks Mystery Series
by John Gaspard**

THE MISER'S DREAM

AN ELI MARKS MYSTERY

John Gaspard

HENERY PRESS

THE MISER'S DREAM
An Eli Marks Mystery
Part of the Henery Press Mystery Collection

First Edition
Trade paperback edition | October 2015

Henery Press
www.henerypress.com

ISBN-13: 978-1-943390-13-7

Printed in the United States of America

ACKNOWLEDGMENTS

Thanks for helping me get this on paper and get it (mostly) right:

Scott Wells, Suzanne, Wayne Kawamoto, Richard Kaufman, Stan Allen, Darwin Ortiz, Joe Diamond, Jim Cunningham, Matt Dunn, Steve Carlson, David Parr, David Gabbay, Joe Gaspard and Amy Oriani.

"In magic, the most suspicious reason
for doing something is no reason at all."
Darwin Ortiz

CHAPTER 1

"I'm a hack."

Holy crap, did I say that out loud? My intention had been to whisper those three words silently to myself, but apparently my brain hadn't properly communicated that goal to my mouth. Consequently, I must have said it out loud, if the stern look from the lady in front of me was any indication. I put a hand over my mouth and cleared my throat, trying and failing to give the impression I had simply coughed. I turned to my right and recognized a puzzled look from Megan.

"Are you okay?" she whispered, effortlessly speaking at the appropriate volume.

I nodded without conviction and returned my attention to the performer who had inspired this brutal self-assessment.

His name was Quinton Moon, and he was killing me.

Quinton was awesome, and not in the flawed and grossly overused current use of the expression. He inspired awe. I was in awe. He awed me, which is no small feat, particularly since we are both magicians. I've seen plenty of magicians in my lifetime. But not one like Quinton Moon.

I had resisted when my Uncle Harry had offered us the tickets because, as a magician, I can honestly say that I may have already seen enough magicians in my lifetime. But Harry had wisely made the offer in the presence of Megan. He had also suggested we dine at Christos in the Union Depot in downtown St. Paul as part of our evening out, and before I knew it, my fate was sealed. Parking was the usual downtown St. Paul nightmare scenario, but dinner was delightful, the hummus to die for, and the wine and the conversation flowed. For a while I almost forgot that my primary goal this evening was to see, of all things, a magician.

Megan declared our walk from dinner to the St. Paul Hotel a "winter wonderland romp," but in reality it was a wet slog through yet another in a series of recent snowfalls. None of the merchants had shoveled and the snowplows had not effectively cleared the streets from the last dusting of snow, so crossing at each intersection became a high-tension thriller all its own. By the time we made it to the classic hotel's ornate lobby, my shoes were soaking, my feet were freezing and my mood was grim. For her part, though, Megan couldn't have been bubblier.

"This is going to be fun," she gushed as we were directed to the single elevator which offered access to the top floor suite.

"You remember we're seeing a magician, right?" I asked as the doors slid shut.

An hour later, my shoes were dry, my feet were warm and I had been transported to a Victorian drawing room and a performance of chamber magic that would, in many ways, change my life.

Quinton Moon appeared as if he had stepped directly out of the pages of a Jules Verne novel. Thick sideburns framed a ruggedly handsome face with piercing green eyes and a warm and inviting smile. It was hard not to like him immediately, but I will say I gave it a valiant effort.

He greeted each guest as they arrived, ushering us to our seats while keeping up a steady patter about the room's history, the night and the snow which continued to gather on the leaded glass windowsills.

The living room of the suite was set with about thirty chairs, all facing the front of the room. The majority of the audience was better dressed than I was, with several gentlemen even sporting tuxes. For his part, Quinton wore a tailored coat, which he removed at the top of the show, revealing a tastefully colorful vest and cummerbund combination.

He was an effortless performer, but I understand enough about the trade to know you only get that relaxed on stage if you've really done your homework offstage. The seventy-minute show was an even mix of illusions I'd seen a thousand times before and tricks I was witnessing for the first time. But in Quinton's hands, even the most clichéd illusions sported a brand new shimmer and shine. Hoary old chestnuts, like The Linking Rings and The Miser's Dream—tricks which are staples of kids' birthday parties, for God's sake—took on an entirely new flavor in his hands, and I watched them all as if for the first time.

The breaking point for me came when he did a seven-minute routine using thimbles. Thimbles! He actually did a routine with thimbles that not only held my attention but transported me. I was transfixed, and my amazement and self-loathing grew concurrently as the evening progressed, until I finally uttered my inner monologue aloud.

"I'm a hack."

The second time I said it (and every subsequent time, of which there were legion), I was able to keep the words inside my head, which I felt was a victory of sorts. But it didn't change how I was feeling, with my primary emotion being one of complete impotence.

Megan, of course, was feeling none of this, but responded to each new miracle with the *oohs* and *ahhs* which are the lifeblood of magicians. She spent most of the performance literally sitting on the edge of her seat, leaning forward in anticipation of each new illusion. And she wasn't alone; Quinton held the crowd confidently in the palm of his hand.

His interactions with the audience members were real and genuine and he was never thrown, even when a trick seemed to go slightly awry.

In fact, he got more out of the mistakes that occurred than I generally am able to get when my entire act goes right. Which is rare. Or hardly ever. Let's call it never.

Speaking in an indefinable accent—was it British? German? Baltic? No, turns out he's Swiss—Quinton was consistently charming and engaging, often seeming to enjoy the illusions as much or more than the audience. His delight was infectious and the act, which was brilliantly structured, built to a final climax that left the audience stunned.

We sat in silence for several long moments before the small crowd burst into applause, giving him an instant and heartfelt standing ovation—a real one, not the obligatory ovations Minnesotans proffer to virtually any performance which safely reaches its conclusion.

As he had done at the beginning of the evening, Quinton spoke personally with each of us as we left, creating an immediate if affable traffic jam pileup at the suite's door. Due to the confined nature of the space, I was able to hear his answers to all the questions put to him while we moved closer and closer to the exit.

"Is this the first time you've done this show?"

"No, I've performed similar shows in London, Zurich, Berlin, and Madrid."

"Why do it in a hotel suite, couldn't you make more money in a large theater?"

"Yes, but then I would miss the—how you say?—*intimacy* of interacting with each member of the audience, such as I am doing now."

"How are you enjoying Minneapolis?"

"We're in St. Paul." (Laughter.)

"What brings you to the Twin Cities?"

"I have a corporate engagement in town and thought this would be an ideal time to present this show as well. Murder a couple of birds, as it were."

And then it was our turn.

"It was wonderful," Megan gushed. "Truly wonderful."

"Thank you," Quinton replied, turning his thousand-watt smile on Megan, and then on me. Megan grabbed my arm and pulled me forward. "This is my friend Eli. He's a magician too!"

I hadn't thought it was possible to feel any worse about myself, but it turns out I was wrong. I suddenly felt about a foot tall. Quinton, however, seemed oddly delighted by the news.

"Not Eli *Marks*?" he asked.

"Yes," I said tentatively.

"Brilliant. I had the very great pleasure of meeting your uncle, Harry Marks, at the show last night."

"Really? He hadn't mentioned it."

"Charming gentleman. We had a wonderful conversation. He even talked me into doing a lecture at your magic store."

"Odd. He didn't mention that either."

"He's quite persuasive."

"He is that."

"I must tell you, it certainly was a thrill to finally meet Harry Marks. Something of a legend, isn't he?"

"He likes to think he is."

"Well, thank you so much for coming tonight. I look forward to seeing you at your shop."

"We can't wait," Megan said before I could respond.

Quinton smiled at her and then at me and then we were out the door.

The drive back to Minneapolis was a quiet one. I did my best to convince myself this was because the roads were treacherous and I needed to concentrate on my driving. But Megan sensed something was amiss.

"He was really good," she ventured at one point.

"Yes. Yes he was."

A few more moments of silence passed.

"Did you enjoy the show?"

"Sure."

Another pause.

"It doesn't feel like you enjoyed it."

"Is this a psychic perception?"

"You don't have to be psychic to sense you didn't have much fun."

She had a point. "It's hard," I ventured, "to watch something that good and not feel bad about it. I mean, if you're in the same business. If that makes any sense."

"But he's not better than you," she said. "Just different."

"No, he's better. A lot better." I turned off the freeway and made a left on 46th Street, moving us as quickly toward Chicago Avenue as the traffic and snow would allow.

"Do you want to hear a joke?"

I turned to look, her adorable face peeking out of a too-big parka, and couldn't help but smile. "Sure. Tell me a joke."

"Okay, let me remember how it goes," she said, biting her lip while working out the joke in her head. "Okay, I got it. How do you climb off an elephant?"

"I don't know. How do you climb off an elephant?"

"You don't. You climb off a duck."

I furrowed my brow and gave her a long look. At least, as long a look as I dared give as the car slipped and slid along the snowy roadway. "Honey, I think you told it wrong."

She shook her head defiantly. "Nope, that's the way I heard it."

"I think the actual joke is, 'How do you get down from an elephant? You don't, you get down from a duck.'"

"That's what I said."

"I don't think that's what you said."

"My way makes just as much sense as your way."

"No," I began and then stopped, glancing at her again. "Are you doing this to take my mind off the show we just saw and my completely understandable feelings of total and utter inadequacy?"

She shrugged. "Maybe."

I couldn't help but smile. "Thanks. It's working. But you still got the joke wrong." Before she could object, I pulled the car into a parking space in front of her duplex.

*   *   *

After a quick kiss goodnight and a final word from her on the subject ("You're still my favorite magician"), I deposited Megan safely at the front door to her duplex and then crossed Chicago Avenue and began the short and slippery trip down the block to my place. The sidewalk in front of Megan's building had been recently shoveled, but the owners of many of the apartment buildings across the street had apparently given up. Due to the frequency and amount of snow we'd received so far this year, it was hard to blame them, but even harder to navigate across their sidewalks.

The businesses on the block had done a far better job of keeping up with the various snowfalls than the apartment houses. Consequently, by the time I hit Pepito's restaurant, I was feeling much steadier on my feet. It was still early enough that the restaurant was going strong, but the Parkway Theater next door was dark and apparently closed for the night.

I glanced up at the theater's marquee and was amused to see it had changed since that afternoon, when it had read *Séance on a Wet Dog Day Afternoon*. Now the letters spelled out *Big Trouble in Little Chinatown*.

The theater had recently undergone a management change and the new manager delighted in putting together what she called Parkway Double Plays, but what my uncle Harry had come to call "Dopey Double Features." These were pairings of movies which had no actual connection to each other except that the words in their titles could fit together in weird and wonderful ways. Other favorite past Dopey Double Features have included *Murder By Death on the Nile*, *Dr. Strangelove and Death*, *Boyz in the Parenthood* and *The Citizen Kane Mutiny*.

Chicago Magic was next door to the theater and I slipped quietly into the store and silently up to my third floor apartment. I stopped briefly on the second floor landing but saw no light under the door, which confirmed my suspicion that my uncle Harry had already gone to bed. I made a mental note to discuss Quinton Moon and his alleged impending lecture in the morning, and then headed up the last flight to my apartment.

I was tired and ready for bed, but old habits die hard and before I knew it I found myself at my desk, scrolling through my new emails, sorting the cream from the spam. As I waited for one particularly large email to open, I glanced out my window and was surprised to see there was still one light burning at the Parkway Theater next door.

My apartment overlooks the projection booth in the theater, and even though it's very much an obstructed view, I have often enjoyed peering into the room from my odd vantage point, trying to figure out what movie is playing by the way the lights bounced off a mirror on the far wall of the booth.

There was no movie running at the moment, but something else immediately grabbed my attention. I stood up to get a better view and confirmed my worst suspicions. Even from this new angle there was no denying my first impression had been correct.

There was a body on the floor of the projection booth, lying in what appeared to be a small pool of blood.

CHAPTER 2

I considered, for one brief moment, not calling the police. Not because I didn't want to do my civic duty, but because I've probably called the police about dead bodies a few too many times in my life. People were beginning to talk. Common sense won out, of course, and I quickly placed a call to 911 and did my best to outline what I had seen. This resulted in the almost immediate arrival of a squad car, and several minutes later two patrolmen and I were peering through my window and trying to determine what we were actually seeing on the floor of the projection booth at the theater next door. We agreed it looked like a body and that the body looked dead.

The patrolmen quickly, in their terminology, "escalated the event" and fifteen minutes later Homicide Detective Miles Wright stood next to me as we stared through the window.

"It's a hell of a thing," he finally said. Wright has the gravelly voice of a lifelong smoker and the yellow teeth to prove it.

"Shouldn't we be, I don't know, *doing* something?" I asked, trying to nudge him toward some form of action.

"Patrol guys are all over it," he said, turning from the window and looking around my apartment. "You are far more inclined toward action than I am. He's dead. It's cold outside. It's warm in here."

He pulled out his glasses and studied the spines of books on the bookshelf. "Besides, the theater is locked up tight. We've got a call into the manager and the patrol guys are working on opening the front door. He'll still be dead when we get in."

He sat down heavily on my couch and took out a pack of gum, offering me a piece. I shook my head.

"What do you think of all this snow?" he continued, as if we were just a couple of guys hanging out, shooting the breeze. "Gotta be some kind of record, don't you think?"

"So you think he's dead?"

Wright glanced at me and then at the window. "Yeah. He looks plenty dead."

I returned to my vantage point and studied the form splayed out on the floor of the booth. I had to agree with Wright—he looked plenty dead. I turned back to the detective, who was seated comfortably on my couch. "Where's your bitter half?"

"You mean better half?"

"You've known him longer than I have."

He nodded in agreement. "Yeah, you were right the first time," he said as his phone began to buzz. "He's on his way." He reached into his coat and pulled out his phone, listening for a few seconds before hanging up. He turned to me as he pushed himself up from the coziness of the couch.

"We're in," he said.

"Okay, it looks like there's 'in' and there's 'in.'"

Wright and I were standing at the base of the stairs to the theater's projection booth. The patrol officers had forced the theater's front door open, and one of them was now struggling with the projection booth's impressive metal door. He turned and looked down at us.

"It's locked," he reported. "There's no keyhole on this side. Looks like it's locked from the inside."

Wright snapped his gum. "Any other way in?"

The patrolman shook his head. "There are some square holes on the front wall for the projectors, but they're barely a foot in diameter. And the window we saw the body through is barred, tiny, and two stories off the ground."

Wright scowled and turned to see the other patrolman approaching. This cop looked new and a little nervous. "Crime scene team is here," the young man reported diligently. "They say there's no way to pull any footprints from out front—too many people have come and gone."

Wright nodded and gestured toward the two exit signs on either side of the theater's large screen. "Take a gander out those two back doors and if you see any footprints, get the team to tent it quick. Otherwise snow will erase all evidence in about ten minutes, at the rate it's coming down."

The young cop nodded and headed down the aisle.

Wright's partner arrived at the same time as the theater's manager, and the contrast could not have been more amusing. Homicide Detective Fred Hutton is tall and wide and grim and humorless. He's a "just the facts, ma'am" kind of cop and doesn't suffer fools (or anyone else, especially me) gladly. He's also married to my ex-wife, which adds a flavor all its own to our prickly, ever-evolving relationship.

The theater's manager was just as tall as the detective, but she wore it better than he did, possessing that willowy stance you see with supermodels. However, at this moment, she looked nothing like a supermodel. Unless that supermodel had been dragged out of bed and forced back to work in the middle of the night to face a dead body, with no time allotted for dealing with makeup or bedhead hair.

If I was remembering correctly, her name was Tracy. We'd had a couple amusing conversations since she took on the job last spring, particularly about the way in which she'd radically changed the line-up of movies at the theater and subsequently made it once again a cool destination. She'd also instituted First Thursdays, a sort of open mic for variety acts, which had pulled my uncle Harry and many of his magician cronies back onto the stage. The Parkway Double Plays were also her brainchild and whenever I thought of a possible title combination, I'd offer it up as a potential programming suggestion, being careful to use her terminology and not Harry's preferred term.

Detective Wright had just finished bringing them both up to speed on the situation when two of the crime scene techs finished their work on the hinges and were able to remove the massive metal door to the projection booth. The techs stepped into the booth and Homicide Detectives Fred Hutton and Miles Wright followed. Their body language told us we were to remain where we were, but by leaning forward, both Tracy and I were able to get a glimpse into the small, square room. Tracy gasped and pulled back.

"That's Tyler," she said in a hoarse whisper.

"The projectionist?"

"Yeah. He worked here when I started. He's been here forever." Tracy backed away, clearly not wanting to see anything else. Oddly enough, my instincts led me in the exact opposite direction, and I took another step closer to the open doorframe.

From this new, slightly improved vantage point, I could see Tyler's body, facedown, sprawled on the floor. A fresh red stain on the rear of his t-shirt suggested a bullet to the back, while a small puddle of blood surrounding the body completed the tableau. Several feet away, also on the floor, lay a really tiny handgun, which the detectives were scrutinizing with great intensity.

Since no one was holding me back, I took two more steps forward, which gave me a better view of the entire room. As the patrolman had said earlier, the front wall of the room had two square holes cut through the concrete, for the projectors' lights to shine through.

Advances in technology must have negated the need for two projectors at some point, as there was currently only one in the booth, though markings on the floor indicated where another projector probably stood for years. A large metal stand with a round, flat plate sat behind the remaining projector, and film was spooled off the plate, across a roller system in the ceiling, and then in (and presumably, out) of the projector.

Against the wall where the missing projector once stood was a wooden stand with a Blu-ray player, mixer, and cables that ran through the other hole in the wall. I leaned to my left, peering around the corner of the booth, where I could see the cables as they snaked out of the hole in the wall. They stretched up to a video projector in the ceiling. This refinement must have been the theater's fledgling move toward digital projection.

I turned to peer back into the booth.

In addition to the projector, there was also a large worktable, a weight-lifting bench with a set of loose weights neatly stacked next to it, and four more different colored weights near what I took to be two large film canisters. Both were open and appeared empty, at least from this angle. Handwritten labels on each of the two canisters read "LAM."

An open-air toilet was wedged into one corner, which probably explained the lock on the inside of the projection booth door. I guessed that projectionists needed to answer the call of nature like anyone else, but don't always have the luxury of heading downstairs to the restroom when the need arose. The base of the toilet looked cracked and moldy, and may have accounted for the small puddles of water I noticed on the floor.

My visual tour of the room was interrupted by an exclamation from Detective Wright. He was pointing to an envelope which lay open on the worktable.

Homicide Detective Fred Hutton moved across the room, just finishing pulling on a pair of latex gloves. He gave the second glove a practiced snap and picked up the envelope, prying it gently open. Even from my distant vantage point, I could see the envelope was full to bursting with cash.

After several minutes of my gawking, the cops had clearly had enough.

Detective Wright instructed one of the patrolmen to escort Tracy and me back to the lobby, where they would join us for brief questioning. We made our way back downstairs and stood around silently for several minutes. Tracy sat in one of the lobby's overstuffed chairs, while I took a position leaning against the candy counter.

"What do they think it is?" she asked, running a hand through her thick, red, bedraggled hair. "I bet it's suicide. If I was handicapping this, I'd put even money on suicide."

"Did he seem like the suicidal type?"

She shrugged. "He had secrets."

"Well, the police haven't said anything," I said. "But it looks like he was shot in the back and the gun was on the floor across the room. I'm no expert, but I think that rules out suicide."

"But didn't they say the room was locked? From the inside?"

"Indeed it was. And therein lies the mystery," I said, looking over as the two detectives made their way into the lobby.

"We've tented the area over the southwest exit door, the one to the left of the movie screen," Detective Wright was saying quietly. "It appears someone stepped out the door, and then turned around and came back into the theater. They left prints in the snow, but the footprints may have been compromised by the falling snow. And, also, by the very act of turning around."

"They stepped outside and stepped back in," Homicide Detective Fred Hutton repeated. "Do you think they saw someone and didn't want to be spotted?"

"That would be my first guess. We're going to do a door-to-door in the morning to see if any of the neighbors saw something."

Homicide Detective Fred Hutton nodded and then surveyed the room, looking first at Tracy and then taking an even longer look at me. "He spotted the body?" he said to Wright. He put a spin on the word "he" that I didn't like and spoke as if I wasn't standing ten feet from him.

Wright nodded. "The window in his living room has a decent view right into the projection booth."

Homicide Detective Fred Hutton grunted and headed across the lobby toward me. "Eli," he said by way of greeting.

"Good evening, Homicide Detective Fred Hutton," I said by way of response. "Or, actually, I suppose at this point I should say good morning."

This produced another nonspecific grunt from him.

Since our initial meeting, when he introduced himself as Homicide Detective Fred Hutton, I have consistently referred to him by his full name and title, much to his consternation and my amusement.

He didn't like it the first time I did it, and likes it even less now. For me, it never gets old.

"Tell me what happened," he said, getting right to the point.

"I don't have much more to add beyond what your partner described," I said. "I came home, glanced out my living room window and saw what appeared to be a body lying on the floor of the projection booth."

"Do you make it a habit to peep into the projection booth?" He had taken out his notepad and was writing small, spidery notes.

"Sometimes," I replied, trying to remove any tone of defensiveness from my voice. "But I'm not sure I would use the word 'peep.' I like to see if I can figure out what movie is playing."

He raised an eyebrow at this. "And how does that work?"

"There's a small mirror on one wall and if you get the angle just right, you can see light bouncing off something or other and sort of get a sense of part of the movie screen..." My voice trailed off and I met his eyes for a moment before looking away. He shook his head with a sigh, and then returned to his note taking.

"And then what did you do?"

It took me a moment to realize we were off my window peeping habits and back onto the body on the floor. "I called 911," I said.

"And what was your relationship with the projectionist?"

This question took me by surprise. "None," I said, perhaps a tad too quickly. "I've never met him."

"You repeatedly and routinely stare into his workspace and yet you've never met him?"

"Not only have I never met him," I said, again working hard not to sound too defensive, "but I've never really even seen him. I mean, completely."

This produced a hard stare from Homicide Detective Fred Hutton, which caused me to stammer a bit as I continued my response. "I mean, I've seen his arms, his legs, I've seen him moving around in there, but I don't think I've ever actually seen his face."

We met each other's eyes again and then he returned to his notebook. "Interesting," he said, scribbling something quickly. "I think that's all we'll need from you for now. We may want you to come down and make an official statement in the next day or two."

"Okay," I said, not sure what the protocol was in a situation like this. "You want me to leave?"

"Nothing would make me happier," he said without humor as he turned and headed across the room to Tracy. She had witnessed his treatment of me, and I could see she was bracing for a difficult conversation.

I pushed against several of the glass lobby doors until I found one that was unlocked. I was about to step into the cold night when I heard one of the crime scene techs come into the room and report to Detective Wright how much money they had found in the envelope in the projection booth.

When I heard the figure, it was all I could do to avoid doing a double-take with an accompanying cartoon sound effect. I successfully squelched the impulse and continued on my way out the door.

CHAPTER 3

"Seventy-five thousand dollars?" Harry gave a low whistle as he stroked his thick white beard.

"That's what the crime scene guy said. I saw a stack of money in an envelope on the table, but I was surprised it was so much. Must have been large denomination bills."

"Must have been. My, you had quite the evening last night, didn't you?"

My uncle Harry and I were having breakfast together in his apartment, as we did most mornings. However, our topics of conversation usually focused on more mundane things, like a new rye bread he was thinking of trying or the need to order more invisible thread for the magic shop. Dead bodies and large sums of cash were, at least up until today, infrequent but welcome breakfast subjects.

The daily breakfast ritual began soon after I moved back into my apartment above Harry's. At the time, I had just gotten divorced and my aunt Alice had recently died. It made sense to return to my boyhood home, if only for a while.

Harry seemed to like the company at breakfast and it gave us an important and valuable opportunity to strategize on ways to upgrade and improve his magic store and its standing in the marketplace.

I should point out we never seized that opportunity, not even once, but instead usually spent the time just reading the paper or kibitzing on topics both obscure and unimportant.

"It sounds like the police have a classic locked room mystery on their hands," Harry said as he headed to the coffeemaker to pour his second cup of the day. He filled the mug to the halfway mark and then added a generous amount of chocolate milk to round out the rest of the cup. "Dead body on the floor, gun nearby, a stack of money on the table and the door locked from the inside. Yes, quite the puzzler."

"Did you know the projectionist? I think his name was Tyler."

Harry sat down and considered. "We were on a nodding acquaintance, I would say," he finally said. "I know he's worked there for years, but I couldn't tell you a thing about the poor devil. You?"

I shook my head. "I don't think I could have picked him out of a crowd," I said.

"Say, speaking of crowds, and on a more upbeat note, how was the turnout for Quinton Moon's show last night?"

I shrugged. "Good, I suppose. I didn't see any empty seats, but it's hard to tell how many more that room could have held," I said, trying to sound as nonchalant as I could.

"Marvelous show, wasn't it?" Harry continued, stirring his coffee so the dark brown liquid transitioned into a milky gray. "Didn't you love it?"

I shrugged again and picked at my toast. Harry leaned across the table. "Are you saying that was not one of the finest magic shows you have ever seen in your entire life?" he said, his voice rising to an incredulous pitch. "Are you seriously saying that? How can you be saying that?"

"I'm not actually saying anything," I snapped. "But you're talking so much, you can't tell."

Harry leaned back in his chair and studied me closely. "Do I sense a visit by the green-eyed monster, envy?" he said quietly. "Is that who has landed at our breakfast table this morning?"

"No," I lied. "I thought he was fine. A nice show. A very nice show."

"Nice? Can you damn him with any fainter praise than nice?"

"I don't know what the big deal is," I sputtered. "It was a good show, very competent, the audience loved it, what do you want me to say?"

"Nothing," Harry said quietly. "You've already said volumes."

Mercifully, my phone chose that moment to beep, signaling the arrival of a text. I pulled it out and gave it a quick look. "It's my agent. She has work for me. I should go call her."

"By all means," Harry said. "Leave your dishes, I'll straighten up. You go call your agent. About your work." He spit out the last three words with a biting precision and then got up and began to clear the table. I took my phone and headed to the door, happy to have an excuse to leave.

Even though I stormed out of Harry's apartment trying to give the impression I had places to go and things to do, as it turned out, I did have at least one place to go. A quick call to my agent revealed the sudden and abrupt need for a substitute magician at a children's magic show. The details were fuzzy, but apparently the scheduled performer had backed out at the last minute, leaving a frantic parent with a room full of kids and no promised and desperately needed child-friendly entertainment.

I am no fan of children's magic shows, because in my hands they generally end up being less about entertainment and more about crowd control. Some magicians can handle the kids with ease and aplomb. For me, it quickly degenerates into a hostage situation, with me as the unwilling victim. However, I wanted to put some distance between myself and Harry, and I really did have nothing else to do that morning. I packed the car and was on the road in less than twenty minutes.

Due to the hurried nature of the request, my agent had failed to supply me with a demographic profile of the group. Not knowing the age range of the audience meant I had to bring not just a few things but virtually everything. I needed to be prepared for any contingency, because experience has taught me a trick that will delight an eight-year-old will completely baffle a five-year-old, sometimes to the point of tears. And then, a trick a five-year-old finds completely enthralling, a ten-year-old will think is the stupidest thing he's ever seen and will be quick to proclaim that, often at great volume. And God help you if the room is full of teenagers.

Consequently, I had over-packed and was ready, I felt, for any eventuality.

I was wrong.

I would have been wise to spend the drive time thinking about what I was going to do for my forty-five-minute act which was twenty-five minutes away. Instead, I spent the trip fuming about how quickly Harry had seen through my feelings about Quinton Moon's performance. The fact was, it was the most astonishing magic show I had ever seen. But something inside made it impossible for me to admit that, at least in front of Harry.

Because this flurry of negative thoughts and self-doubt had clouded my brain, I think I could be excused for not noticing the red flags of danger as they appeared, one right after another.

The first indicator something was amiss was the complete lack of cars in the parking lot at the party's location, Pirate Pete's Pizza Peninsula. With a kid's birthday party in progress, the lot normally would have been filled to overflowing with SUVs and minivans, but there were only a handful of cars dotting the large space.

I encountered the second red flag when I entered the building, passing a prominent and hastily scrawled "Closed for Private Event" sign which hung crookedly on the door. What was striking was the volume, or actually lack of volume, that I experienced when I walked into the entertainment complex. Pirate Pete's consists of a ridiculously large video game arcade, a bowling alley, indoor putt-putt, a performance stage and outsized dining area. Noise levels—including the sound effects from all the video games, the rumble from the bowling alley, the screaming of kids and constant thumping of bass-heavy music—usually combine to create a wall of sound as you walk into the place. However, on this day, I was greeted by blessed, eerie silence.

The third red flag was actually more of a red fire hydrant: a short, muscled bullet of a man I'd come to know only as Harpo. With his short-cropped red hair and imposing stance, he was the first human—to use the term loosely—I encountered as I entered the building. My heart sank when I saw him, because the appearance of Harpo was a clear harbinger I was once again going to come face to face with—

"Ah, there he is, the man of the hour! Welcome, Mandrake, welcome."

I followed the sound of the thin, reedy voice, finally spotting its thinner, reedier owner.

Mr. Lime was seated on a chair in the large and empty dining area, looking like a pale, skeletal waif set adrift in a sea of colorful tables. I forced a smile onto my face and headed toward him, fording the large sandbox area which acted as a moat of sorts between the play zone and the food area. If I had been crossing an authentic moat to do battle with an actual dragon, I think I would have felt better about my odds.

"Welcome to my version of a surprise party," he said with a too-wide smile, making his tight white skin seem even tighter and whiter.

"The surprise being, there is no party?"

"Exactly." He gestured to a chair across the table from him and I sat reluctantly, like a child forced into an impromptu meeting in the principal's office. Assuming, of course, the principal was a grinning, aging sociopath.

Our paths had crossed three times earlier that year and I still knew nothing about the man, not even his real name. In addition to his criminal activities, which he only alluded to, he was a rabid movie fan. At our first meeting, he proposed the name Harry Lime as a plausible substitute for the real thing. The charming but immoral Orson Wells character from *The Third Man* had seemed a reasonable analog, and from that point on he had become Mr. Lime in all of our brief but terrifying encounters.

His delight in assigning movie nicknames was applied without prejudice to all comers. His silent bodyguard, houseboy, chauffeur or whatever the hell he was, had been given the name Harpo as a nod to the great silent comedian. And I was dubbed Mandrake, in honor of the comic strip magician of the same name.

"I'm glad your schedule was free this morning," Mr. Lime said. "Can Harpo get you a soft drink of some kind? They have one of those machines which appear to offer hundreds of selections. I myself," he continued, gesturing to the bright plastic cup in front of him, "am happily partaking of a Diet Vanilla Cherry Coke, of all things."

To prove his point, he picked up the cup and took a sip from the colorful straw. His skin was so translucent, I swear I could see the dark liquid through his cheeks as it moved out of the straw and into his mouth. He looked just as old as he had when I first met him several months back, and that was really, really old. Thin strands of white hair covered his pale scalp, and his head balanced atop his wiry shoulders like a ghoulish bobble head.

"This is a unique place to meet," I said by way of a conversational icebreaker.

"Thank you, thank you," he said, taking the comment more as a compliment than intended. "I thought a birthday party would be a good ruse, and this seemed as likely a place as any. In fact, I think technically I own this establishment," he added as he looked around the large space, as if for the first time. "But I suspect that would be very hard to prove."

"By design?"

"Exactly."

Feeling more cocky than I had any right to, I pressed the question. "Mr. Lime, what exactly do you do? I mean, for a living. We've never discussed that."

"I'm not sure I understand the question," he said without a hint of sarcasm.

His apparent naiveté stumped me for a second. "All right," I said, searching for another way into my query. "For example, when you fill out your income tax form, what do you list as an occupation?"

This produced a gruesomely large smile, during which he bared all of his large, yellow teeth. "Income tax form? You are a funny young man, Mandrake. You really are."

He laughed a ragged, phlegmy laugh and then took another long sip from his soda cup. The straw made a slurping sound as it sucked up the remaining liquid and in an instant Harpo was at his side, replacing the empty cup with a full one and then disappearing as quickly as he had appeared. Mr. Lime seemed to take no notice of any of this and focused his attention entirely on me.

"I understand you had a bit of an occurrence last night," he began.

For a brief instant, I thought he too was going to launch into a lecture about what a freaking great magician Quinton Moon was. But then I realized he was referring to the murder at the movie theater. Oddly enough, that felt like a much more comfortable conversation topic.

"I suppose I did," I said. "It's not every day you look out your window and see a dead body."

For some reason this produced another slight smile on Mr. Lime's thin lips. "No, I imagine for you that is a rare incident. But as you've doubtless assumed, that's what I've brought you here today to discuss. If you don't mind?"

Never in the complete history of time has a question been more rhetorical. "Sure," I said while nodding agreeably. "It's your party."

"Yes, I suppose it is." He took another sip of his Diet Vanilla Cherry Coke. "Walk me through what happened. What you saw, what you did, what you said." He gestured expansively with one hand while gripping the soda cup with the other.

I sat back in my chair and began. Just as I had done with Harry an hour before, I recounted the key moments of the previous evening: discovering the body, calling the police, watching them break into the projection booth, and the tableau they found when the door was finally removed.

When I finished, Mr. Lime looked off into a corner of the room and smiled thoughtfully. He clucked his tongue. "It looks as if our friend the projectionist got himself into a bit of a situation."

"Did you know Tyler?" I wasn't sure if the floor was open for questions, but Mr. Lime turned and once again smiled his toothy death mask at me.

"We had an oblique connection, yes," he said. "But I should point out, while I have no actual correlation to the man's death, I do have an interest in it. Let's call it something more than curiosity."

He leaned toward me, resting his weight on his arms as they rested on the table.

I couldn't see his limbs through his black suit coat, but if they were as bony and frail as the rest of him, I worried for a moment his arms might give way under the strain.

"There were two film canisters on the floor?"

"Yes," I said.

"Open?"

I nodded. "Open and, apparently, empty."

"Tell me again what was written on them."

"Each had a white label stuck on it," I said carefully. "With handwriting on each of them. One was labeled 'LAM #1,' and the other was labeled 'LAM #2.'"

He looked at me for a long moment and then leaned back in his chair. He picked up his cup and took another long, thoughtful slurp through the straw. "That is fascinating," he said, his voice just above a whisper. "So very fascinating."

He didn't seem poised to share why it was so fascinating, and I decided not to pursue it. I was weighing my next question, but before I could present it he snapped out of his reverie.

"Okay, Mandrake, let's do this. Why don't you do me a trick and then I'll lay out my plan, such as it is."

I was startled by his sudden change in mood and energy. "Do a trick?" I repeated.

He nodded with enthusiasm. "Yes, I believe it is traditional for magicians at birthday parties to perform tricks. That is still the custom, am I right?"

I couldn't help but agree, but the sudden request put me momentarily on the spot. I had left all my gear in the car, planning to come in and determine the age range I was dealing with first. Consequently I had nothing on me I could use for an impromptu trick. At the same time, I knew in my gut if I went out to the car now, my fight or flight impulse would switch to flight and I'd be halfway to Canada before I knew it. And as I looked across the table at Mr. Lime, I recognized there was no way that could end well for me. He was as deadly as he was old, if that makes any sense.

I quickly surveyed the space to see what was available and was thrilled to spot several small tin buckets in the sandbox moat which circled the eating area. One of those would be perfect for a quick rendition of The Miser's Dream. Plus, having just seen Quinton Moon perform an exquisite version of the effect last night, I realized this would be an ideal opportunity to see if I could emulate his approach to the trick on the fly.

I walked over and grabbed one of the cleaner buckets, stopped by the change machine to get some coins, and headed back to Mr. Lime, who was leaning forward in keen anticipation. Say what you will about him, the scary old guy was a great audience for magic.

Many magicians perform The Miser's Dream to music, but Quinton had done it in complete silence, which only intensified the magic. Currently the only sound in the room was coming from the refrigeration units behind the counter and a slight, persistent wheezing from Mr. Lime.

I began the routine as I remembered Quinton doing it, reaching up to the empty space in front of me and attempting, again and again, to pull a coin out of the air. On the third try it appeared between my fingers and I held the coin over the bucket, letting it drop with a resounding clink onto the bottom.

While there are countless variations on it, the basic premise for The Miser's Dream is just what I demonstrated: pulling coins out of thin air (or from behind someone's ear or out of their nose) and dropping these coins, one after another, into a tin bucket or other similar container. The bucket fills up magically with all these coins, just as a miser might dream, and then at the end you reveal...

You can go a lot of different ways at that point. In most versions, you do a final move of some kind and call it a day. But Quinton created a different and striking ending: He poured out all the coins, scooped them into his hands and immediately poured them back into the bucket. Then, with a final flourish, he turned the bucket over and only one coin tumbled out. He picked it up and held it up in the air. A moment later it vanished, leaving him exactly in the same position in which he started.

Quinton's rendition was truly a thing of beauty and as dramatic a piece of magic as I had ever seen. Since I was familiar with all the moves he made—with the notable exception of the disappearance of all the coins at the end, about which I didn't have a clue—it felt like a simple process of recreating each of the steps and in so doing, recreating the routine. Simple in theory, but the further I got into the routine, the more I realized there was clearly something missing. I was successfully completing all the steps in the same sequence he had performed them, but something felt imperceptibly off. I plowed ahead gamely, but when I noticed Mr. Lime suppress a yawn, I felt the routine nearly collapse around me.

I made it through to the conclusion and improvised a quick ending, producing an oversized coin from behind his ear, a hoary cliché, but it was all I could think of. I stood back and waited for his applause. And I waited.

The room was deathly silent, with the only sound coming from the compressors in the kitchen. Mr. Lime had stopped his gentle wheezing and before I had glanced over at him, I wished as deeply as I could that he had left at some point during the routine.

Sadly, he was still seated across from me and he looked no happier than I felt.

"So," he said finally, after I had set the bucket down on the table. "That happened."

"Sorry you didn't enjoy it."

He shrugged ineffectually. "Perhaps it's my age. Do children appreciate that trick?"

"Some do," I said. "Children are notoriously harsh critics."

"Yes, so I've heard. One of the myriads of reasons I never had any." He moved the bucket aside on the table and gestured for me to sit again.

"Mandrake, about the murder of our projectionist friend," he said, his voice taking on a tone just above a whisper. "I believe I have some information and insight which might be of value to the law enforcement community. If I may bend your ear for just a few more minutes, I will share with you an offer I would like you to extend to them."

CHAPTER 4

"The Minneapolis Homicide Division does not take offers or make deals."

"No, but the Minneapolis District Attorney's office does, so shut up and let him talk."

After combing through City Hall, I had finally come across Homicide Detective Fred Hutton and Assistant District Attorney Deirdre Sutton-Hutton in the midst of eating their lunch in the building's cafeteria. After the kind of playful banter you'd expect one to exchange with one's ex-wife and her new husband, I explained the reason for my visit.

"Wait, who is this Mr. Lime?" Homicide Detective Fred Hutton asked, holding up a hand to bring the conversation to a dead stop and turn it in a direction more to his liking. "And why should we listen to him?"

"You remember, his name came up earlier this year during the Dylan Lasalle murder investigation," Deirdre explained, and then turned back to me. "We couldn't find a trace of the man during that investigation, Eli. He was vapor. And yet you say he called you again out of the blue?"

I shook my head. "No. Just like he did last time, Mr. Lime posed as a potential client, called my agent and booked me to perform at what turned out to be a bogus event. A kid's birthday party, no less."

"You hate doing birthday parties," Deirdre said, sounding almost sympathetic.

"They are the worst. But work is work," I replied. "Like Harry always says, follow the money."

Before we could continue this discussion on the microeconomics of being a working magician, Homicide Detective Fred Hutton jumped in. "And this guy claims to know who killed the projectionist, Tyler James?"

I shook my head again. "No, but he does have a theory as to why he was killed, which I understand is more than you folks currently have."

"The Homicide Division is pursuing several important leads," he said with great diplomacy.

"In other words, you have nothing," I translated. He just stared at me, so I turned to Deirdre. She nodded.

"Let me tell you what he told me, and then I'll lay out his offer," I said. I gestured toward their uneaten food. "You may want to eat while I talk. I'd hate to see your food get cold."

"We're eating cold sandwiches," Homicide Detective Fred Hutton said dryly.

"Well, then I'd hate for them to get warm," I shot back. "Anyway, Mr. Lime said Tyler James has made a good living for years as a movie memorabilia broker."

Deirdre, who had just taken a bite from her sandwich, raised an eyebrow and reached for a napkin. I held up my hand and began to elaborate.

"You see, as a broker, Tyler acted as a middleman. If you were looking to buy an expensive, original movie poster or you had a rare film print to sell, Tyler would handle the deal. If you were selling, he'd find a buyer. If you were buying, he'd find a seller. However," I added, "Tyler also offered services which other brokers avoided."

Deirdre was still chewing, so she gave me a shoulder shrug, gesturing that I should continue. Homicide Detective Fred Hutton just stared at me in his patented bovine manner, chewing slowly and methodically.

"The first was that Tyler was more than happy to look the other way if the piece he was brokering was warm or perhaps even hot. He didn't seem to mind who the rightful owner was, only how much commission he could make on the sale.

"The other service he offered," I continued, "was he was willing to work anonymously. The buyer didn't need to know who the seller was and vice versa. In some instances, even Tyler didn't know who he was dealing with."

Deirdre had finally finished chewing. "How did that work?"

"Bogus email accounts. Cash drops. Wiring money to and from offshore accounts."

"And Mr. Lime thinks this was a deal gone bad?"

I nodded and then eyed Deirdre's potato chips, suddenly remembering breakfast had been a long time ago. She pushed the plate in my direction and I grabbed a couple chips and quickly scarfed them down.

"Perhaps Tyler was completing a deal in the projection booth with a customer," she began to theorize. "Something went south and the killer shot Tyler and left him to die in the booth."

Her husband was shaking his head slowly from side to side as she spoke. "Doesn't make any sense," he said. "The killer left empty-handed, leaving the money on the table and the gun on the floor."

"And somehow locked the door from the inside on his or her way out," Deirdre added.

"That's just the thing," I said, taking the opportunity to grab more potato chips. "Mr. Lime doesn't think the killer left empty-handed." I glanced at the pickle slice on her plate and then up at Deirdre. She gave me the nod, and I didn't need to be told twice.

"Remember those two empty film canisters next to the weight bench?" They both nodded at me. "If the film which was in those canisters is the one Mr. Lime thinks it was, the killer left with something *very* valuable indeed."

"What does he think was in there?" Deirdre asked.

"Oh, only the most famous lost movie of all time."

*   *   *

"It doesn't look all that amazing."

"I didn't say it was amazing, I said it was famous. And lost. And therefore valuable."

At my behest, we had moved our impromptu meeting up to Deirdre's office, where I availed myself of her computer and the internet. Moments later I was clicking through a series of still photos from the classic 1927 silent movie, *London After Midnight*.

"It is generally believed the last surviving print of this Lon Chaney movie had been destroyed in a fire around 1967," I explained, as I pointed out the Man of A Thousand Faces in one of his least seen yet most iconic performances.

Wearing a black top hat and a coat which seemed to open like a pair of wiry bat wings, Chaney peered back at us from the computer screen. Long, stringy hair flowed from under the hat and his eyes were deep rimmed, wide and bulging.

But the standout feature—the primary reason the image possessed its haunting quality—was his broad, wicked smile and his teeth, each of which appeared to have been sharpened to a razor point.

"Okay, but if the last surviving print of the movie was destroyed in a fire," Deirdre said, "then what was Tyler selling?"

I turned away from the computer and looked up at her. It was odd to be sitting at her desk, but no odder than laying out the terms of a deal from a wispy ghoul like Mr. Lime to my ex-wife and her cop husband. I pressed on.

"Apparently, there's been a rumor floating around for years that a German film collector had a copy, which was seized—along with all his other assets—by the Nazis during the war. Somehow the film print made it to Switzerland, where it was purchased by a buyer on the black market. He sold it to someone who sold it to someone else, who sold it to someone else."

"Then it's not really a lost film if this copy exists," Deirdre began, but I cut her off.

"That was exactly my point to Mr. Lime. But it was stolen by the Nazis and should, by all rights, be returned to the original owner's family in Germany. Whoever has it now can own it but can never admit to owning it."

"It's stolen property," Homicide Detective Fred Hutton said matter-of-factly.

"That's right," I said. "They can't claim ownership, they can't screen it publicly, they really can't get any of the benefits of owning the only print of the most famous lost movie of all time."

"Except the satisfaction of owning it," Deirdre offered.

"Exactly," I said.

"But is it worth killing for?"

"Apparently it was to someone."

"Here's Mr. Lime's offer," I began.

We had all shifted positions in Deirdre's office. I was now seated in one of the two chairs in front of her desk. She was in her rightful place behind the desk, while her husband had taken up a bored position, leaning against a windowsill.

Deirdre had a dish of hard candies on her desk. The earlier pickle and potato chip combo had not sated my appetite but instead intensified it. I considered pulling one or two candies from the dish, but they'd been in that bowl as long as I'd known Deirdre. I suspected if I attempted to pluck one out, I would instead pull out the entire sticky messy mass.

"Because of his familiarity with the world of local black market movie memorabilia," I said, "Mr. Lime believes there are four likely suspects in this case."

"Including him?" Homicide Detective Fred Hutton muttered under his breath from his sullen position across the room.

"He insists he was not involved in this transaction in any way, and I for one am inclined to believe him."

"Why?" Deirdre had noticed my longing look at the candy dish. She reached into her desk drawer, produced a granola bar and tossed it my way, as if mollifying a cranky toddler. I gratefully grabbed it out of the air.

"For one, I don't believe he's ever lied to me in the past." This produced a derisive grunt from Homicide Detective Fred Hutton. I acknowledged it and continued. "The other reason is, why? Why would he pull himself into this investigation if he were involved in some way?"

"Because maybe he's insane?" Deirdre suggested.

"Oh, there's no question he's crazy. But he certainly isn't stupid. And his offer is so...benign, I guess would be the word," I said, trying to best capture the nature of his request. "It's so benign that, in the long run, I don't see how it can hurt. And if nothing else, it will give you four names to look into, which I understand are four more than you currently have."

Deirdre leaned back in her chair thoughtfully, then turned and looked at her husband across the room.

Their silence said volumes.

He gave her a nearly imperceptible nod and she pivoted her chair back in my direction.

"Okay, what's the offer?"

"The way he laid it out to me, it's simplicity itself. He said, 'Tell Woodward and Bernstein...'" I stopped and looked at their blank faces, realizing I had left out a key piece of information. "I should explain. Mr. Lime is big on movie-themed nicknames for people. He calls his mute assistant Harpo, he calls me Mandrake. He calls you two Woodward and Bernstein."

Deirdre gave me a long look. "Why?"

"Because you're investigating this, so in his mind you're Woodward and Bernstein from *All the President's Men*. Trust me, I lobbied hard for Nick and Nora Charles from the *Thin Man* movies, but he was adamant." I looked at both of them and the puzzled looks I got in return told me it was time to move on.

"Anyway, after he gives you the suspects' names and you interview the four people, he wants you to allow me to talk to them as well. After you're all done."

"He wants you to talk to them after we talk to them?" Homicide Detective Fred Hutton spat out the words. "Why?"

I shrugged. "To be honest, I'm not entirely sure why he keeps picking me. He says he likes my perceptions."

"And that's it? He gives us the names, we give you access?" Deirdre's tone told me she was highly suspicious of the simplicity of the deal.

"That's it."

"Why?" she said, repeating her husband's previous question while dragging the word out to several syllables.

"I don't know. Something about this whole thing is sticking in his craw," I said, not really certain the rail-thin old monster actually even had a craw.

"Okay," Deirdre sighed, leaning back in her chair. "What's the next step?"

I smiled. "Do you still have that big flowerpot out on your balcony?"

Her eyes narrowed to slits. "Yes. I still have the flowerpot. It's covered in snow, but I have it."

"If you agree with these terms, you need to put a flag in it."

"A flag?"

"Yeah. Nothing elaborate. A stick with a handkerchief on it will work fine."

"Why?" I had to give Deirdre credit. She continually found new and curious ways to draw the word out.

"Because that's how Woodward, or was it Bernstein?" This stumped me for a second. "I think it was Woodward. Whatever. That's how Woodward communicated with Deep Throat in *All the President's Men*."

She gave me a long, penetrating look. "I put a small flag in the flowerpot on my balcony and he'll give us the four names?"

I nodded. "What could be simpler than that?"

Her response was typically short, sweet and utterly obscene.

CHAPTER 5

"How much of your life do you think you've spent shuffling cards?"

The question was a good one, though hardly original. It had come up numerous times over the years at the back table of Adrian's, where the remaining Minneapolis Mystics spent much of their days chewing the fat and the occasional burger.

It's not the sort of question you'd expect from a card man or even a coin man, but in this case it came from a ventriloquist. Consequently, it was greeted with the same degree of patience and tolerance one would grant to a dog who suddenly spoke English but not very well.

I had taken a temporary seat at the table, awaiting Megan's arrival for a dinner date. She works down the block at the store she owns and runs, Chi & Things, and since Adrian's is situated between her shop and Uncle Harry's, it has become a frequent post-work hangout for dinners that often extend well into the evening.

"I can't begin to fathom how many times I've shuffled a deck of cards," my uncle Harry said as he began to answer the question posed by Gene Westlake.

As a ventriloquist, Gene was not considered to be a core member of the Mystics, which counted among its number mentalists, magicians, coin men and card sharks. Others who dabbled in the variety arts—jugglers, clowns, and other "circus geek acts" as the Mystics called them—were not generally offered membership to the exclusive group. But Gene's skill as a ventriloquist was just this side of magical, and he was also a terrible poker player who bet high and often, so he was ultimately if grudgingly welcomed into the group.

"But consider this, if you will," Harry continued, as he warmed up to the topic. In addition to Gene, two other Mystics were currently in attendance and both turned to listen as Harry launched into a mini-lecture. "When you shuffle a deck of cards, you change the order of those cards."

"Isn't that the point?" This came from Abe Ackerman, who sat directly across from Harry.

"Yes, but did you know this: Every time you shuffle the deck, they obviously can land in any order. How many different orders do you think they can end up in?"

Abe grunted and glared back at Harry. "What am I? A mind reader?" The question was particularly ironic, as Abe had made his living—and it had been a good one in his day—as a mentalist in the Kreskin mold.

Coin man Sam Esbjornson stopped rolling quarters across the backs of his fingers, set the coins gently on the table and scratched his chin thoughtfully. "Let's see, there are fifty-two cards, so there are fifty-two possible orders, times fifty-two for each card..."

His voice trailed off. Harry looked to Gene Westlake, who shrugged. Gene glanced down at the small suitcase which sat on the floor next to him. "Any ideas, Kenny?"

"Hell if I know," came a muffled voice from inside the case. "Next, ask me if I care."

"The number of possible sequences for the cards is a big, big figure," Harry said to the group, pointedly ignoring the remark from the suitcase. "In point of fact, it's the number eight, followed by sixty-seven zeroes. To put it in perspective for you," he continued, picking up cards off the table and quickly shuffling the deck, "it is not only possible but highly likely that the order I just put this deck in—via this single shuffle—is an order that has never occurred before and might never happen again."

He fanned the cards dramatically, showing the faces of the cards.

"So, in short, you're saying you've shuffled a lot of cards," Gene Westlake finally said, bringing something resembling closure to the topic.

It was circular conversations such as these that had driven my late aunt Alice to dub the group The Artful Codgers. Given their average age and temperaments, this was an apt description of the old coots. My interest in the conversation was momentarily derailed by the arrival of Megan, which for me is generally a happy occurrence. However, in this instance it was less so, as she entered the bar with none other than the dreaded Quinton Moon practically hanging on her arm.

"Look who I found wandering around outside." Megan was bubblier than I would have liked.

Quinton chuckled good-naturedly. "When Harry proffered his invitation to stop by, I misheard the name of the pub and thought I was looking for an establishment called Hadrian's," he explained to the table. "Not sure exactly what I was looking for. Perhaps the Pantheon and some chaps decked out in Roman togas, I suspect."

"Hadrian was a Roman Emperor," Megan said to me in a terrible stage whisper.

"I know that," I lied.

"I'm glad you finally found us," Harry said, getting up and extending a hand.

"Couldn't have accomplished it without the help of this fetching lass," Quinton replied, taking Harry's hand firmly.

"Let me make introductions all around," Harry continued, mercifully pulling Quinton away from Megan's grasp. I stood up and stepped back while Harry played the good host and Quinton the delighted guest, repeating each name as it was presented and smiling warmly at every greeting.

"And of course you know Eli and Megan," Harry concluded. Quinton removed his black, broad-brimmed hat and gave a deep bow to Megan and then extended a hand to me.

"Good to see you again, Eli," Quinton said with a wide smile. "I hope you and Megan will be joining us for dinner," he added, gesturing to the table.

"Sure—" Megan began, but I cut her off.

"Thanks, Quinton, but I promised Megan a dinner date tonight, and I can't renege on that. Plus, I think you've got a quorum back here in the corner." I took Megan's arm and began to pull her away from the group. "Have a lovely meal."

"But—" was all Megan could get out before I had steered us toward a table at the other end of the room.

"You don't want to spend the whole night listening to a bunch of stuffy old magicians going on and on, do you?" I asked rhetorically as we set our menus down.

"That's how we spend every night," Megan replied.

She had a point, but I chose to ignore it. Was it my imagination, or was she staring longingly at the table across the room?

Before I could explore the idea further, my phone beeped, signaling the arrival of a text. I scanned it quickly.

"That was quick," I said as I put the phone away. "Deirdre just got the names of the suspects."

"What names? Who's a suspect?"

I outlined my meeting with the terrifying Mr. Lime and his subsequent offer to the DA's office.

"Is this dangerous, Eli?" she asked. "If it's dangerous, I don't want you to do it."

I shook my head. "Hardly. I'm just talking to some people and then reporting back to Mr. Lime. Although I'm not quite sure how," I added, realizing not for the first time I had no actual method of contacting the scary old man.

"I don't know," she began doubtfully, but I cut her off.

"It's a mystery, Megan. I'm a magician. We love creating mysteries, we love solving mysteries."

"I think you've already had enough experience with mysteries," she said. "A couple of which, I'm sure you remember, were life-threatening. I don't want to see you get hurt. Or worse," she added, her eyes going a little wide at the thought.

"This is nothing like those other times," I said, rationalizing quickly. "I'm just going to talk to some people and gather some perceptions. It will be fun. Besides, unlike those past experiences, I had no personal connection to Tyler James. He's well outside the danger zone."

"Danger zone?" Megan repeated skeptically.

"That's an actual term," I said reassuringly. "Or maybe a song from *Top Gun*."

Before Megan could respond, there was a burst of raucous laughter from the back of the room. We both turned and looked, seeing Quinton Moon in full raconteur mode, standing by the table, putting the final tag on whatever story he had been telling.

"Then Tamariz says something in Spanish, and suddenly *I'm* the one holding the jumbo Queen of Hearts and he has my wallet!" This produced another explosion of laugher from the Mystics. Quinton then punctuated the story by imitating some quick strokes on an imaginary violin, in typical Juan Tamariz style.

I turned back to Megan, but she was still transfixed by the table in the back and, I assumed, the way too charming Mr. Moon. I frantically scanned the room before landing on a possible distraction in the form of a very tall redhead standing by the bar.

"Hey, Tracy!" I said, my voice landing somewhere between normal and a shout. "How's it going?"

The theater manager was apparently picking up a to-go food order, along with a handful of pull-tabs. She turned at the sound of her name, finally spotting us at our table by the far wall. Tracy waved and I returned the wave, signaling she should head over.

The appearance of the tall, athletic woman shifted Megan's attention as I had hoped. "Who's that?" she asked.

"That's Tracy," I said. "You know, she's the manager at the movie theater."

"Oh," Megan said, watching her as she approached our table. "Wow, she's pretty."

I made quick introductions all around.

"It's nice to meet you," Megan said genuinely. "How are you doing? Eli told me about the projectionist, what was his name?"

Tracy nodded. "Tyler. I didn't really know him, but it was quite a shock. I'm handling his duties as well as my own until we can find a replacement." She turned her full attention on me. "I'm guessing this whole thing must have been pretty weird for you. I never got the full story. You looked out your window and saw...what? Tyler getting shot?"

I shook my head. "No, I really only saw his body on the floor. I think whoever did it was gone by then, or on their way out."

"Weird. The whole thing is just ultra weird," she said. "Plus, it looks like it will be dinner in the booth for me tonight and for the foreseeable future," she added, holding up her to-go bag.

"Now you have to be the manager *and* be the projectionist," I said. "That's a lot."

"As luck would have it, tonight's movies are on Blu-ray, so it really just comes down to hitting a button, setting the volume, and checking in every few minutes to make sure it hasn't locked up or anything." She glanced at one of the television screens over the bar. "Are you guys watching the game tonight?"

I had no idea which game she was referring to, but since there would not be any chance we would be watching any of them, I shook my head. "Nope, just here for dinner."

"The point spread is wild on Green Bay, isn't it?"

I nodded enthusiastically, signaling my complete agreement. In reality, I had no idea to what I was agreeing. I had a vague notion of where Green Bay was, but no understanding of what a point spread might be.

"Hey," I said, suddenly remembering a recent brainstorm. "I've got three more candidates for your double features."

I almost added Harry's "dopey" adjective, but thought better of it at the last second.

"Your Parkway Double Plays," I said, gesturing toward an empty chair.

"Lay them on me," Tracy said as she took a seat, her mood brightening at the change in topic.

"Okay, the first one is *The 39 Stepford Wives*," I began.

Tracy smiled and nodded. "That works."

"Yeah, I liked it too," I said. "The second one is a bit longer. *One Flew Over the Sterile Cuckoo's Nest*."

This one actually made her laugh. "Oh, that would be a fun night. We'll have to put the whole audience on suicide watch."

"And the third one is the longest one of all: *Bob and Carol and Ted and Alice Doesn't Live Here Anymore*."

"Yikes," Tracy said. "Let's hold off on that one until I can hire a new projectionist. I've got to do the actual letter hanging on the marquee now, and that one might be the end of me. But it's a good one."

Megan nodded along with us and added, "Oh, I have one. *A Night in Casablanca*." She waited for our excited reactions, which did not materialize.

"That's just one movie, hon," I said. "It's supposed to be a double feature."

"It is," she explained, her enthusiasm undampened. "It's the Marx brothers' movie, *A Night in Casablanca*. And it's the Humphrey Bogart movie, *Casablanca*."

Another long pause. "How would people know that?" I asked.

Megan considered the options for a moment. "I don't know," she finally said. "I suppose you'd have to tell them when they buy their tickets."

"We could do that," Tracy said, putting a positive face on the idea. "Good idea. Thanks, Megan. We'll add it to the list," she said as she stood up. "Enjoy your dinner."

"You too," I replied.

She got about five feet away and turned back, shifting her weight from foot to foot. "Say, how well do you know the police detective who came to the theater?"

"Which one? The tall one with no personality or the short one with no personality?"

She moved back toward us slowly. "The tall one. The reason I ask, it seemed like you knew him."

"That I do," I said sagely. "He's married to my ex-wife."

Tracy took a dramatic step backward. "Oops. Sorry," she said. "Awkward."

"Not a problem," I said, putting up a reassuring hand. "That's old news."

"Okay," she said, once again moving closer. "The reason I ask is he seemed to think it was weird I didn't really know anything about Tyler. Like I was lying or something. I tried to explain I've only been in town about six months and that Tyler really kept to himself up there in the booth, but I got the impression he thought I was hedging and he wasn't buying it."

I nodded.

"Not buying it," I explained, "is the go-to emotion for Homicide Detective Fred Hutton. Some people are convinced it's his only emotion."

She smiled at my attempt at humor and then turned serious once again. "The thing is, I remembered today times when Tyler met up with a guy in the lobby and they went up to the booth. It was all so low-key it really didn't stand out at the time. But I figure I should call the detective about it, right?"

Her intonation suggested the best answer I could give her would be "no."

"Sadly, yes," I said.

"He's going to think I'm an idiot."

"Yes, but he thinks everyone is an idiot. You can't take it personally. Do you remember what the guy looked like?"

Tracy scrunched up her face in thought. "I don't know. Middle-aged. White guy. Well-dressed. Your standard, boring middle-aged white dude." She set her to-go bag down on the table and leaned against the chair, shaking her head. "I'd just rather not go to the police if I don't have to."

"He's really not a bad guy," I said quietly. "I mean, deep down he's pretty okay." I turned to Megan for support on this argument. "Didn't you once say Fred has a caring aura?"

Megan considered this for a moment. "I think I said it was on the warm side of cool," she said, then quickly added, "but deep down, I think Fred's a good guy."

"Okay," Tracy said, not entirely convinced. "But if I do have to go talk to him, would you mind coming along? Moral support and all?"

I turned to Megan, thinking she'd find a quick and reasonable excuse to keep me from spending any more time than absolutely necessary with this leggy beauty. But instead, Megan was nodding in agreement.

"Sure, Eli would be happy to," she said with complete sincerity.

"That would be great," Tracy said. She thought about it for a moment longer, then picked up her to-go bag. "Anyway, thanks. Have a nice night."

She moved toward the door, missing the wave Megan gave her as she walked away. I turned to Megan, who was back to studying the menu.

"You're okay with me shuttling her to the police station?"

"She's been through a lot. It would probably help," Megan said without looking up from the menu.

"A beautiful woman, emotionally vulnerable. New in town, no friends to speak of. None of that is an issue?"

"What sort of issue?" Megan said, finally looking up from the menu. Her clear blue eyes and radiant complexion showed no indication of even a hint of jealousy.

"Never mind," I said. Even if I had wanted to pursue it further I couldn't, as the waitress choose that moment to arrive at our table. We turned our attention to ordering what would ultimately be a fine if quiet dinner.

*   *   *

When we finished eating, the Minneapolis Mystics and their special guest, Quinton Moon, were still in the throes of their own lively evening of wine, food and stories.

I would have been fine just slipping out of the bar unnoticed, but Megan insisted we stop back and say goodnight to the group, who were in the midst of another loud round of laughter and drinks as we approached their table.

Quinton stood—of course he did—and kissed Megan's hand before giving me a firm and manly handshake.

"I hope to see you again quite soon," he said to Megan, and then turned his steely eyes on me. "Both of you, I mean."

"Oh, I hope we do," Megan said a little too quickly and emphatically for my liking.

"Until then, I bid you goodnight." It might have been my imagination, but it seemed like he clicked his heels together at the end of his statement. For my part, I wanted to put as much distance between him and Megan as I could.

"Yeah, catch you later," I said, taking Megan's arm and steering her toward the front door.

The cold night was made even chillier by my mood as we crossed the street, walking up the hill to Megan's duplex.

"There's something about that guy I don't like," I finally muttered, half aloud and half under my breath.

"What?"

"Nothing," I said, recognizing the more I complained about him, the less attractive it would make me. And the more attractive it would make him. A classic no-win situation.

"We should find time to have dinner with Quinton while he's in town," Megan said. "Just the three of us. I think you two have a lot in common."

I bit my lip for a second, sorting through possible responses.

"Sure," I finally said. "As long as it doesn't interfere with me helping Tracy."

"Oh, I don't think it will," she said with a smile. "Aren't you coming in?"

I thought about it for a moment, seething a bit at her interest in Quinton and her complete lack of interest in the threat posed by the attractive theater manager. Not that there was an actual threat, of course. But the fact that Megan saw no risk with Tracy—when all I saw were warning bells and sirens with Quinton—was making me a little insane.

"No," I said, scrambling for some plausible deniability. "It's late, I'm tired, I have to get up early, I told Harry I'd help him with inventory."

I would have continued with several more items in the list, but I seemed to have satisfied her. She gave me a warm kiss and touched my cheek.

"Okay, we'll talk tomorrow. Be safe walking home," she added as she unlocked the door.

"It's just across the street and down the block," I said.

"I know that. Be careful," she said as the door swung open. "And I'll email Quinton about getting together for dinner," she added as the door swung shut.

"No problem," I said to the closed door. "Want me to invite Tracy?"

Of course there was no response, which was just as well. I turned on my heels and attempted to storm away, but the slippery conditions sucked the intended drama right out of my unseen exit.

I wasn't really giving the outside world my full attention as I stepped out into the street through a gap in the mounds of shoveled snow that lined the sidewalk. As I cautiously negotiated the icy patches in the pavement, I turned to see headlights barreling toward me on the slick and slippery street.

The car was making no attempt to slow down on the slick road. In fact, I got the distinct impression it was speeding up as it raced toward me. I scrambled to get out of the way, but the frozen, polished street didn't afford much traction. I considered turning back, but that option didn't look like it would provide any stronger footing. I made a last-ditch attempt to dive out of the careening car's path, and thought I'd been successful until I felt its side view mirror slam into my hip and rocket me to the icy pavement.

I hit the ground hard as the car torpedoed past me, my shoulder slamming into the roadway. I rolled over in time to see the car burn through the stoplight at 48th Street, no brake lights in evidence, before it disappeared into the snowy darkness of Chicago Avenue.

CHAPTER 6

"You must have the police on speed dial by now."

"Sadly, you're not the first person to make that suggestion. However, in this rare instance, I was not the one placing the call."

Harry looked up from his position behind the counter. Given the events of the previous night, I had chosen to sleep in and skipped our traditional breakfast. He'd eaten without me, unlocked the shop, and was ready to face the day. I had wandered down the stairs moments before and was still in a bit of a sleepy daze.

"Who placed the call? An alert citizen?" He put a spin on the last two words which bordered on sarcastic.

"Someone in one of the apartments happened to be looking out and saw the accident. From their perspective, it really looked like the car hit me, so they called 911."

"But you were unscathed?"

I shrugged. "I'm a little scathed. I've got a black and blue mark in the shape of Peru on my hip, and my shoulder is pretty sore, but I seem to be otherwise unharmed." I touched a hand tenderly to my hip and quickly pulled it away. "Relatively unharmed."

"And the culprit? Was he duly apprehended?" Harry made some minute adjustments to a row of thumb tips, and then began to sort and re-box some playing cards left over from a demonstration the previous afternoon.

I shook my head. "The cop I talked to said they found the car, crashed into a light pole about a quarter of a mile away. It had been stolen and abandoned."

"Stolen and abandoned," Harry repeated softly, raising one eyebrow. "Remarkable."

"He said it had one of those auto-starters which turns the car on when the temperature drops below a certain point. It was parked about a block away and the owner hadn't locked the car."

"Foolish."

"A crime of opportunity is what he called it."

"And there you were, standing in the way of opportunity."

"I guess so," I said as I sat on one of the stools. I sighed deeply and looked around the shop.

"Other than that, how was your evening, Mrs. Lincoln?" This was a favorite expression of Harry's and it never failed to produce at least a smile, which it successfully achieved on this particular morning.

"It was okay, I suppose," I finally said, deciding not to go into greater detail.

"I must say, you missed the boat when you declined Quinton's dinner invitation. He was delightful and the evening was a treat, a treat, I tell you."

Harry suddenly clapped his hands together and stepped around the counter to face me. "In fact, the sly bastard even pulled off the ice block trick."

He knew this would pique my interest, and he was correct. "Max Malini's ice block trick? The one he did for Dai Vernon?"

"The very one."

Malini's ice block trick was legendary in magic circles. According to those who were in attendance, a couple hours into a dinner with Vernon and several other magicians, Malini was doing some innocent coin tricks at the table. At the conclusion of one effect, for which he had borrowed another diner's hat, he lifted the hat to reveal an actual block of ice, completely frozen, sitting on the table.

"With a block of ice?" I continued. "An actual block of ice?"

"The very same." Harry pulled up another stool and hiked himself up on it. He leaned in close and spoke in a conspiratorial tone, despite the fact we were the only two people in the store. "It was a thing of beauty. He was doing some very fine coin work, nothing we hadn't seen but with some divine twists on the old techniques. Really elegant stuff. Even Sam was impressed. He actually whistled."

Being the resident coin man in the Mystics, getting more than a grunt from Sam Esbjornson when you performed a coin trick in front of him was considered the highest of praise.

"He whistled?" My tone suggested I recognized hyperbole when I heard it, but Harry immediately began to shake his head.

"Like a train he whistled. Anyway, Quinton's in the middle of a routine and he asks to borrow a hat, so I gave him mine."

Harry's hat was legendary, a fine wide-brimmed black fedora that had traveled more of the world than I was likely to ever see.

"I handed him my hat, he set it over the coins on the table and what do you think was sitting there when he pulled it away?"

"A block of ice?" I said this tentatively, not wanting to believe it was true.

"Sure as I'm sitting here. An actual, freezing cold block of ice."

"How big was it?"

"It fit under my hat, but just barely. Frozen as the day is long." Harry shook his head, smiling at the memory. "It was a thing of beauty, Buster, a thing of beauty."

I felt a pang of regret, probably similar to the one felt by any magician who had declined the dinner invitation with Malini on that fateful night so long ago.

"Sorry I missed it," I said quietly. "Sounds like quite an evening."

"Oh, it was one for the record books," Harry said as he climbed down from the stool and headed back behind the counter. "I can only imagine what miracles he has in store for us at his lecture this Saturday. Oh, by the way, that theater manager from next door stopped by earlier. Looking for you."

I twisted around on the stool, exacerbating the tender spot on my hip. "Really?" I asked, trying not to wince. "What did she want?"

"She wanted you," Harry said.

"What for? For what?"

"No details were forthcoming. I said I'd let you know she was looking for you. Which I have now done." He studied me for a long moment while I considered what this might mean. "She said she'd be at the theater all morning," he added.

"Thanks," I said, still considering the implications. "Well, shall we get started on inventory?"

Harry gave me a long, penetrating look. "I suspect our inventory project will suffer if we are lacking your full attention. Why don't I give it a start while you conduct your business next door?" I started to object, but he held up a hand. "Our inventory has sat here untabulated for months. I believe it can wait a tad longer without suffering undue negative consequences."

I could tell there would be no further discussion on the topic, so I headed next door without even stopping to grab my coat.

I was surprised that the first of the several doors I tried opened immediately. I stepped into the quiet theater lobby and stopped, listening for any sounds of human habitation. I could hear voices, but after a moment it became clear it was a radio playing somewhere within the confines of the theater.

"Hello?" I said both loudly and tentatively. A moment later, my call was echoed by a distant "Hello?" Seconds later, Tracy peered around a corner, a smile breaking across her face when she saw it was me.

"Oh, hi," she said, as she crossed toward me quickly. "Did I leave the door unlocked?" she said as she sailed past me and turned the bolt on the glass door. Not only did she turn the bolt, but also the latches at the top and the bottom of the door. She gave each of the other doors a test push, to ensure they were also locked.

"Harry said you stopped by," I began and then realized I had nothing to add to that thought, but I plowed ahead anyway. "Earlier this morning."

"Yeah," she said, turning away from the final door once she was satisfied it was secure. She realized I had just observed her check five doors right in a row.

"Sorry," she said with a shrug. "I think this whole Tyler James thing has me a little spooked.

"Understandably."

She ran a hand through her hair, which today looked properly combed and coiffed. "I wanted to let you know I went down and talked to the homicide detective this morning, first thing."

"How'd it go?"

She playfully swatted the question away with her hand. "Piece of cake," she said. "In fact, I think I bored him."

"I'm glad it wasn't the ordeal you thought it might be."

"Not at all."

We stood there awkwardly, having quickly exhausted our supply of conversational gambits. And then a thought occurred to me.

"You know," I began, glancing around the lobby, "as long as you're here, I'm wondering if I could ask a quick favor?"

"Sure thing."

"It has to do with the murder," I continued slowly. "This is hard to explain, but for reasons I don't completely fathom, I'll be talking to a number of suspects in the case this week. It might be helpful if I took a closer look at the crime scene."

She broke into a wide smile. "Look at you. Who are you, Encyclopedia Brown?"

I shook my head. "More like Wikipedia Brown. I get some of the facts right, but people keep changing them on me." This joke got the response it deserved, which was small, so I continued. "If now isn't good, I can do it another time."

She shook her head and began to glide through the lobby. "Not a problem. The police finished their work up there. However, no one has stopped by to reinstall the projection room door they took off."

"I wouldn't hold my breath on that," I suggested.

"Yeah, I figured as much. Anyway, go on up and snoop to your heart's content. I'll be in my office, placing Help Wanted ads online." She gestured to the right and I headed up to the booth, while she turned to the left, moving toward what I assumed was her office.

We both turned back at the same moment, laughed self-consciously when we caught each other doing it, and then continued on our respective paths.

The house lights were on in the auditorium, but it was a dim climb to the top of the stairs to the projection booth. The large metal door had been set awkwardly against the back wall and the booth consisted of an open doorway with inky blackness beyond.

I reached an arm slowly around the doorframe and felt delicately for the light switch, hoping against hope the lights weren't controlled by a string dangling somewhere in the middle of the dark room. My fingers fumbled and then found pay dirt. I flipped one of two switches and the fluorescent lights hummed to life in the small space.

And it really was a small room, much smaller than I had remembered. Hence the term booth, I thought as I stepped through the entry and took the room in. The body was gone, of course, as was the envelope of money on the worktable. The police had also taken the two film canisters, which made me wonder for a moment how the killer had transported the film reels out of the building. I suppose in his, or her, haste, they grabbed the most valuable item in the room and made a dash for it, leaving both the cash and the canisters.

There was a dark brown stain on the ground, but I noticed the toilet was no longer leaking, as no water puddles were visible on the floor.

I turned and surveyed a bulletin board on the wall behind me. It held take-out menus from nearby restaurants and an old newspaper article about the previous owners of the theater, a nice couple that I only remembered vaguely from my childhood days haunting the theater. Also tacked to the board was a photo strip, one of those four-snapshot affairs you get from photo booths which used to turn up at county fairs and have now found new life at weddings and parties with a budget.

The photo showed a man and a woman intertwined, making a series of faces at the camera. I assumed the guy was Tyler James, at a younger point in his life, but the woman didn't spark any recognition in me. I studied the photo strip for a long time, trying to read something from their multiple, goofy expressions, but the only lasting impression I got was they appeared to be drunk or high. Or both.

I stepped across the room and looked out the window on the far wall, with its dull view of the side of our building. Glancing up, I could see I had left the light on in my living room, but the window offered a far less expansive view of my space than my window offered of the booth. I stared up for several seconds, but the only valuable information I took away was that my living room ceiling was in desperate need of repainting.

I turned and surveyed the booth from this new angle, hoping to see something—anything—which might spark an idea. I scanned the room for several long seconds, but nothing jumped out at me. Whatever secrets the room had, it was keeping them to itself. I moved past the large projector, which blocked access to one of the square holes that looked into the auditorium. The other hole had only the Blu-ray cart in front of it, providing enough space for me to lean over it and peer down into the theater.

It was a long way from the booth to the screen, farther than I might have guessed. The curtains were open, revealing the large blank white screen, with a small stage platform in front of it.

Red exit lights shone on either side of the screen, reminding me there was one other location in the theater I should check out if I wanted to be thorough in my ersatz investigation.

*   *   *

I parted the curtains which led to the exit on the left side of the screen, stepping immediately back into darkness. My hand groped in front of me until I felt the door, which opened with a quick push of its center bar.

Sunlight poured in and I squinted at the sudden brightness. I stood in the doorway while my eyes adjusted to the light, thinking the killer hadn't had to deal with this sudden change in light levels. It would have been dark, with only the alley lights and the reflection of light off the snow providing illumination. Of course, on a bright, moonlit night, that can be more than enough light to see quite a distance.

The view from the exit doorway didn't offer any immediate answers as to why the killer had stepped out, or why he then turned around and stepped back into the theater. Perhaps he had seen someone. Or perhaps someone had seen him. Whatever it was, it was enough to force him back into the theater in search of another form of egress.

Retracing those steps, I moved back into the building, once again parting the curtains and stepping into the auditorium as the exit door slammed shut behind me. My eyes reacted to the sudden low level of light and I squinted into the large space. My attention was drawn back up to the booth.

I had forgotten to turn off the lights, which were visible through the two square holes in the back wall, as well as through the now doorless entryway. That meant another hike all the way back up there. I grumbled to myself as I started up the aisle.

"You solve the mystery?"

I looked over to see Tracy, silhouetted in the lobby doorway.

"Not even close. And, like a moron, I left the lights on up in the booth."

"Don't worry about it," she laughed. "I have to go up there and test tonight's discs. Want me to unlock the lobby doors for you, or do you have more clues to ferret out?"

"Don't bother, I'm done here," I said. "I'll just go out the back," I added, gesturing to the exit over my shoulder. "Thanks for letting me play detective."

"Come over and play with me whenever you like," she said with a laugh as she turned and headed back toward her office.

I considered the implications of this offer for a moment and then quickly made my way back to the magic shop, this time via the alley. It was a short walk, but I really wished I had brought my coat.

I entered the magic shop's back room, expecting to see Harry in the midst of counting and cataloging the hundreds of products we carry. His filing system, such as it is, is just this side of haphazard, with most of the products stored and labeled in a manner that makes sense only to him. Or not.

But instead I discovered him seated at his desk, his feet up, happily paging through a book. He looked up when he heard me enter.

"Buster, this is wonderful. Simply wonderful."

I didn't recognize the book he was reading. "A new book?"

"Yes, certainly, but also an instant classic. Quinton Moon gave it to me. It's an advance copy of his new book on magic theory. Don't worry," he said, probably reacting incorrectly to the pained expression on my face, "you can read it as soon as I'm done with it."

"What happened to inventory? I thought it was a priority."

"Priorities shift," he said without looking up. "We'll get to inventory later. Or tomorrow. Or later tomorrow."

Before I could comment on the likelihood of that alleged event, my phone twittered. I pulled it out and scanned the incoming text, finishing up my reading with a small exclamation.

"Fan mail from some flounder?" Harry asked as he licked his index finger and delicately turned a page in the book. The question was one of his favorite phrases from the old *Rocky & Bullwinkle* cartoons he had watched with me when I was a kid, laughing at jokes it would take me years to comprehend.

"The police have finished their first interview and now it's my turn. And it's with Clifford Thomas."

At the sound of this name, Harry lowered the book. "Clifford Thomas? You're going to talk to Clifford Thomas? *The* Clifford Thomas?"

I re-looked at the text from Deirdre. "That would appear to be the case," I said.

Harry's eyes twinkled. "Any chance you could get a book or two autographed for me?"

CHAPTER 7

Harry's "book or two" turned into five, all hardcovers, which I lugged under my arm as I made my way up the immaculately shoveled sidewalk in front of Clifford Thomas' Summit Avenue home.

The lumber barons who built St. Paul had erected giant tributes to their wonderfulness on Summit Avenue, in the form of block after block of truly impressive mansions. The one Clifford Thomas called home was both typical and atypical. It was certainly large and imposing, but it also possessed a certain whimsical charm, including cast iron bats built into the fence that surrounded the house, and two decapitated snowmen in the front yard.

The house included a turret and a widow's walk, the latter of which had been decorated with a large Santa Claus figure. The illuminated leg lamp from the movie *A Christmas Story* was visible in the front window.

Given the level of his publishing success, I wouldn't have been surprised if it was the original prop from the movie. In fact, given how rich Clifford Thomas was, that could have been Santa himself taking a shift up there on the widow's walk.

A former newspaper reporter and freelance critic, Thomas had made his name as the author of a series of mystery and thriller novels, all set in Minnesota and each featuring a clue-laden and weather-related title. Under my arm, I held Harry's copies of *Blizzard Watch*, *The Lake Effect*, *The Night of Black Ice*, *Polar Vortex*, and his latest bestseller, *The Endless Killing Frost*.

I had been surprised Clifford Thomas answered his own phone and was equally surprised when he answered his own front door. Despite being in the dregs of winter, he sported a healthy tan that appeared to have come from the sun, rather than a bottle or tanning bed. Perfect teeth formed a perfect smile as he put out a large, warm, and soft hand.

"I'm Clifford Thomas, you must be Eli Marks," he said, gesturing with his free hand that I should step out of the cold and into the massive foyer.

His introduction was unnecessary, as his face was just about as well-known as his books, at least around these parts. No Salinger-esque reclusive lifestyle for the Twin Cities' own Clifford Thomas. His face adorned local magazines, he appeared frequently on the local PBS fundraising telethon, hosted celebrity-packed charity events and was said to personally hand out candy to trick-or-treaters each Halloween.

Needless to say, he offered full-sized candy bars to the kids, not the loathsome "fun size."

"I'm surprised you greet guests yourself," I said. "I imagine you get a lot of fans knocking on this door."

"I do get a lot of fans who come to the house. Some I let in, some I don't."

"Depending on your mood?"

"Depending on the fan," he said with a smile and a wink. "Oh, don't bother taking your shoes off. I have dogs."

I was willing to take him at his word, but the surroundings belied his assertion. The immaculate wood floor showed no obvious evidence of canine occupation. He ushered me into the foyer and it did not disappoint. The lumber baron who built the house clearly had access to only the best timber and displayed it stunningly across the walls, the stairs, the banister and even an inlaid wood ceiling.

Clifford moved energetically toward a bookcase that lined one wall. "Can I get you something to drink while we talk?" he asked, looking over his shoulder at me.

"I'm good," I said, not entirely sure why we were walking at full speed toward a bookcase. Before I could form the question, the answer appeared. The bookcase slid open, parting like the doors on the Starship Enterprise. I may have been mistaken, but the process might have even included the *swish* sound effect from the TV series.

Clifford turned and beamed as we entered the room. "I have to spend my money on *something*." He laughed by way of explanation. "And who doesn't want a secret room behind a set of bookcases?"

"I can't speak for the population at large," I said as we entered the big, airy room. "But it's something I've wanted since I was, like, five. Please tell me you don't also have a bat pole to the Bat Cave."

"If I did, would I admit it?"

"Probably not."

The room appeared to be a mix of library, office and sitting room. One wall consisted of large, leaded-glass windows, the corners featuring a bit of stained glass. Two other walls were lined with actual bookcases, while a large writer's desk took up the center of the room. Atop the desk was a vintage IBM Selectric typewriter, and next to it a stack of typing paper, along with various correspondence.

Clifford must have recognized the five hardcovers were weighing me down, for he gestured to the desk while he scooped up the typewritten pages and straightened them into a neat pile. "Returned and remaindered?" he asked, gesturing to the stack of books I'd lugged in.

I shook my head. "My uncle, he's a fan. He was hoping for an autograph. Or five."

"Not a problem." He smiled as he made a final adjustment to the neat stack of paper. He looked up and caught me watching him.

"The latest novel?"

He shrugged. "Maybe. I'm in the midst of rereading and editing. Not sure if it's ready to go or not. Let me tell you, Eli, novel writing can be a real bear. Plus being on deadline is a headache all its own. I'm being pressured to turn it in, but happily I've reached a point where I can say they'll get it when they get it and have the clout to back that up."

"That must drive your publisher a little crazy."

He shrugged. "They've learned to live with it. They know they'll get the book—and the all-important title—when I'm ready to hand it over."

I glanced down at the classic Selectric, which was in pristine shape, not beginning to show any of the wear and tear you'd expect to find. "You know, I had read somewhere that you still write on a typewriter, but I always thought it was just PR."

"It's both true *and* PR," he said, gesturing to an antique couch as he took a seat in a matching high back chair. "Like it or not, it's all PR." There was a moment of silence while we both settled in.

"All right, Eli, I understand we're here to talk about murder."

His bluntness took me by surprise. "Yes, I suppose we are."

He straightened the seam of his pressed trousers and I saw for the first time that while his shirt and pants could easily have been hand-tailored, for footwear he preferred the nostalgic look and feel of plain old, bright red Jack Purcell sneakers. These contrasted nicely with the Rolex on his wrist.

"Our friends in Homicide filled me in on the details of the murder of Tyler James and gave me the impression I was under consideration as a possible suspect. I understand all that. What I don't understand is how you fit into this. They said you found the body, but that doesn't naturally lead to conducting interviews, does it?"

I shook my head. "I think there is no precedent for this. All I know is I'm supposed to talk to the suspects after the police have finished with them."

"Oh, sad to say, I don't think the police have finished with me. You see, I knew Tyler James well, and had made a handful of purchases through him. I told the police as much."

"That doesn't necessarily mean anything."

He shrugged. "Perhaps, perhaps not. We'd had some heated negotiations in the past, Tyler and I. I'm sure at least one of those arguments was witnessed by others. Plus, of course, I have no alibi for the night of the murder. I've convicted people in my books with far less compelling evidence."

"How do you feel about that?"

He smiled at me wryly. "Is this a therapy session?"

"I'm not sure what this is."

"Honestly, I feel intrigued," he said, settling back into the chair. "I have written more than my fair share of locked room stories, but this is the first time I've found myself as a character thrust into the midst of the mystery."

"Any thoughts on a solution?"

"You mean as a mystery writer as opposed to a murder suspect?"

"Whichever works."

"They say the difference between fact and fiction is fiction has to make sense. Sadly, real life doesn't always work out that cleanly."

He smiled and continued. "Eli, I love locked room mysteries. That's why I write them with," he gestured around the room, "no small amount of success. I think their appeal lies in the fact that each of us, in our experience, is a victim of our own locked room mystery. We're locked into this thing called life, we're doomed, and we end up dead. With no real understanding of who killed us and why."

"That's very philosophical."

"The best mysteries are ultimately primal. I suspect your uncle would agree with me," he said. "As for this case in particular, one or two elements don't quite make sense to me."

"Such as?"

"For one, if in fact Tyler was in the midst of a transaction involving *London After Midnight*—a mouthwatering possibility, if it's true—why did it go south? All the elements of the sale were in place. What went wrong?"

I considered this. "Clearly something."

"Clearly. The other odd element is simply the amount of money. While $75,000 is still, even in this day, a lot of money, I believe it's far below the market value—or perhaps I should say black market value—of that movie."

"A down payment?" I ventured.

"In fiction, these are questions which would demand to be answered. In real life, we may not be so lucky." He glanced at his watch. "Eli, it's coming up on lunch time."

I was on my feet before he could continue. "I understand. I've taken up enough of your time."

He waved a hand at me. "On the contrary, I was going to ask if you'd like to continue this conversation over lunch. I was just going to walk to the club, assuming another blizzard hasn't descended on us while we spoke," he added, turning to inspect the weather conditions through the large windows.

"It would not surprise me," I said, not sure if I should stay standing or return to my position on the couch. "This is the only winter in memory in which I was actually concerned about coming down with snow blindness."

Clifford suddenly turned from the windows and tilted his head to one side, his eyes narrowing. "Snow blindness," he said slowly. "Snow blind. I like that. I like that very much." He jumped up and moved quickly to his work desk.

He yanked on a black knob on the front of the desk and a small, wooden board slid into view. From where I stood, I could see a sheet of paper had been taped to the surface and the sheet was covered with handwritten scribblings. Clifford grabbed a pen and added a notation to the sheet.

"Snow Blind," he said with satisfaction. "Oh, that's a good one. Thank you, Eli."

He slid the board closed and then looked over, recognizing the look of confusion on my face.

"Oh, I keep a running list of possible book titles," he said, gesturing toward the desk. "I've learned that whenever I think of one, I have to write it down or else it will disappear into the ether, never to return. Such is the life of a writer," he added with a smile. "Now let's go get some lunch and talk a bit more about murder."

* * *

I admit to having a preconceived notion—okay, let's call it a prejudice—about the Summit Club. It's a legendary institution in the Twin Cities, with an exclusive membership and a storied history. My impression of the place had always been that when really rich people wanted to make moderately rich people feel inferior, they would invite them to the Summit Club.

Situated on Summit Avenue and overlooking downtown St. Paul, the club completely lived up to its reputation. I felt instantly out of place the moment we walked through the massive front door. To be honest, my deep feelings of inferiority kicked in as soon as we approached the massive building, which was half mansion, half quasi-castle and one hundred percent imposing.

Clifford Thomas had not been kidding when he suggested we walk to lunch. The club was less than a block from his own mansion, and upon arrival I got the immediate impression he was a frequent, perhaps daily, visitor.

We were quickly settled into what I assumed was his regular table, right next to a large set of windows presenting a stunning view of downtown St. Paul below and the river and rolling hills beyond. Within seconds I was handed a daily menu on what felt like real parchment, while the waiter set a tumbler of something with ice in front of Clifford. The waiter, an older rail-thin man with a feathering of white hair across his otherwise bald head, stood by silently while I quickly scanned the options on the menu, finally landing on something I recognized.

"A BLT," I said, handing back the menu and trying to get comfortable in the chair, which had apparently been designed without comfort in mind.

"And to drink?"

I glanced over at Clifford who was sipping his unknown concoction and I immediately decided not to blindly emulate him, as that might lead to actual blindness or at the very least passing out in the foyer.

"Hot tea would be great, thanks."

The waiter nodded and moved away as quickly and quietly as he had arrived.

"Aren't you eating?" I asked.

"He knows what I want. I'm a creature of habit in most things, but especially lunch."

"This place is impressive," I said, scanning the room, which held maybe twenty small tables and currently about ten other diners.

"I believe that is its sole ambition," Clifford said. He smiled and looked around the room, where the quiet buzz of conversation seemed to magically stay at exactly the same volume. "My ex-wife hated this place. She called it The Elitist Club."

I had forgotten he even had an ex-wife, and might not have known about her if not for my late aunt Alice's reading habits. "Oh, yes. My aunt Alice used to read her books."

"Why did she stop?"

"She died," I said.

He gave me a sympathetic nod. "As good a reason as any to stop reading someone's books," he said. "But not the reason I stopped reading hers."

"She writes mysteries too, right?" I ventured.

"That she does. The Mother Goose Murder Series," he said flatly. "She has done quite well for herself. Lives in Manhattan, on the park. Last I heard she was dating a police detective."

"That's funny," I said.

"Haven't seen the humor in it yet," he said, smoothly handing off his empty glass as the silent waiter placed a new one on the table in front of him.

"No," I said, trying to pull myself out of this unforeseen hole. "I mean, I have an ex-wife and she's also involved with a police detective. Married to him, actually."

"Ah," he said taking a sip of the fresh drink. "Is that why she's your ex? A crowded bed?"

I nodded. "Yes," I said, not sure I enjoyed his turn of phrase.

"My marriage fell victim to something just as primal," he said, his gaze falling on the skyline over my shoulder. I waited, not sure if I was meant to delve further. He continued without me. "Jealousy. Simple jealousy. I can admit it now. I thought I should be the famous writer in the family, but fate clearly had other plans."

I nodded, but at this point I wasn't sure he was even really still talking to me.

"When she wrote the first book, *The Mother Goose Murders*, I thought it was a lark. You know, a passing phase. That is, until her book rocketed past my latest on *The New York Times'* bestseller list. Then came *Murder at St. Ives*, and *Simple Simon: A Taste for Murder*." He didn't exactly spit out the titles, but his tone made it clear he had little love for them. His eyes shifted back to me. "And suddenly she's the one on the book tour, she's the one making movie deals, she's the one everyone wants to see and touch and purr over." He took another long sip.

"But," I said quietly, not sure I was really part of this conversation, "your books are bestsellers. You have movie offers. You're..." I couldn't think of the right words. "A big deal," I finally said.

He clucked his tongue. "Of course, I knew that on a conscious level, but that's not where jealousy does its best work. No, Eli, it's a persistent little devil, eating away at a relationship, destroying the underpinnings before you even realize the level of damage it's doing." He looked up to see the waiter had returned, with a sandwich for me and a bowl of soup and another drink for Clifford.

"Heed my advice," he said in conclusion, as he stirred the soup absently. "Guard against jealousy at every turn. If not," he said with a laugh as he gestured around the grand, impressive room full of millionaires, "someday you may end up like me."

"I had the strangest dream last night."

Clifford was still talking, but we were no longer seated within the warm confines of the Summit Club. After a long, long lunch that mostly consisted of drinks for Clifford, he had wisely decided he needed a nap and we were in the midst of making the short trek back to his house. His gait was unsteady and I kept one hand near his elbow as we navigated the light snow which had fallen during our afternoon sojourn.

"I dreamt I had killed someone," he said as we crossed Summit Avenue. My ears, buried as they were under my stocking cap, perked up, and I did my best not to make any sound of surprise as we made a left, heading down the block toward his mansion.

"I mean," he continued, "in the dream, I had this vague memory of killing someone, but I had somehow blocked it out. But when I woke up, the feeling of the dream stayed with me. Has that ever happened to you?" He turned toward me and I shrugged.

"I'm not sure I know what you mean."

He stopped in the center of the sidewalk. "I think it's a fascinating feeling—to suddenly have the sense you've committed this horrible crime, but it's only a vague feeling and you have no actual memory or proof of the incident. It exists—if it exists at all— in the never-never land of dreams." He looked around to get his bearings, spotted his house and continued toward it, with me one step behind on the narrowly shoveled walk.

"Like a repressed memory?" I offered.

"Yes," he said, turning to look over his shoulder as we walked. His eyes were narrow slits and he appeared to be having trouble focusing them. "I think that might be the premise for the next book," he added as he turned back and continued toward his house. I followed and nearly collided with him when he suddenly stopped and pivoted around.

"And I'll use the title you gave me," he said loudly, clearly excited by the sudden flow of ideas. "*Snow Blindness*. That's perfect. I have to go write this down. Eli, never forget to write the good ideas down. There are some who say good ideas never really go away, but in my limited experience that's hardly ever the case."

With renewed energy he spun around and increased his pace, making it difficult for me to catch up to him. I doubled my speed and caught up as he climbed the steps to the massive front door. I stood at the bottom of the steps and looked up as he inserted his key in the lock. He turned to me as he pushed the door open.

"Thank you, Eli," he said, smiling down at me. "Thank you for a most productive afternoon."

"Sure," I said. "About the books I brought for my uncle—"

Too late. The door shut with a thudding finality and then all was quiet.

I looked up at the dark house, as one light popped on in what I guessed was the library we had sat in earlier. The only other light came from the Santa on the widow's walk. From this low angle, there was nothing jolly about this old St. Nick. The gray light of dusk and the dim bulb inside the plastic figure gave his features a decidedly menacing appearance.

The snow continued to fall lightly as I quickly headed back down the walk, past the decapitated snowmen, realizing for the first time just how cold and dark the day had turned.

CHAPTER 8

"You may need to reassess your definition of 'crowded,' in terms of its relationship to this store."

It was a convoluted thought, but I knew exactly what Nathan meant. A perpetually low-energy children's magician, Nathan had a slow, thoughtful way of speaking which could be lulling in its monotone cadences. His perceptions may have been slow in coming but were nearly always dead on, and his thoughts on what now constituted a crowd were no exception.

In the past, when we referred to Chicago Magic as being "crowded," we were likely referring to a sudden rush of customers amounting to at most five people. Five was a crowd, six would be thought of as crushing, and with the exception of a handful of magic club meetings when I was a kid, I couldn't remember when we'd had more than a dozen people in the store at the same time.

A quick and likely inaccurate head count on my part totaled at least twenty-five people, and the jingle of the bell over the door signaled the arrival of even more patrons.

"You're going to need to put out more chairs," Nathan said without recognizing the understatement he was making.

"Hell, we're going to have to buy more chairs," I said. "I'll go over to the bar and see what I can borrow. I think we're going to have to move this whole thing into the shop in back. Can you head back there and make some room?"

Nathan nodded. He turned left while I turned right and twenty minutes later the back room was set with a charmingly mismatched array of chairs. Every blessed one of them was occupied, along with a line of people in SRO positions against the back wall.

"This guy must be pretty good," Nathan murmured quietly. "You've seen him, right, this guy we're seeing?"

"Who?" I asked, having lost track of his question as I did a quick head count, giving up after I passed thirty heads.

"This magician. Quinton Moon. He's supposed to be great, right?"

I turned sharply to Nathan, expecting to see a wicked leer, but there was no sense of taunting in his expression.

"Yeah," I said. "We saw him the other night. He's not bad."

Nathan nodded slowly and looked around the room. "This is quite a crowd for being not bad," he said with typical understatement.

As if on cue, at that moment the back door swung open and Quinton strode in, looking like Dr. Zhivago as the wind swirled a circling cascade of snow around him. He wore a long, gray duster and his dark hair was swept back in a styled-but-not-too-styled casual look.

Harry, all bundled and blustery, stepped in behind him, his eyes growing wide at the sight of the mob which occupied our normally empty back room.

"You're late," I whispered to Harry as the adoring fans slowly approached Quinton, seeming to bask in his glow.

"We stopped for breakfast and then we gave him a quick spin around the lakes."

"We?"

As if in answer, the door opened again, revealing Franny Higgins and, right on her heels, Megan.

Franny is a tiny bird-like woman, so small that Megan nearly towers over her.

Both are psychics, with Megan still floundering in her amateur status while Franny makes a good living as a phone psychic, putting in banker's hours and rarely offering psychic observations outside of her nine-to-five schedule.

In the past several months, she and Harry have been spending more and more time together, which has been as charming to watch as it was puzzling.

A staunch debunker of psychics throughout his career, I was surprised to see Harry seemed to be able to set all that aside in his growing relationship with Franny. For his part, Harry saw no real conflict.

"Your late aunt Alice was a dyed in the wool Republican," he told me. "Besides cancelling out each other's votes at every election, I made that work for over fifty years. This is hardly any different."

Megan caught my eye at that moment and I set aside my musings on Harry's relationships.

"Hi there," I said, looking from her to Franny and Harry, who were both helping Quinton with his coat. "The three of you picked up Quinton this morning?"

"Harry asked Franny to drive and she was afraid it was too slippery," Megan explained. "I volunteered. Of course, then we ended up being early because it wasn't slippery at all, so all four of us went to breakfast and then took a quick detour around a couple of the lakes. Q wanted to see them."

"Q?"

She laughed. "He said I could call him Q. People call him that. I thought it was cute."

I struggled to quickly craft a James Bond joke out of all this, but sadly came up short.

"Q, huh," I said, working hard to keep anything resembling a tone out of my voice. "How was your breakfast?" I continued as casually as possible.

"Not bad," she said, all innocent. Or perhaps I was imagining it. Or not. "How was yours?"

I shrugged. "Half a stale Pop Tart and a piece of leftover pizza. And orange juice," I said, turning and pretending to be interested in something across the room.

"Breakfast of champions," she said.

We stood silently side by side for several more seconds.

"Are you staying for the lecture?" I finally said. "Or have you had enough of Q for one day?"

"Hardly," she laughed. "He's a real charmer. But no, Franny needs to get to work, I need to open the store, and I really don't want to know how he does any of those amazing illusions."

This gave me pause as I immediately registered that, in her mind, Quinton did *amazing illusions,* while I assumed I merely made my living doing *little tricks.*

"Okay, then," I said, glancing at my watch without noting the time. "We should probably get this party started."

"All right, I'll see you later."

I turned, planning to plant an oh-so-casual kiss on her cheek, but she was already halfway across the room. She joined Franny and after exchanging some pleasant words with Harry, they headed toward the door.

"Ladies. Ladies." A voice stopped them in their tracks. They turned to see Quinton.

He momentarily abandoned his flock and pushed across the room to give, I assumed, his goodbyes to the two women. I couldn't hear what he said, but given how Megan giggled and how Franny swatted him playfully on the arm, I gather it was nauseatingly charming. I stood there glowering and would have continued doing that for several more minutes if Nathan hadn't broken my concentration.

"Wow. Everybody loves him and he hasn't done a thing yet."

"That might be his best trick," I said through gritted teeth.

"If it is, I hope he teaches it this morning."

I am ashamed to admit it, but on some level I was really hoping the lecture would be a bust. I'm not proud of it, but there you have it. However, once again I was foiled, and once again he was brilliant.

Quinton performed for about forty-five minutes, offering one stunning illusion after another, without repeating anything he had done at the show earlier in the week. The audience of geeky magicians sat spellbound for the entire act, *oohing* and *ahhing* as if on cue at all the right moments.

Like he had done with his chamber show, this performance was an equal mix of old chestnuts polished into new life...and brand new effects which stunned me into a stupefied, grumpy silence. The final piece he introduced with, "This one is still rather new. I've only been working on it for fifteen years." This produced a laugh and then stunned silence as he performed a Three Card Monte routine with oversized playing cards that was absolutely mystifying.

The applause at the end of his act was long and passionate, and as they had done at the hotel show earlier in the week, the audience jumped to their feet. I imagined he must be getting tired of standing ovations. I'm sure I would be if that happened with any regularity at the end of my act. Or, for that matter, ever.

With the performance behind us, next came the lecture at which I assumed he—like many lecturing magicians—would offer some tidbits without providing any real information or insight into how he achieved his effects. And once again I was wrong. With an openness and candor which surprised me, he walked us through each illusion, freely giving up the details on every move, every sleight and his thinking behind what really works in a performance setting. His ideas were original, his approach was cutting-edge, and after the third explanation I was ready to trash my entire act and get a job at Trader Joe's washing the produce.

As I stewed, I also silently wished he had done his version of The Miser's Dream today, so I could learn how he made all but one of the coins vanish from the bucket in the final phase of the trick. As a fellow magician, I knew it was something I could take him aside later and ask. Given his open nature, he would very likely give me all the details and more. And yet, I didn't see myself ever stepping forward and asking that question.

For that matter, I could have put the same question to one of the Mystics, Sam Esbjornson, who did his own variation on The Miser's Dream. He didn't conclude his version with the disappearing coins, but odds were he would have a clue as to its solution. Yet for some reason my pride wouldn't let me ask, while my ignorance continued to drive me nuts.

As Quinton began the explanation of his Three Card Monte routine, I was surprised to see Harry, who had been sitting on a stool we'd grabbed from the store, get up and quietly step out of the back room. I followed him into the store, pulling back the curtain after stepping through it. Quinton's voice, now muffled, could be heard vaguely from the back room. He was talking about the value of time misdirection and his theory on the importance, in magic, of separating the cause from the effect.

"You had enough as well?" I asked Harry as we stepped into the shop.

Harry turned. He looked surprised to see I had followed him out.

"What's that?"

"You had enough of the lecture?" I repeated. "Me too. I mean, enough's enough, right?"

Harry shook his head. "On the contrary, I think it's the best lecture I've ever witnessed. Ever."

I furrowed my brow. "Then why did you leave?"

"He's about to explain his Three Card Monte routine," he began.

I nodded as I cut him off. "Right, and you already know how it's done. Pretty simple trick, really." In truth I had absolutely no idea how he had accomplished the illusion.

"On the contrary," Harry said. "It's such an amazing trick, I truly don't want to know how it's done." He registered the puzzled look on my face.

"Eli," he continued, "it's not often I can be fooled these days, and so when those opportunities arise, I pounce on them." He slid open the curtain which led to the upstairs apartments. "It's been an eventful morning," he said as he turned to me. "Be a dear and give Quinton a ride back to his hotel when this is all done, will you?"

He didn't wait for a response, and was out of sight before I had mustered even a plausible excuse to avoid the dreaded chore.

Having nothing else to do, I was reluctantly going to head back into the lecture when my phone began to buzz in my pocket. I had turned off the ringtone for the duration of the lecture, so I was forced to actually look at the phone to see who was calling.

"Morning, sunshine," I said, summoning an unnaturally cheery disposition, which was in sharp contrast to my actual mood. "What can I do for the District Attorney's office on this chilly, snowy Saturday?"

"How did it go with Clifford Thomas?" Deirdre said sharply, sidestepping any traditional greetings.

"How did it go?" I repeated. "Fine, I think. I didn't gather much insight, if that's what you mean. I had a nice sandwich and got to watch him get drunk."

"I'm taking it he didn't confess?"

"If he did, he did it so obliquely it sailed right over my head."

"Figures." I could hear rustling paper through the phone. "We have two more people you can talk to," she continued. "The conversations we had with them were no more enlightening than the one you had with Mr. Thomas. Can you write this down?"

I moved behind the counter and after some digging through drawers seemingly crammed with everything *but* paper and pen, I finally put together the proper set of tools.

"Shoot," I said and quickly scribbled down the names and phone numbers as she rattled them off. I read back the phone numbers to ensure accuracy.

"Anything else to report?" I asked as I stuffed the slip of paper into my pocket.

"Not much," she said with a sigh. "Information is coming in dribs and drabs. Turns out the projectionist was using a false name."

"Really," I said. "So he wasn't really Tyler James?"

"No, he took an imaginative leap from his actual name."

"Which was?"

"James Tyler."

"He gets points for simplicity. Anything else of note?"

I could hear her flipping through some more sheets of paper. "Fred brought the theater manager in for more questioning," she finally said. "Nothing to report there. Noteworthy background, though. Turns out she was a champion NCAA athlete."

This gave me pause. "But," I finally said, "Tracy's not black."

This produced a very familiar sigh from the other end of the line. "Not NAACP, you moron. NCAA. National Collegiate Athletic Association."

"Oh," I said. "My mistake," I added, fully cognizant of the fact that Deirdre had a personal understanding of my lack of sports knowledge. "Did she have any connection with Tyler? I mean James. Whatever."

"We checked, but her story holds up. They met when she took the job at the theater last spring. Before that she was playing ball for an international team in Japan."

"And Tyler. James. The projectionist," I finally settled on. "He'd been at the theater for years?"

"Fifteen years. No family to speak of. We searched his apartment and came up with some items that, if they aren't hot, are certainly warm. His bank accounts suggest he was doing a good business."

"Until the other night."

"Yes, his business took a sharp downturn the other night."

A pause while I searched my mind for any other pertinent or impertinent questions. "You still have one person to talk to off Mr. Lime's list?"

"That's right. And now you have two people to talk to."

"Looks like we both have work to do," I suggested.

"Whatever," was all she said, and then she hung up.

*   *   *

As he had done at his performance earlier in the week, Quinton took time to talk to each member of the audience at the conclusion of the lecture. This process started in the back room and gradually transitioned into the store proper, primarily because Quinton kept answering questions by referring people to products we sold in the shop. Before long, he was behind the counter, demonstrating products with consummate skill and, in the process, ringing up considerable sales for us.

"You should hire him full-time," Nathan suggested as we marveled at Quinton's skill with the customers. "Not only is he making money for you, but he didn't even bring any products of his own to sell."

Once he pointed this out I realized Nathan was correct. Magicians who toured the country giving lectures always, repeat, *always* had products to sell. They could range from simple photocopied lecture notes to books, DVDs, and even custom tricks and gaffs.

Quinton had none of these wares to proffer, but was instead doing a great job selling the items we had in the store—some of which had sat on the shelves for months or even years. If nothing else, he was certainly going to make the task of inventorying, when we finally got around to it, a lot easier.

As the crowd began to finally dwindle, I noticed one kid of about ten or eleven who was shyly standing off to one side of the store, surveying the action. It looked like he was gathering up the courage to approach Quinton, but he kept not making the move. I sidled up alongside him.

"Waiting to talk to Mr. Moon?" I asked quietly.

"I don't know," he shrugged. "Maybe." He kicked at the carpet with his tennis shoe and looked everywhere but at me.

"You know, when I was your age, I had a chance to meet Dai Vernon. Do you know who that is?" I figured he might know Criss Angel or David Blaine, but would be unlikely to know Vernon.

"The Professor, sure. And it's Dai," the kid said, pronouncing the name so it sounded like "day."

"Excuse me?"

"You said Dai," he continued, pronouncing it so it sounded like "dye." "People who knew him on the West Coast only pronounced it that way. But his true friends from the East Coast pronounced it 'Day.'"

I considered this for a moment. "I met him on the West Coast."

"Sure thing," he said, still looking nervous and avoiding my gaze.

"Look, I'm trying to give you a motivational pep talk. Do you want it or not?"

"I suppose," he nodded and I continued.

"I was about your age and my uncle had taken me to The Magic Castle in Los Angeles. The night we were there, Dai Vernon was sitting in his regular chair in the lounge. I knew who he was, I wanted to talk to him, but I was terrified. I mean, it was Dai Vernon," I said, consciously conforming to the kid's preferred pronunciation of the first name.

"What'd you do?" he said, finally looking up at me.

"I gathered all my courage and walked up to him and said, 'Professor, can you tell me what I'm doing wrong on my top change?'"

The kid's eyes went wide. "What did he say?"

"He said I was doing everything wrong," I said, letting the phrase settle in. I then repeated it, doing my fairly accurate impression of The Professor's nasally twang. "'You're doing everything wrong.'" Scratch any magician who spent any time with Vernon and he'll give you his own impression.

The kid smiled, either at the story or at the impression. "Really?"

I nodded. "Yep. Then he spent an hour showing me how to do it right. I'm really glad now I was brave enough to do it back then."

"And how's your top change?"

"Still sort of sucky." This made him laugh and then he saw a break in the action with Quinton. I gave him the slightest of shoves and he moved forward, gaining confidence as he crossed the shop. For his part, Quinton saw him coming and bent down to receive his question. He then spent the next fifteen minutes answering it for him.

It was a full two hours later when Quinton and I stepped out of the front door of the shop and I turned to lock the door. Harry hadn't come back downstairs so I made the executive decision to close up the store for the rest of the day.

I figured—given the size of the turnout for the lecture—every possible customer we possessed had already been in the store that morning and was unlikely to return.

"You are quite the demonstrator of products," I said as I pulled the door shut and waited to hear the reassuring *snick* of the lock slipping into place. I used my key to turn the deadbolt.

"Am I? Well, I did a stint as a magic demonstrator at Harrods while at University," Quinton said, turning up the collar of his long coat to the sharp wind which was whipping down Chicago Avenue. "Haven't done it for years, so I was a tad surprised at how quickly it all came back."

My mind toyed with a quick riposte about riding a bike and Bicycle brand playing cards, but I once again came up short. I headed toward the car, but in this mentally clouded state, I nearly collided with a ladder in the middle of the sidewalk. Quinton reached out and pulled me to safety.

I looked up to see a figure in a parka near the top of the ladder, adding large black metal letters to the theater's marquee. While the jacket did a great job of obscuring the figure inside it, when I saw the reach she had in extending her arm to add a letter to the marquee, I knew it had to be Tracy. Although I know literally nothing about basketball, I had to imagine that long arms would be something of an advantage in the game.

"Are you still short a little help?" I asked loudly, suddenly wondering to myself if tall people take offense when you use the word short around them.

She glanced around, wondering where the sound had come from, and then looked down at us. Her face was visible through the faux fur that enveloped the hood of the parka.

"I've learned that theater managers are like mailmen," she said, looking remarkable upbeat despite the cold conditions. "Rain, sleet, snow, hail. No game is ever called on account of weather."

I stepped back and surveyed her work. Currently it read: *Guess Who's Coming*.

"Guess Who's Coming," I said out loud slowly. "Clearly the first feature is *Guess Who's Coming to Dinner*."

"That is the favorite," she said, digging through the box which hung on one of the ladder's rungs and pulling out another letter. "Are you ready to double down on the rest of it?"

"Not quite," I said, squinting at the marquee, as if that action would somehow make me smarter. I turned to Quinton, who was watching this exchange with a bemused smile. "The theater runs these oddball double features," I explained, but he waved it away.

"Oh, yes, your uncle mentioned it when we drove by the theater earlier today. At that point, the marquee read, let me think..." He snapped his fingers. "It was *Gone With the Mighty Wind*." He looked up at the marquee again and hummed softly for a moment. "How about *Guess Who's Coming to My Dinner With Andre*?" he suggested.

"And we have a winner," Tracy said with a laugh. She descended two rungs of the ladder and put her hand out. "I'm Tracy, by the way."

"Well, Tracy By-The-Way, I'm Quinton Moon, and it is a sheer delight to meet you." He shook her hand, adding in a quick pat with the left hand to complete the action. Somehow he was able to turn every moment into a James Bond charm-fest.

"Quinton gave a lecture on magic this morning in the shop," I said, in a weak bid to stay in the conversation.

"I'll bet that was fun," Tracy said, her wicked smile visible within the confines of the parka hood.

"More likely tedious," Quinton said. "I prattled on at length, not at all sure what I said."

"He's being modest," I said, for some reason feeling the need to take on the role of his PR person. "The audience was spellbound."

"Oh! And that's another possible double feature for you, if I'm allowed to suggest," he said, his eyes twinkling. "*Spellbound For Glory.*"

Tracy laughed and I joined in halfheartedly. I had to admit it was a pretty good off-the-cuff suggestion.

"Thanks," she said. "I'll add it to my ever-growing list." She started to re-climb the ladder, then turned back when she reached the top. "Nice to meet you. Stop by anytime for some free popcorn."

"I will happily take you up on that kind offer if my schedule permits," he said with a tip of his hat, using the British pronunciation of the word "schedule" which I usually find charming, but not at present. "Good day."

He looked to me for direction as to where we were headed. I pointed him toward my car and we started to trudge toward it, my self-loathing-filled grumblings lost in the sound of traffic on the street.

"She seems like a charming girl, don't you think? I mean, she's no Megan, but delightful nonetheless."

I winced at his mention of Megan and nearly missed my turn onto the freeway. "Tracy?" I said, feigning ignorance. "I don't know her all that well, but yes, she seems nice."

"But no Megan," he repeated definitively.

"Yes. I mean no." I merged into traffic and then attempted to merge this conversation into a different direction. "You have a corporate gig this week?"

"Yes," he said. "An insurance group. Wonderful people."

Another pause which may or may not have been awkward. I was no longer able to adequately judge. For his part, Quinton seemed content to look at the snow landscape as it sailed past his window.

"They certainly loved your lecture," I finally came up with. "It was nice of you to take the time."

"Happy to do it," he said, turning away from the window. "You know what Arturo de Ascanio y Navaz said about magic."

Of course I didn't. I didn't even know who he was talking about. "Ascanio?" I said, butchering the name.

"You know. He created the Ascanio Spread."

"Oh, right," I said, really having no idea if this was a card move or something you put on toast.

"I'm paraphrasing," he saido, ignoring my blathering, "but he said something to the effect of 'Magic is like gardening. It requires constant attention.' I've found that to be, essentially, true.

"But enough about magic for one moment," he continued, shifting in his seat to give me his full attention. "Your uncle mentioned you were part of a murder investigation. That must be fascinating."

"Yes," I said slowly. "I think you could say I'm officially on the far edge of the periphery of the case."

"And a locked room murder, no less. That must be enthralling. Can you give me the pertinent particulars of the case?"

I glanced over at him and he raised an eyebrow at me. I considered my options. "I'm not really sure I'm at liberty to discuss the details," I said, enjoying the officious sensation the statement provided.

"Oh, understood," Quinton said quickly. "Completely understood. However, judging from the details your uncle provided..."

He then went on to outline each and every facet of the case, which Harry must have presented in minute detail. As it turned out, Quinton Moon knew exactly what I knew about the murder investigation, and for all I knew, probably more.

"I've had some experience in my travels," he continued, "with the buying and selling of rare and precious artifacts. In my case, it's generally been in the magic realm, you understand."

"Sure," I lied, not fully understanding. "Such as..." I said, gesturing for him to fill in the details.

"Oh, all types of miscellanea and ephemera. A blooming orange tree illusion, reputed to belong to Thurston," he said offhandedly. "Some letters from Houdini to his brother. The gun that killed Chung Ling Soo."

He turned and looked out the window as we wound our way through the streets of downtown St. Paul, which was snowy and quiet.

"In this world, Eli," he continued, "I've learned for every soul who has something they treasure, there is almost always someone else who wants to take it from them. Often by whatever means necessary."

I wasn't sure how to respond to this statement, or if a response was even required. I was still sifting through conversational options as I maneuvered the car through the circular drive in front of the St. Paul Hotel.

"Anyway," I said, falling back on our earlier topic, "thanks again for coming to do the lecture."

"And thank you," he said, taking my hand in a warm grip, "for the fine transport. I am sure beyond all measure my path will cross yours and Megan's in the not-too-distant future."

I suppressed a wince at his continued mention of Megan, but before I could compose a response, he was out of the car and on his way into the hotel.

As he strolled up the long red carpet which led to the gilded front doors, I wasn't in the least bit surprised he seemed to be on a first name basis with the valets and bellmen, all of whom he greeted like long-lost friends. He was truly warm and convivial with each and every one of them.

God, he was annoying.

CHAPTER 9

"I'm a very moral man. Except, of course, when it comes to collecting."

"Is that what you told the police?"

"Not in those words." Chip Cavanaugh said this with a winning smile which I suspect had gotten him out of many a scrape in the past.

We were in the sunken living room of his penthouse apartment off Mears Park in downtown St. Paul. His phone number was the first of two Deirdre had dictated to me, and I called him after dropping Quinton Moon off at his hotel. Chip said he was available to chat right then and his apartment was only blocks away, so it seemed like the stars had aligned for this conversation.

Before going into the building I had done some quick research on Chip Cavanaugh, via my phone.

I saw at once why the name was familiar; as the middle son of one of the richest families in the Twin Cities, I had heard about him virtually my whole life, even though we were likely about the same age.

Like another local family, the Pillsburys, the Cavanaugh name had become synonymous with the business they ran—in their case, a large, privately held bank, the old and prestigious Cavanaugh Bank in downtown St. Paul.

A quick Google search of Chip showed him at various charitable functions over the years, always with a different beauty on his arm and the same self-satisfied smirk on his face. The photos which weren't from charity events generally showed him at the helm of a large boat on Lake Minnetonka, or captaining a yacht in some far-flung sea race, with rich white guys fiercely competing against other rich white guys.

I didn't come across any scandals, just article after article about how Chip, of all the Cavanaugh children, did surprisingly little except travel the world, sail boats and look after the family's massive art collection.

Despite being a confessed lover of art, there was precious little on display in the impressive large, white-walled living room. In addition to the three blank walls, the apartment also sported a floor-to-ceiling window which offered a stunning view of downtown St. Paul, with the frozen river visible to the left and the dome of the Cathedral up and off in the distance. And distance was something I was keeping from that window. I am no fan of heights, less so in the last few months, but still enough that I avoided them whenever possible.

"Come, look at the view," Chip suggested after he had taken my coat and offered me a drink. "After all, I'm paying a fortune for it," he added with a laugh. He was shorter than I had anticipated, but solid and muscular, probably from years of playing lacrosse and water polo, or similar sports I couldn't afford and didn't understand.

"Thanks, but I'm good here." I decided to not go into any explanation of my recent panic attacks in high places, or of my months of therapy, which had basically devolved into the therapist finally throwing up his hands and suggesting I simply stay away from high places. I had heartily agreed with this clever plan of action, bid the good doctor farewell, and had since really suffered no serious setbacks using this common sense approach.

"Suit yourself. So, what's your connection to this case?" Chip asked as he crossed the room and took a seat in a matching chair across from the couch. Despite the frigid air outside, he was dressed as if for a tropical party, sporting leather sandals, khakis, and an understated Tommy Bahama shirt. Just like Clifford

Thomas, he had a tan, which was not only out of season but also appeared to have been gathered on a faraway beach. "The cops weren't entirely clear on your involvement in this whole brouhaha."

"Neither am I," I admitted. He saw me glance at a bowl of nuts on the table between us and pushed it in my direction. It had been a long time since breakfast and somehow lunch had eluded me. The amount of nuts I grabbed balanced on that delicate fulcrum between the most I thought I could politely take, while being the very least amount I wanted to eat.

"Friend of the victim?" he offered.

I shook my head, sorting the peanuts from the almonds from the cashews as I quickly arranged them in the order I planned to eat them. "I found—or I guess saw—the body," I explained between bites.

"So you're a person who's interested in the persons of interest?" he suggested with a twinkle in his eyes.

"I think that's the case," I agreed.

"Like Thompson, the reporter."

"Excuse me?"

"Thompson, the reporter in *Citizen Kane*. Trying to develop a post-mortem picture of the late Tyler James by talking to people who knew him."

"Yes, I suppose that's what I'm doing," I agreed. "So, why are you a person of interest?"

He shrugged. "According to the police, because I used Tyler James' services in the past. My collecting is focused mostly on the art world, but from time to time I have shown an interest, some would say an obsessive interest," he added with a laugh, "in the world of movie memorabilia."

"What sort of things did you buy through Tyler? James. James. Tyler." I gave up on the whole name thing and ate some nuts.

"The police asked that same question," he said, still smirking.

"And what did you tell them?" I was down to the cashews and wished I had taken more.

"I sort of took the fifth on that one," he said. "You know, the one about self-incrimination?" I was chewing, so he continued. "From time to time, I purchased some treasures from Tyler which were not actually on the market. So to speak." Again the smirk.

I looked from Chip to the huge window behind him, noticing for the first time a particular skyscraper which was dead center in the view. The home base for the Cavanaugh Bank.

"I understand you're in charge of buying art for your family's bank's collection?"

"I oversee those purchases," he said. "Primarily because my brothers have not taken a very strong interest in the arts or collecting."

"You're more active in collecting?"

More sneering. "Much more active."

I couldn't help glancing around the room at the bare, stark walls. He watched me, his smile getting even wider.

"And you have a personal collection?"

"I do."

"Where do you keep it?"

He shrugged. "Around."

While probably in his late thirties, Chip's attitude was that of a teenager with a very funny little secret he was keeping from the world. Or from me. He ran a hand casually through his thick head of hair and settled back farther into his chair.

There was a long pause as I considered where to take the conversation next. He continued to chuckle throughout. I felt enough time had passed, so I took a second handful of nuts, nudging as many cashews as possible into my hand. "You said earlier you're a very moral man, except when it comes to collecting. What did you mean by that?"

He leaned forward, seeming engaged for the first time since I had arrived. "Mr. Marks, do you collect anything?"

"You mean besides debts and parking tickets?"

"No, I mean seriously collecting something. Like stamps. Coins."

"Hmmm," I said, thinking about it. "When I was a kid, I remember I loved *Mad* magazine and I tried to collect all the issues. That is, until I found out how many of them there were and how much the older ones cost."

"Sadly, scarcity drives the economics of these things," he said.

"Then, of course, I had to own the entire set of Tarbell."

"Tarbell?"

"It's a set of magic books, *The Tarbell Course in Magic*. Eight volumes total. There's a saying in the magic community that if you think you've invented a new idea, look in Tarbell, because you probably haven't."

"And did you ultimately collect the full set, all eight books?"

"I did," I said. "And they're still on my bookshelf. If I were a better magician," I added, thinking about Quinton Moon, "I would take them down and study them more often."

"See, you understand the joys of collecting a group of things—a set. There are many people out there like that. Completists. For me, the fun comes in collecting something singular. Where there is one and only one."

"Art?"

"Art, yes. Movie memorabilia, by all means. Whatever catches my fancy."

"What might catch your fancy?"

"You mean hypothetically?" His arch tone matched his eyebrows as he practically winked at me.

"Sure," I said, playing along. "Hypothetically."

"Hypothetically then," he said, turning to his right and gazing at the white wall on the far side of the room, "I'd love to be the one who owns Picasso's *Le Pigeon Aux Petits Pois*." He saw my puzzled expression and kindly translated for me. "The Pigeon With Green Peas."

"Never heard of it. What's stopping you?"

"It was stolen in 2010. The thief says he panicked and threw the painting in a dumpster."

"A dumpster?"

"That could happen," he said with a shrug, then turned his head to the left and got a dreamy look in his eyes. "I'd also love to have Van Gogh's *View of the Sea at Scheveningen*."

I was about to ask the obvious question, but he beat me to it. "Also stolen," he said without looking at me, still staring at that point on the blank wall. "2002," he added.

He continued to gaze almost lovingly at the wall. I felt for a moment like I was intruding on something…intimate.

"How about movie memorabilia?" I asked, hoping a new category might pull him from his reverie. He turned back to me.

"That's a very limited area in my mind," he said. "Not a lot of Holy Grails out there. With one exception, of course." He smiled broadly and then whispered, "Rosebud."

"The sled from *Citizen Kane*? I thought there were more than one of those out there."

Chip shook his head. "They made three for the movie. They shot two takes of the final shot of the sled going into the fire, so two of them were burned."

"But didn't somebody famous buy the third one? Like Spielberg or something?"

"He may think he bought it, but word on the street is the one he got is a fake."

"Which means?"

He looked over my head, at the blank wall behind me. "Which means, it could still be out there. Somewhere." Again, a long, loving gaze, which was just this side of creepy.

"But this sort of collecting doesn't really make sense, does it?"

"How do you mean?" He didn't look at me and I could tell I still didn't have his complete attention.

"These are all things that, if you had them, you could never tell anyone you had them. Right? Being stolen and all."

He continued to stare at the wall. "I could make my peace with that," he said. "Sometimes, just the having is all."

"How about *London After Midnight*? Does it have any interest for you?"

"The police asked that very same question," he said, turning back toward me. "However, as I remember, it was phrased differently and their tone was nowhere near as nice as yours."

"Did you have any interest in it?"

"I'll tell you what I told the police: Tyler approached me, as I imagine he approached a lot of people. He said he might have access to the only surviving print of the movie. And he wanted to know if I was interested."

"Were you?" I heard the siren call of the bowl of nuts and reached forward, taking another handful from the side of the dish which seemed to offer the greatest number of cashews.

"I considered it," he said. "But in the end, I didn't pursue it. Which I also told the police," he added.

"Why not? You'd have the only one."

"True enough," he agreed. "But a bunch of film reels doesn't hold the same visceral, visual appeal for me. In order to get any real pleasure out of these things, I need to be able to see them, physically in front of me. A film print, as alluring as its unique individual status may be, just doesn't do it for me."

"And that's what you told the police."

"Essentially. To be honest, I'm not sure they understand my need to collect, so I didn't go into much detail with them. Certainly not as much as I've told you." He flashed a smile which was both sincere and sad. I got the sudden impression that behind the smile he was actually sad most of the time.

"All right then," he continued, visibly putting his cheerful self front-and-center. "Anything else?"

"Sure. One last question: Does your family belong to the Summit Club?"

He thought about this for a moment. "Belong? I think that's too weak a word. My great-grandfather was one of the founding members. Not that I spend much time there. A little too stuffy for my liking. Mr. Marks, is that all you needed?"

The fact he stood up while saying this suggested if this weren't all I needed, it would have to suffice, as it was all I was going to get.

I stood up and moved toward the door, with Chip Cavanaugh right behind me.

"I have to admit," he said, "I still don't fully understand your role in all this."

I stopped at the door and turned. "To be honest, Mr. Cavanaugh, I don't either. But the sense I'm getting is that, for your part, you had virtually no role in this."

"That's what I tried to explain to the police. However, I must admit you seem more open to that scenario than they did."

"That sounds like a compliment, so I'm going to say thank you." I reached for the door handle, but stopped when he put his hand on my arm.

"Eli, you seem like a man I can trust. I'm a pretty good judge of character and that's the sense I'm getting."

"Thank you," I said again slowly, not at all sure where this was headed.

"You want to see something?" His voice was low and his tone conspiratorial. He smiled at me and I think he even winked.

"Maybe," I said without conviction.

He moved past me to the other side of the doorframe, reaching toward the light switch plate. Instead of flicking the final switch in the row, he gave it a slight pull and the entire plate opened on a hinge, revealing yet another row of switches recessed in a small opening.

"This is just between you and me, okay?"

I nodded slowly, glancing down at the door handle and quickly calculating how fast I could pull the door open and dart down the hallway.

He turned back toward the room and looked at the white wall to our left. He glanced at me and tilted his head in the direction of the wall. As I turned, I heard him flip a switch and suddenly the wall disappeared. It was there one moment and gone the next. I realized it was not an actual plaster wall, but glass that had, by some electronic means, been frosted white, giving the impression of being a solid wall. Now, after the switch had been flipped, I saw it was a wall of clear glass, encasing another wall about two feet behind it.

On the center of the wall was a large, framed painting. It looked cubist to my uneducated eye, primarily because much of it was made up of gold and gray cubes. The word *Café* was written in the top right corner. From this distance I didn't see any pigeons, and even though I couldn't see the signature, it somehow felt like a Picasso painting. Given the way Chip Cavanaugh was looking at the framed piece, it most likely was.

After a long moment, Chip tilted his head toward the wall on the right and I heard him flip another switch. The frosted glass was immediately transparent, revealing another large framed painting on the interior wall. It showed a ship in the distance, the seashore and dark figures in the foreground. The thick swatches of paint and wavy lines screamed Van Gogh, but again, what do I know?

I looked at Chip Cavanaugh, but he did not return my look. Instead, he gazed longingly at the painting. He exhaled, caught my eye, and then tilted his head at the wall behind me. I turned just as the frosted glass disappeared and found myself face to face, as it were, with a piece of movie history.

Hanging on the interior wall, inches away from me (albeit, behind a thick pane of glass) was a small, fragile-looking child's sled.

I read the name stenciled on the front of the sled, unconsciously slipping into a hoarse whisper as I did so.

"Rosebud."

On the drive back to Minneapolis, I considered the two suspects I'd met so far. Both rich, both eccentric, both living in what appeared to be their own little worlds.

Each used his considerable wealth to fuel his hobbies and each seemed obsessed enough in their little worlds that stepping outside it in the name of murder—while not likely—still didn't seem completely out of the question.

Throughout it all, I couldn't help think of a plaque we had trouble keeping in stock in the small section of Chicago Magic devoted to gag gifts. Amid the fart spray and fake dog vomit was a series of posters and plaques which sold far better than most of the magic tricks we were ostensibly there to sell. The bestseller, hands down, was the image of a quartet of rotund animated men, each holding their sides with laughter. The side-splitting caption above them explained their mirth-filled state: "You want it when?"

But the plaque I couldn't shake from my consciousness after spending some time with Clifford Thomas and Chip Cavanaugh was a perennial favorite found in offices across the land. It read, "You Don't Have To Be Crazy To Work Here. But It Helps!"

Based on these two most recent encounters—coupled with other odd experiences in the past year—I was getting the sense you didn't have to be crazy to be rich, but it certainly helped.

I was still mulling this over when I pulled my car into a slushy spot in front of the magic shop. Dusk had fallen and the street seemed unusually dark, even for a late January afternoon. I had just opened the car door when my phone buzzed on the seat next to me. The caller ID read Unknown Caller and I considered letting it go to voicemail, but it was cold outside and the car was still warm, so I shut the door and answered the phone. This is how decisions are often made during long, cold Minnesota winters.

"Mandrake, how does life find you on this fine snowy evening?"

Any warmth I had been feeling left my body at that instant, driven by a primal and Pavlovian response to the voice of Mr. Lime, which had taken hold of my central nervous system without even stopping to ask permission. I cleared my throat and struggled to sound relaxed and at ease. I was neither.

"Mr. Lime, good to hear from you," I said with what sounded to me like forced cheer. "How are you doing?"

"What a coincidence. I called to ask you that very question," he said, his thin, reedy voice sounding far more substantial than my own. "I understand you were quite recently the victim of what they call a 'near miss.' I hope you are suffering no ill effects from the encounter with an errant automobile."

"How did you hear about that?" I asked, immediately recognizing the futility of the question.

"I have my fingers in a number of pies," he said and I could see him smiling at the metaphor. "Some stickier than others. I must say, my boy," he continued, sounding much avuncular than I would have preferred, "when I asked you to take on this endeavor, I did so thinking it would not put you in harm's way. Please accept my apologies. It has never been my wish to see harm come to you."

"You and I have that in common," I said.

This produced a low chuckle from the other end of the phone and then silence. I waited it out for a moment and then had to fill the quiet gap.

"So..." I began and was immediately cut off.

"The good news, of course, is you are unharmed," he said, once again seizing control of the conversation. "The other news is an incident such as the one you experienced often means you're heading in a productive direction."

I considered this for a moment. "But," I said, as a thought occurred to me, "when the car tried to run me down, I hadn't talked to any of the suspects yet."

"True enough," he said with another low chuckle. "But you had said 'yes' to the enterprise. And sometimes, in this world, just saying 'yes' can set the wheels in motion. As it were."

Another pause and another attempt by me to fill it.

"So..." I repeated and once again this was enough to jumpstart the conversation.

"Be assured, I will investigate further," he said. "For the time being, I suggest you maintain your course. Keep an eye peeled. As they say, 'there be dragons here.' And sometimes they be right."

There was the sound of a click and then once again nothing. I truly couldn't tell if he had ended the conversation or not. "So..." I ventured again, but this time the only response was silence.

*   *   *

I was still considering his opaque warning as I navigated the steep, snowy mounds which separated the street from the sidewalk. I wasn't really paying attention to much more than where my feet were landing, so it took a moment for me to realize the standard form of lighting, which generally blanketed the front of the store in the early evening, was not currently providing illumination of any sort.

The marquee for the movie theater, which normally lit up several doors on either side of the cinema, was dark, as was the theater lobby. I checked my watch, thinking I might have completely lost track of time, but it was only 7:10 p.m. Under normal circumstances, the theater should have been open for business by now.

The ladder Tracy had been using earlier in the afternoon had been haphazardly abandoned, splayed across the doors to the theater. The box of black metal letters, which had hung from the ladder, had been pushed to the curb, with several letters protruding from the snow.

However, the most unsettling element—which was visible even in the dim light—was what was staining the icy sidewalk beneath the marquee. Partially frozen, but still sticky and viscous, was a disturbingly large pool of blood.

There be dragons indeed.

Chapter 10

"I don't have all the details, but my understanding is that someone—person or persons unknown—pushed or pulled the ladder from beneath her while poor Tracy was atop it. She landed on the sidewalk, sadly breaking her fall with her head." Harry was standing in the doorway to his apartment, just putting on his coat, while he brought me up to speed on the events of the afternoon.

"Is she okay?"

"That is still an open question," he said, shutting the door behind him and heading down the narrow stairway toward the shop below. "Megan was the one who found her. She called 911 and then when the ambulance came, Megan accompanied them to the hospital. I thought she would have called by now with a report, but my cell phone has been oddly silent."

"It's lucky someone was there," I said as we made our way through the dark shop. "I think I should go down to the hospital and see how she's doing."

"I'm not entirely sure which 'she' you mean, nor do I wish to know, but that's an excellent notion," Harry agreed.

For a moment, I wasn't actually sure either.

We parted ways in front of the shop, with me heading back toward my car and Harry headed, I assumed, next door to Adrian's for a spot of dinner and some camaraderie with whichever members of the Minneapolis Mystics were in attendance that evening. However, as I pulled away from the curb and performed a neat U-turn in the middle of Chicago Avenue, I was surprised to see he had bypassed the door to the bar and was heading farther down the sidewalk. The stoplight was in my favor, so I didn't have time to think about it as I continued down the barely plowed street toward the hospital.

There was no answer the several times I tried Megan's cell phone while I drove, but that seemed reasonable, as many hospitals limit the use of cell phones in some key areas. I imagined the Emergency Room was one of them.

What was intended to be a quick check-in at the front desk took longer than anticipated, when I realized to my chagrin that while I knew Tracy's first name, I had never bothered to learn her last. The front desk attendant was kind enough to perform a computer search using only the first name and moments later I was in the elevator, on my way to the third floor.

Finding the room proved to be easier than anticipated, as I immediately spotted Megan as I exited the elevator. She was chatting with a man dressed in traditional blue hospital scrubs standing in front of the door to a patient room.

"Oh, Eli," she said, breaking into a sad smile. "You must have heard." She grabbed my arm and pulled me into the conversation, giving my hand a warm, steady squeeze.

I looked at the doctor and recognized him immediately. Redheaded with a thick ginger beard, he had written out a prescription over a year before which I still carried in my wallet. It read, "Don't get hit on the head anymore." A quick glance at his name badge confirmed my memory.

"Dr. Levine, I'm Eli Marks. You saw me after I got a concussion last year."

"Have you stopped getting hit on the head?"

I couldn't believe he remembered the specific incident, so I assumed this was a standard line he gave to any patient who had taken a blow to the head.

"I do my best every day," I said.

"Good to hear," he said. "As I was just telling Megan here, your friend Tracy is a very lucky lady. She took quite the fall and amazingly broke nothing but her noggin."

"How badly?"

"There was so much blood," Megan added.

"Head wounds are notorious gushers," Levine said. "She's got a nasty concussion and we're watching for internal bleeding, which is why I want her to stay the night. We did an initial CAT scan and didn't see any evidence of epidural or subdural hematomas. But I want to keep an eye on her for the next twelve to sixteen hours."

He glanced down at the chart he was holding and then looked up at us. "That being said, she could have easily broken an arm, a leg, her back," he continued, then paused and added, "even her neck."

As if on cue, Megan and I both turned to look into the room, where Tracy lay motionless.

"Has she been conscious at all?" I asked, addressing my question first to the doctor and then adding Megan. "Did she say what happened?"

"She's been in and out," Megan said. "I asked her if she saw what happened and all she said was someone knocked the ladder over. She didn't see anyone."

It struck me for the first time that someone had tried to run me down just a few feet from where Tracy had fallen.

I flashed back on the two of us standing outside the projection booth, leaning in to see Tyler's body and the evidence which lay around him.

Megan must have seen the puzzled look on my face.

"What's wrong?"

I shook my head. "Nothing," I said, trying to put my thoughts into words and giving up. "Nothing at all."

I was still thinking about that coincidence as we made the short drive back to our neighborhood.

"Lucky thing you found her," I said, breaking the silence which had enveloped us since leaving the hospital.

"If it hadn't been me, it would have been someone else. I mean, people walk up and down that sidewalk all day."

"Still, you were there. You made the call. Speed is imperative in these things," I said.

"It was a good thing I had my phone. Because as you know, I don't always carry it."

We both smiled at this admission, as my inability to reach her by phone had been an ongoing sore point in our relationship. She shook her head, then the smile faded away.

"Oh, Eli, there was so much blood. Who would do something like that, I mean, just run up and do that?"

I shook my head. "Lot of wacko people in the world," I said, patting her leg ineffectually, the physical equivalent of saying "there, there."

The mention of blood brought me back again to Tyler's body in the projection booth. I searched for a connection with Tracy's fall and with my literal run-in with a car the other night and came up short on both fronts.

"How's everything at the store?" I said, trying to steer us into more innocuous territory.

Megan's store, Chi & Things, occupied the corner of Chicago and 48th Street and offered a full complement of crystals, aromatherapies, healing balms and other holistic tchotchkes and doodads.

Megan had inherited the entire block from her grandmother and took over the empty corner shop, making her first fledgling attempt into the often stormy and unpredictable waters of retail. The inheritance also made her my landlady, a fact which never ceased to amuse me.

"It's okay. We've had a sudden influx of used New Age books," she said, apparently relieved to be talking about something more mundane. "Without an equal increase in sales of new New Age books."

"People are unloading old books, but not buying new books?"

"I guess," she said. "I have no idea what it means." Several more moments went by, and then Megan made a conversational stab of her own.

"Anything going on in the magic shop?" she said.

I considered this. "We finally had a black guy come in and ask if we had any black thumb tips," I said. "That was nice. So I was able to prove to Harry it had made sense to make that small investment in our inventory."

"That's great," she said with a tad more enthusiasm than was really required. "How many did he buy?"

I thought back on the encounter. "None. But I feel it was a small, inclusionary victory for the world of Chicago Magic."

"Oh, absolutely."

We drove in silence and then she suddenly perked up. "Oh, I forgot to tell you. At breakfast with Q, he said I could be part of his stage act this week. He's going to cut me in half or thirds or something. Isn't that cool?"

"Excuse me?" It took great effort on my part, but those were the only words I could make my mouth produce which weren't inflammatory or obscene or both.

"He's doing a corporate show this week and said he was looking for an assistant for a trick of some kind, a Ziggy or a Zaggy or something."

"Zig Zag?" I suggested through gritted teeth.

"That's it, Zig Zag. He says it's like sawing a woman in half, but different."

"Yes, it's a very famous effect. A staple among magicians," I said coldly. "And you're going to be part of his act?" I continued as calmly as possible.

"Yes, I think it's downtown somewhere on Thursday night."

"You are going to be part of his act," I repeated. "You who have vehemently and heatedly objected if I ever accidentally revealed or even hinted at how a trick is done. You who, and I am quoting here, 'Never, ever wants to know how a trick is done.' This same person is going to rehearse and perform the Zig Zag as part of Quinton Moon's act. Did I get that right?"

I think my tone must have gotten through to her, for her response was now as cold as mine. "I don't understand what the problem is," she said sharply. "You've asked me to help out with your act in the past."

"Yes, and every time—let me repeat, every single, blessed time—you have declined, on the grounds that you, and again I quote, 'don't want to know how the trick is done.' But apparently you have no such compunction with Mr. Hot Shot Eurotrash magician."

"Who? Oh, right," she said, realizing I was talking about Quinton. "Eli, I don't see why you're getting so upset. Do you want me to say no?"

"I would love for you to say no," I said quickly.

"Fine, I'll say no," she said as I pulled up in front of her building.

"Is that what you want?" I said, trying to take some of the emotion out of my voice.

"No, but apparently it's what you want."

We stared at each other for a long moment and then she turned and stepped out of the car.

"I'll think about it," she said.

"Good—" But she never heard my final words, as the slamming of the car door cut off the rest of my sentence.

"How would you feel if your girlfriend performed in another magician's act?"

"I don't have a girlfriend."

"Hypothetically, then."

Nathan considered the question thoughtfully.

"If I had a hypothetical girlfriend, I'd be so grateful I probably wouldn't mind if she performed in another, hypothetical magician's hypothetical act." This conclusion reached, he looked across the counter at me. "But that's not the answer you were looking for, was it?"

We were hanging out in the magic shop and I had brought him up to speed on Quinton Moon's breach of magic etiquette.

Harry hadn't gotten up yet when I stopped in for our morning breakfast ritual. He begged off for "just a few more minutes or maybe an hour" of sleep, so I ate a bowl of Cheerios over the sink and opened the store early. Nathan stopped by to refill his stock of balloons for a kid's party, complaining how nowadays the kids were always asking for weird animal breeds when he took requests.

"I understand not every kid is going to make my day easier by asking for a wiener dog," he explained. "But what the heck am I supposed to do with a request for a Golden-Doodle?"

We commiserated about this and Quinton's betrayal for several minutes and could have continued for several more when we were interrupted by a phone call. I knew it was from my ex-wife before I had even taken the phone from my pocket, signaled by the ringtone I'd assigned to her: The Stones' "It's All Over Now."

"We're visiting the final suspect Mr. Lime provided later this morning," she said without any greeting or fanfare. "How did it go with Mr. Cavanaugh?"

I thought back on the sad millionaire and his hidden and highly-suspect art collection. "Nothing to report except to say he's a bit of an odd duck. But you probably already gathered as much. Who was it who said that quote about the rich? 'They are different from you and me.'"

"I think it was Fitzgerald."

"Barry or Geraldine?"

"No, you movie geek idiot. F. Scott. And he was right. They are a whole different breed. And if you don't believe me, wait 'til you meet the next one on your list."

"What do you mean?"

"Just wait," was all she said before hanging up.

CHAPTER 11

"You have not met a serious collector, my friend, until you've come face to face with a comic book collector."

I felt I had, in fact, come face to face with a couple of serious collectors in the past week, but the large crowd which browsed excitedly throughout the Glendower Comics store seemed to establish the veracity behind his statement.

"Are you having a sale today?" I asked, surveying the large crowd with something akin to envy.

"Today? No, this is pretty typical. You should be here on a Wednesday."

I looked over at him and he answered my question before I could ask it. "New comics always come out on Wednesday," he explained. "When does new magic come out?"

I had only been talking to Randall Glendower for five minutes but we were already at a point in our relationship where he felt it was okay to kid me about the lowly status of magic in the world today, at least compared to the seemingly endless popularity of comic books.

Randall was, to put it kindly, a striking individual.

Nearly as round as he was tall, he was wearing a multi-colored t-shirt which gave him the appearance of a beach ball with stubby legs.

His head was covered with a shaggy mess of dirty blond hair, which morphed seamlessly into a disheveled, dirty blond beard, providing his head with an odd, shaggy nimbus.

Glendower Comics took up the prime center spot in a block-long strip mall in Bloomington, a first-ring suburb best known as the home of the Mall of America.

The store was a bright explosion of color and images and posters and toys, with a dizzying amount of inventory and a large, t-shirted staff. Classic rock played through the speakers and was interrupted on a nearly constant basis by the ringing of cash registers.

"Let's go down to my office to talk," Randall suggested as he started waddling toward an adjoining room. "It's a little tough to have a real conversation in this environment."

It would have been equally difficult to have a conversation in the next environment as well. The second room was full of gamers, seated at long tables around game boards and playing cards and figurines. Some gamers were in the midst of heated, but muted, play, while others sat quietly painting their game pieces or reading up on the latest strategy. The room had the look and feel of a gothic library and was in stark contrast to the circus-like feeling of the main room. Randall continued forward toward a door on the far wall and moments later we had descended a wood-paneled staircase and entered the strangest environment yet.

"Is this your parents' basement?" I asked, looking around at what appeared to be a large-scale version of the basement of a suburban geek kid.

"Almost exactly," he said, beaming with pride. "I've supersized it, of course, but it's exactly what it looked like when I was a teenager, right down to the same harvest gold shag carpet."

"As a teenager you had life-sized models of Yoda, C-3PO and R2-D2?" I asked, gesturing to the trio of figures looking back at us from the far corner.

"Actually, no, but I dreamed about it," he said with a laugh as we moved through the room. "I have more resources at my disposal these days."

The source of those assets was visible in the next room, a small, dark office with a computer desk, keyboard and two large monitors. He gestured me into an overstuffed armchair as he settled into the seat in front of the screens.

"The comic book store, the game store, it all pretty much just breaks even. This," he said, pointing to the website visible on one monitor, "is what pays for everything else."

By "this" he meant the GeekintheKnow website, the most-visited and most-debated site on the internet for information, rumors and opinions on the latest and greatest movies, TV shows, comic books, graphic novels and games of interest to geeks, fan boys and other mere mortals.

"And it all started in your parents' basement, right?"

Randall nodded. "That's the legend, but in this case you can print the legend, 'cause it's true. Just me and a laptop, recycling—and early on, manufacturing—rumors about the top upcoming genre movies."

"And now," I said, "an empire."

He nodded in thoughtful agreement. "I suppose so. Never underestimate the power of anticipation and disappointment as a valid economic model."

He'd lost me with the last statement and my face must have indicated this confusion, so he pointed at the website on the screen.

"Sixty percent of the content on the site is about movies and TV shows that are in production, or might be in production, or might go into development, or might, might, might. Endless energy is exerted by our readers as they conjecture and debate and argue about how a project might turn out, or why a project is doomed to failure, or the finer points of why a particular project should never even have been considered."

He reached under the computer desk and popped open a cabinet door, which revealed a small refrigerator within. He rummaged around and pulled out a soda for himself and then gestured to me.

I nodded and he tossed a can to me before continuing his explanation. I was surprised to see it was a vintage brand I hadn't seen since I was a kid.

"Where'd you find this?" I asked, turning the can over and inspecting it. It looked exactly like I remembered. "I thought they stopped making it like twenty years ago."

"I got a bottling plant in Thailand to start manufacturing them for me. I sell them on the internet to cover costs, but that's basically a break-even proposition."

He turned his attention back to the computer monitors. "Anyway, what 'might be' takes up about sixty percent of the site. The other forty percent of the content consists of readers complaining about those same movies and TV shows once they've been completed; how they don't live up to their expectations, how the story has been mangled, or—again—how they never should have been made in the first place." He took a long sip from his pop can. "Anticipation and disappointment," he declared with a satisfied sigh. "The yin and yang of internet success."

"That's a unique business model," I said.

I held the can an arm's length away and popped it open. A mild but manageable amount of soda sprayed harmlessly into the air. "But how does a person make money at it?"

"The bulk of the income comes from advertising," he continued. "You know, banners and pop-up windows. Plus anytime a reader clicks on a link, we harvest that information and sell it to advertisers. We also take a small percentage from sales on the Marketplace."

"Marketplace?"

"That's a section on the site where people can sell memorabilia or put up requests for things they're looking for. If a sale happens, we get a small cut."

"Would someone like Tyler James place items for sale in the Marketplace?"

Randall shrugged. "He might have, but most of what passes through the Marketplace would be pretty small change for a broker like Tyler."

He leaned forward with sudden speed and hit some keys on the keyboard. One of the two screens instantly switched images, becoming a window into a series of moving lines and flashing red dots.

"These are real-time metrics of traffic on the sites and sub-sites," he said, pointing to the ever-changing lines and blinking lights. The cosmic light show on the screen was mesmerizing and it was apparent the site was far more popular than I had imagined.

"It's very busy," I said, not taking my eyes off the screen.

"Oh, this is nothing. I can make it spike like mad if I want." He got a devilish look in his eyes. "For example, we've got a rumor we're releasing today for one of the studios. There are plans to remake a famous movie," he said, going on to name the classic film.

I gasped. "That's ridiculous," I said, feeling outrage beginning to grow from deep within. "That movie is a classic. To touch it, to remake it, that's the dumbest thing I've ever heard."

My voice had risen an octave and I turned to Randall, who was beaming at me.

"Never underestimate," he said, "the power of anticipation and disappointment." He tapped some keys on the keyboard. "Let's see what happens when we release that rumor," he said, giving one key a final flourish as he tapped it.

We waited for several long seconds, quietly looking at the metrics screen. For a moment I thought nothing was going to happen.

And then the lights started to flash. Lines spiked up. More red lights. Lines went higher. The screen began to resemble a pinball machine on overload. I turned to Randall. I'm sure my mouth was hanging open.

"And that," he said, leaning back in his chair, "is how I can afford to do business with someone like Tyler James."

"Did you do a lot of business with him?"

Randall shrugged. "A little here, a little there. I mean, he presented more stuff to me than I ever bought. But he knew where my interests lay and wasn't afraid to let me know what was out there."

"Did he approach you about *London After Midnight*?"

Randall nodded. "He did indeed, and I told the police that."

"Really. Even though it was technically stolen merchandise?"

"I didn't care about that," he said, finishing his soda and reaching into the fridge for another. "If my offer had been accepted, I planned to turn it over to the National Film Registry or the Library of Congress and let them deal with the paper trail."

"You didn't want to own it?"

"Oh, sure, what are you, nuts?" He laughed. "Of course I wanted to own it. But I didn't *need* to own it. I really just wanted to make sure it was preserved, so people could actually see it."

"But your offer wasn't accepted?"

He shook his head, still clearly disappointed by the outcome. "I got outbid."

"Can I ask what your bid was?"

"Half a million. Ten percent down."

"That means the winner offered $750,000, with $75,000 down."

"That's what I'm guessing, and the police seemed to agree."

Our conversation was interrupted by a jittery, squeaking sound coming from down the hall. I leaned toward the doorway and was surprised when a small, brown, excited monkey suddenly came leaping into the room. It jumped past me and climbed up into Randall's lap, causing him to nearly spill his soda on the computer keyboard. He set the can aside and turned his attention to the pint-sized creature, which was about the size of a tiny dog.

"You have a monkey," I said, stating the obvious.

"Yes, this is Jinx. He's a Javan macaque monkey."

I squinted at Randall and his little friend. "Isn't it illegal to own them? As pets?"

"It sure is, but he's not a pet. Jinx is the Managing Editor for the site. He's on the masthead. He gets a paycheck and everything."

"I suppose that makes all the difference."

The small creature ran up one of Randall's arms, across the back of his neck and down the other arm, with Randall laughing the entire time. He looked over at me, grinning as widely as he had since I met him, and keep in mind, he'd been grinning a lot. "Eli, as a kid, didn't you ever want a monkey?"

"Only always."

"Me too." He sat back, stroking the monkey's tiny head lovingly. "You know, it's weird. There were so many things I wanted when I was a kid, and now I have them all and you know what?"

"What?"

"It's great. Just great."

The two of them together looked like a Norman Rockwell painting, if Rockwell had ever attempted to capture a warm, heart-tugging human/simian relationship. Randall gave Jinx a quick kiss on the head and the monkey returned the buss with what sounded to me like a happy squeak.

On the metrics screen, the lines continued to grow and the lights continued to flash like a freaked out pinball machine.

Chapter 12

As I left the comic book store and crossed the parking lot, my head was still vibrating with the heavy thump of blaring rock music and chiming cash registers, so I think I can be excused for not hearing or feeling my cell phone ringing in my pocket. I finally recognized the familiar sensation before the call went to voicemail and clicked on the phone despite the announcement on the screen that this call was coming from yet another Unknown Caller.

"Hello," I said too loudly, still trying to regain my auditory balance after the sensory overload of the store.

"Hi, Eli, sorry to bother you." The voice was familiar, in the "I'm pretty sure I've talked to you before, but probably not on the phone" sense. "It's Tracy. You know, from the theater. Next door."

"Tracy, yes, hello, how are you?" I sputtered, overcompensating for no apparent reason, trying to remember the last time we'd spoken and then remembering the image of her unconscious in the hospital room. "I mean, really, how are you?"

"I'm okay," she said unconvincingly. "They've released me from the hospital, so that must mean something."

"That's great," I said, fumbling for my keys with my spare hand and hitting the unlock button on the car key.

"Yeah, well, that's why I'm calling. I'm sorry to bother you, but I'm at the hospital and they won't let me take a cab home and I don't have my car and so I'm kinda stuck here."

"Okay," I began as I slipped into the front seat, but she was still talking so I stopped.

"I called Megan, because, you know, she had come to the hospital with me. And she's not able to leave her store, but she suggested I call you instead."

I was just about to close the car door but stopped in mid-motion. "She suggested that, did she?"

"She did. She said something like, 'I bet he'd love to pick you up.'"

There was a silence between us as I quickly sorted through the mental haze I suddenly found myself in.

If the situation were reversed, I would never—ever, in a million years—suggest Megan pick up Quinton Moon from anything or anywhere.

Yet here was Megan, volunteering me to act as chauffer for this attractive, single woman. Was this some sort of trust exercise, or was Megan simply lacking the jealousy gene in her DNA, making her an even better person than I had already suspected?

I'm not sure how long I sat there considering this, but eventually Tracy must have thought the connection had broken.

"Hello?" she said tentatively. "You still there?"

I snapped back to the present moment so quickly I nearly gave my brain whiplash. "Yes, sorry, just driving," I lied. "I'll be there in twenty minutes."

"I'll bet this wasn't how you expected to spend your afternoon. Sorry to make you change your plans."

"Not to worry. The truth is, I rarely have anything resembling a plan, let alone the plural."

This made Tracy smile, not for the first time on our short drive from the hospital to her apartment. "That raises an interesting question: what's a typical day for a magician?"

I shrugged as the light changed and I touched the accelerator. "Sadly, I don't really ever have an agenda. My day is just mostly dealing with crap as it comes in."

"Not unlike the life of a theater manager."

I glanced away from the road for a second to look at her. She looked normal if a bit pale. A white bandage above her temple was almost completely covered by a knitted stocking cap, which held her wild red hair in place. "And how did *that* happen? I mean, you becoming the manager of a movie theater?"

"It was certainly not by design," she said with a smile.

The awkward feelings I'd had at the start of the drive were beginning to dissipate, but it still felt odd. Tracy was a decidedly attractive woman, but I wasn't aware of any amorous feelings on my part or, for that matter, on her part.

I was starting to believe Megan's innate trust in me was completely justified.

"You were an athlete. Playing ball in Japan," I began, hoping this would help coax the story out of her. "And now you manage a movie theater. Connect the dots for me."

"It's not a typical path, is it?" she said with another wide smile. If nothing else, the brief drive with me had gone a long way to perk up her mood. "The short version is my eligibility ran out at school at the same time I got an offer to play with a women's league overseas. I figured, what the hell, and before I knew it I was suited up and playing in front of cheering throngs of Japanese fans."

"And how does that connect to Minnesota, the Land of Ten Thousand Lakes?" I asked, gesturing around with one hand to indicate her present location.

"Nothing very inspired, I admit. My contract ran out and I had to go *somewhere*," she said, also gesturing with one hand to indicate our present location. "I'd heard great things about the state, I'm a big Prince fan, and so I figured, what the hell?" She looked out the window at the snow-covered landscape around us. "Of course, it was early summer when I got here and, believe me, it looked a whole lot better in June than it does now."

"Yes, Minnesota is a fickle mistress. She lures you in with three wonderful days of summer and then whacks you upside your head the rest of the year."

"You're funny," she said with a smile.

"Oh, I bet you say that to all the funny people," I said and then stopped. Okay, this definitely felt like flirting, but it was too late to pull it back.

"This is me," she said, pointing to a three-story apartment complex on the right. I pulled into the short driveway which led to the front door and lobby. As the car came to a stop, she turned to me, her big green eyes sparkling. "Can I repay your kindness with a cup of tea and some homemade but admittedly not great chocolate chip cookies?"

Her smile was as inviting as her offer. I sifted through all the responses which flooded through my brain and was about to land on one when I noticed the mailman just heading toward the apartment building. He was sorting through a thick handful of mail as he walked and didn't see a patch of ice in the center of the sidewalk. He hit the ice at full stride and his feet nearly jerked out from under him, but he was able to right himself at the last moment. He looked down at the offending ice patch and then checked the sidewalk ahead of him before continuing on his now slower course toward the front doors.

A phrase moved up through the distant corners of my brain, suddenly appearing out of the depths of my consciousness. "If you don't want to slip..."

I had a sudden memory of my late aunt Alice, a lovely but firm presence throughout my teen and young adult years. It was one of her favorite phrases which she returned to time and time again whenever I found myself on the outer edges of getting into trouble.

"If you don't want to slip," Aunt Alice had always said with conviction, "don't go to slippery places."

"Slippery places," I repeated out loud.

"What's that?" Tracy asked, looking around, clearly not sure who I was talking to.

"Oh," I said, snapping out of my reverie. "I was just thinking, this time of year there are a lot of slippery places."

Tracy nodded in agreement, as it was a hard statement to argue with.

"Thanks for the offer," I continued, putting both hands on the steering wheel to provide a visual indicator I wasn't getting out of the car. "But I've still got some more errands to run."

"I'll give you a rain check," she offered, then added, "or a snow check. If that exists."

"Sure thing. Feel better."

"I feel better all ready," she said. She suddenly leaned over and gave me a quick kiss on the cheek, and then just as quickly climbed out of the car. "Sorry, sometimes I'm impulsive," she added before swinging the door shut.

Out of habit I watched to make sure she made it to the front door safely and noticed as she deftly sidestepped the patch of ice which had nearly done in the mailman.

Then I backed down the driveway, feeling like I had just narrowly missed a dangerous patch of metaphorical ice myself.

I found a parking spot in front of Chicago Magic and sat in my car for several moments, writing, rewriting and then re-rewriting a quick text to Megan. I gave the words one final read, my index finger hovering over the SEND button.

I got Tracy safely home from the hospital, per your request.

I considered—again—eliminating the "per your request" portion of the text, decided to keep it, thought about deleting the whole thing and starting over, and then took the plunge and pressed SEND.

I sat in the car, grateful not for the first time I had opted for the seat warmers, looking at my phone, trying to will it to reply. It was slow in coming, so I turned my attention to the theater marquee, which still read *Guess Who's Coming to My Dinner With Andre*. Then my hand felt the phone vibrating with a response. I unlocked the screen and read Megan's one word answer.

Tnks

I studied those four letters for way too long, looking for hidden meanings and striving to determine what tone of voice had been used to compose this maddeningly succinct reply. Rather than dwell on it, I opted for action and quickly typed a response I hoped would elicit a more detailed response.

I'm back at the store.

Again the response seemed to take if not eons then certainly hours to appear. It actually arrived in less than a minute and when it did, it provided even less information than the last text. Her response consisted of a single letter.

k

I stared at the letter far longer than was necessary and then stared out the car's side window for inspiration for a response. I'd been in the car so long that the windows had begun to fog over, which was fine, as inspiration was nowhere to be seen. In desperation, I typed two keystrokes and hit SEND.

:)

I don't know how long I waited for a response, but it never came and I finally gave up, shut off the car and trudged through the snow and into the store.

I found Harry alone in the shop, seated on his trusty stool, paging thoughtfully through Quinton's magic book. He held a pen in one hand, which suggested he was actually making notes in the margin, which he only did with the best books in his collection. He glanced up at me as I entered.

"Back from interviewing a person or persons of interest?"

I nodded. "Did that this morning. And then I picked up Tracy and brought her home from the hospital."

This statement garnered his full attention and he looked at me intently over the top of his reading glasses. "Did you now?"

"Yes," I said, trying to sound nonchalant but not getting anywhere near it. "Megan suggested I do it."

Upon hearing this, he actually closed Quinton's book. "Did she now?"

"Yes she did."

"I see." He glanced down at his watch. "Well, since you're here," he began, but I waved the thought away with my hand.

"Inventory, absolutely. Let's get to it," I said with cheer that wasn't entirely forced. I clapped my hands together, looking for the best place to begin.

"Actually, I was going to say that since you're here, perhaps I'll take this opportunity to take a short nap. If you don't mind watching the store?" He lowered himself carefully from the stool and picked up a bookmark off the nearby counter, inserting it neatly into the book.

"No problem," I said. He began to walk toward the curtains which led to the stairs to our apartments. "Harry, are you feeling okay?"

He turned back. He looked tired, but he hadn't lost any of the twinkle in his eyes. "Never better. Just need a nap."

"Okay," I said, deciding not to push the issue. He got almost to the curtain and then my voice stopped him again. "Harry?"

He turned, apparently not in the least annoyed at the second interruption to his impending nap. "Yes?"

I wasn't sure how to phrase my question, and after one or two false starts, I finally blurted it out. "Do you think my act is any good?"

He gave the question a long moment of serious consideration. "Eli, I don't know. I liked it when I saw it, but I really haven't seen you perform it in years."

"It's essentially the same," I said.

"It is? That's problem one," he said, stepping away from the curtain and crossing to a counter, where he placed a hand to steady himself.

"How is that a problem? You're always railing against magicians who are constantly changing their acts."

"That's true, but an act is a living, breathing entity. It should change and evolve as you change and grow, just not on a whim."

"You're saying I'm not growing as a magician?" A defensive tone had begun to creep into my voice, and I did nothing to mask it.

"By no means. I would never be so presumptuous. But I will say this: I'm a retired magician and I'll bet I still practice more than you do."

"What for?"

"To tune up the act, like a car. Take the engine apart and see if you're getting the most out of each piece. Look at each effect, each move, each sleight, each segment. Really ask yourself why you're making this move here or saying that line there."

"But you always say, 'If it's not broken, don't fix it.'"

"I do indeed," he said with a smile. "But from time to time, I think you have to check under the hood to see if, in fact, anything *is* broken."

I began to answer him but realized he was right. "You think I'm skating by?"

"That's not for me to say; that would be your call. But now that you've asked, I would have to say—if your act hasn't changed in years and you spend virtually no time practicing—yes, you are skating by. And skating on thin ice."

I narrowed my eyes, not entirely certain what was meant by this last remark. "How do you mean?"

"You know what Ed Macauley said."

I shook my head. "Who's Ed Macauley?"

"A basketball player of some repute."

"Harry, since when do I know anything about basketball? You should be having this conversation with Tracy over at the theater."

"I'm not sure what that means," Harry said with an arched eyebrow. "But Mr. Macauley said, and I'm paraphrasing here, anytime you are not practicing, remember someone somewhere is practicing. And when you meet him, he will win."

I felt my jaw clenching up. "So you're saying Quinton Moon is beating me?"

He seemed surprised by my mention of Quinton. "I'm saying nothing of the kind. What I'm saying is a good magician is like a swan gliding across a lake. All you see is grace and beauty, but his feet are working like mad under the surface. With the best swans, no one ever sees the effort. But the swan would never look graceful without it."

"My act is like an awkward swan?"

"I haven't a clue. I haven't seen your act in years. But I'd be happy to sit with you and critique it at any point." His tone was warm and, in his own way, loving. I felt my jaw begin to unclench.

"Not just now," I said. "But I may take you up on that."

"It's a standing offer," he said, heading back to the curtain. "After my nap, do you care to join me in a spot of dinner?"

I shook my head. "I think I'll stay in tonight," I said.

"And practice?" he said with a wicked smile.

"Probably."

"Atta boy." He disappeared through the curtains.

I stayed in the shop until closing time, and then spent the rest of the evening in my apartment, practicing my act for the first time in I can't remember how long. I started looking at everything I'd been doing for years and asking myself why I did it that way.

It was much harder than I had anticipated and, when I finished for the evening, sleep did not come easily. When it finally did, most of the night consisted of me dreaming that I was dreaming.

Clifford Thomas provided a running commentary for this dream within a dream, during which he kept repeating his bizarre story about dreaming he had somehow repressed a murder. And then, still dreaming, I would wake up and not be entirely certain that the story wasn't about me. Then I would fall back into the dream within the dream and it would all repeat.

When I finally woke up for real, I felt more tired than when I had gone to bed. I lay there for a long time, unrested and unnerved, then finally convinced myself the day ahead couldn't be any weirder than my night had been.

True to form, the universe took that challenge and met it head on.

CHAPTER 13

"Mr. Marks, welcome to BuyMax. Have you been offered a beverage?"

Sherry Lisbon asked the question in such a manner that it came out more like a potential accusation against her assistant than a warm, hospitable offer directed toward me. I'll say this for her, she knew how to establish an immediate tone for a meeting.

As a corporate magician, I've met my share of CEOs and you can set your comic bungling stereotypes aside; the ones I've met have been dynamic, magnetic and surprisingly sharp. Their focus may be on the bottom line, but most have known how to carry a conversation and how to win over a room. Some have even been remarkably warm and funny.

This last was not the case with Sherry Lisbon, the CEO of BuyMax. The snowy and icy view through her large office windows was warmer than the hand which shook mine.

Her steel blue eyes were colder than the skating rink visible through the window on what must have been a corporate-built manmade pond.

Her well-coiffed hair was so blonde it might have been white, but that could have been a trick of the light. She wore a tailored skirt and coat combination which was accessorized with a variety of bracelets and rings emblazoned with stones of various colors. Around her neck was a simple gold necklace, which she touched unconsciously after shaking my hand, perhaps reassuring herself I hadn't lifted it in some well-practiced pickpocket move.

Of the four possible suspects I had met, Sherry Lisbon was the biggest puzzle and that was clearly by design. Clifford Thomas was a flat-out local celebrity and Randall Glendower was an internet sensation, so research on those two—if I had needed it, which I hadn't—would be deep and plentiful.

Chip Cavanaugh's presence on the internet was less pervasive. The Cavanaugh Bank empire was publicly owned (albeit a huge percentage of the company was still owned by the family), and so finding out about him had been a relative ease. In fact, I had been able to accomplish it with my phone while parked in a visitor spot outside his downtown condo.

Sherry Lisbon was something else altogether. BuyMax was a privately held company and a little digging on my part demonstrated just how private it was. The company website was designed to sell products of all shapes and sizes and make that process easy; it also seemed designed to tell you as little about the company and its owner as possible.

Mission accomplished, I had decided that morning, after spending two fruitless hours trying to get a sense of my next and final interview subject.

"The police warned me of your visit," she said with a smile but no humor, gesturing to a seat in front of her desk as she returned to the rich leather chair behind it. There was nothing on the desk's surface, not even a piece of paper, a pen or a phone. Given how barren it was, I wondered for a moment why it needed to be so large. I lowered myself into one of the two chairs facing the desk.

"Yes, thank you for seeing me on such short notice," I began, settling into the chair uncomfortably.

"They gave me the impression the visit was mandatory; however I can't imagine how such a request could be effectively enforced."

Her words were clipped and she sounded angry, but her face revealed no emotion. In her late forties, she had high, strong cheekbones and a long, thin neck. If surgery had been involved to create her look, it was an impressive and invisible job.

"It can't be," I said with my most sincere smile. "Which is why I appreciate you taking the time to talk to me."

"Mr. Marks, I can tell you what I told them," she said, getting right down to it. "I certainly knew Tyler James and had done some business with him in the past. Their arrival to question me was the first I had heard of his death."

"That must have come as quite a shock," I suggested. She stared at me as if I had just begun speaking a foreign language, so I blabbered on. "I mean, finding out about his death that way."

"We weren't close in any sense of the word," she said, throwing a glance at her assistant which spoke volumes. The young lady hightailed it out of the room so quickly that, had this been a cartoon, she would have stirred up a small dust cloud in her wake. "I reacted as I would to the loss of any vendor."

"And how is that?"

She looked at me with the closest thing to an emotion she had revealed thus far, if slight puzzlement qualifies as an emotion. "How is what?"

"How do you typically react to the loss of a vendor?"

"You get a new vendor," she said.

It wasn't as if I was being scolded, but it felt darned close. Having not been scolded in, I don't know, twenty-five years, it took me a moment to recognize the feeling. I didn't like it any more now than I had when I was a kid.

She continued to stare at me.

Somewhere I heard a clock ticking, even though none was visible in the room.

"What sort of business did you conduct with Mr. James?" I ventured. "Buying or selling?"

"Exclusively buying," she said as she spotted a piece of invisible dust on the desk and removed it with great care and unnecessary precision, being it was invisible and all.

"What sorts of things did you buy?" I continued, feeling like I was coming toward the end of a painful and rather futile game of Twenty Questions.

"I honestly don't remember," she said. "I buy lots of things. That is, in fact, my business."

She made the slightest nod to TV monitors on the far wall, which silently projected the live images from studios around the country or around the world. There were a lot of monitors and on each one of them, in a different BuyMax studio, a plethora of products were being presented for sale. All the screens were silent, but the scrolling text on each screen represented a diverse variety of languages, many of which I recognized but none of which I could read.

I turned back to her. "I thought you were in the business of selling?"

She shook her head oh so slightly and I thought I recognized the slimmest trace of a smile cross her lips. "I'm in the business of selling in order to provide me with the resources to be in the business of buying. Sometimes I sell the things I buy, often at a significant profit. Sometimes I simply keep what I have purchased." The change in subject seemed to suddenly energize her. "Tell me, Mr. Marks, do you shop?"

"I'm sorry?"

"Do you, from time to time, visit a department store or perhaps our own Mall of America and move from store to store with no other intention than to discover something to buy? Or peruse the internet with no other goal than to find a treasure you never knew existed but now must own at all costs?" I was about to attempt to form an answer, but she cut me off. "No, you don't strike me as the type." She gave me another long look which felt sort of piercing. "No, not the type at all."

"What type do you think I am?" I asked, trying to sound confident in the boldness of my question. I doubt it fooled her for a second.

"You, like so many people—mostly men, but not confined to one gender—are targeted buyers. You need something, you find it, you buy it and then you're on to something else."

"But that's not how you do it?"

"No, that's not my approach. For me, there is nothing more fulfilling than finding an object—a rarity, a one-of-a-kind item—and swooping in and plucking it away." She hit the word "plucking" with such force I felt myself jump. Just a little.

"Does it matter what it is?"

She shrugged. "Sometimes. Not always."

"For you, it's the swooping. And the plucking."

This produced, for the first time, an actual smile. "I suppose you could put it that way."

"Is that what you did with Tyler James? Swooped and plucked?" Saying it out loud made it sound vaguely dirty, but if she was offended she kept it to herself.

She turned toward me. It felt like she was either starting to warm up to the subject or to me. I desperately hoped it was the subject.

"Tyler and I used to play a little game," she said. She stared me down, like she was teasing me to ask more.

"A game?" I worked hard and succeeded in keeping my voice from cracking. "What kind of game?"

"Sometimes he would find himself in a situation with two bidders, each going after the same object, tooth and nail. Each one outbidding the other. An escalating battle, as it were. If Tyler was feeling like a bad boy—and he often was a bad boy, don't think for a second he wasn't—he might get in touch and allow me to enter the fray."

"To swoop?" I suggested.

"Yes, to swoop in at the last second and outbid them all."

"And pluck."

"Yes." Again, almost a smile but not quite. "Swoop and pluck." She basked in the recollection for a long moment.

"Why?" I asked, breaking the silence. "Was it something you wanted?"

"Was what something I wanted?"

"The thing you outbid them on?"

"I have no idea. I often had no idea what I was bidding on."

Now it was my turn to feel like someone was speaking a foreign language. "Then why do it?"

"I really can't explain," she said, her voice dropping to just above a whisper. "But, Mr. Marks, let me share this with you: there are few pleasures on this earth equal to stepping in at the last second and taking something someone else desires. I mean, something they really, really want. An object. A relationship. A person."

She turned and looked at me. Her eyes were cold, yet they somehow burned into me. "You should try it sometime. You might be surprised just how pleasurable that can be."

Mercifully, our interview concluded moments later and I was quickly and efficiently escorted back out the way I had arrived, through a maze of cubes and TV monitors and white noise.

Dusk had come and the thermometer in my car put the temperature at a frigid fourteen degrees, but it felt balmy compared to the arctic chill I'd felt in Sherry Lisbon's office. I had turned back as I exited and I caught her eye. The look she gave me was decidedly predatory but, and I might have been imagining this— and I hope I was—there was a sexual component which was both undeniable and frightening. I tried to convince myself I was imagining it and I think I almost succeeded.

Once the car started, I immediately switched on the seat warmer and cranked the heater up to full. However, I didn't start to feel any real warmth until I was nearly home.

CHAPTER 14

The recent snowfall meant parking restrictions were now in place again on Chicago Avenue, with parking allowed on the even side of the street only, to make way for the snowplows. Consequently, I had to park my car way up the hill from our shop, wedging my car into a narrow spot and hoping my tires would be able to get me out of it when the time came.

The marquee was blazing at the Parkway Theater and people were just entering the lobby for the first show. I looked up at the marquee and was annoyed to see it read: *Spellbound For Glory*. I had given Tracy easily a half-dozen title possibilities—better ones, in my admittedly biased estimation—and yet she had chosen to program the very first option Quinton had tossed off in what I felt was a casual and slapdash manner.

Tracy was visible in the lobby and if she hadn't been in the midst of a conversation with a pair of customers, I might have stepped in and...and what? Told her I was miffed that she took one of Quinton's suggestions over mine? If I wanted to win some sort of pettiness award that would certainly be the way to do it. I gave the lobby one last look, long enough to see she seemed to have recovered completely from her fall as she conversed in an animated fashion with the couple, their backs to the door.

I continued down the sidewalk, digging in my pocket for my keys and silently berating myself for my current state of mind. My visit with Sherry Lisbon had put me in a sour mood and I wasn't feeling particularly upbeat about any of my fellow human beings.

Thinking of her led me to thoughts of Chip Cavanaugh and his sad and illicit art collection. And then I thought of Clifford Thomas, who was using alcohol to fight demons of his own, including his jealousy of his ex-wife's success.

Of the four alleged suspects I had interviewed—if interview is even the right word—the only one I felt any real connection to was Randall Glendower and his silly movie-and-comic-book-obsessed lifestyle. Unlike the other three, he was the only one who seemed to be getting any real healthy joy out of his wealth, even if it was expressed in a decidedly child-like manner.

"Are you locked out?"

A voice pulled me out of my reverie and I turned to see Megan trudging toward me. She was bundled up in a mismatched stocking cap, scarf and mittens, the odd combination creating a pleasing knitted mosaic. I smiled in spite of myself, which triggered a smile from her, and after a moment we stood there beaming at each other, our breath visible in the frigid air.

"No, just lost in my thoughts. You done for the night?" I asked, gesturing to her store down on the corner.

"Yes, and not a moment too soon."

"Tough day?"

She nodded. "Tough customers. For all their talk of peace and light and positive energy, some days New Age customers can be a real pain in the ass."

"Don't mince words, Megan. Tell me how you really feel."

She continued, either not recognizing my sarcasm or simply not caring. "Here's a few of the words I'm not going to mince: sanctimonious, self-involved, narrow-minded, narcissistic, clueless and condescending."

"Suddenly my day is looking like a bed of roses."

"Even a thorny bed of roses would be better than the day I had. But I refuse to take bad karma home with me." She waved her mittened hands in front of her face, symbolically brushing away the events of the day, then shut her eyes for a moment of either quiet meditation or continued silent cursing. Or both.

"Peace and light and happiness," she whispered and when she opened her eyes, all the anger and frustration had apparently lifted and she looked to be her normal, smiling self.

"That's better," she said, and then added suddenly, "I've missed you."

"I've missed you too."

"If you're not busy," she continued, flirtatiously, "would you have any interest in coming over to my place for dinner?"

"You're going to make me dinner?"

"Well, no, obviously you would make it. But you can do it at my place and we can eat it together."

"I can't imagine a better plan," I said, pocketing my keys and taking her hand. She gave my hand a warm squeeze through her mitten and we turned and began the trek back up the hill toward her duplex.

As we passed the theater I glanced into the lobby to see that Tracy was still in deep conversation with the same couple. This time she saw me and waved me to stop, crossing quickly to the glass doors.

"Hey, Eli," Tracy said, holding open the door with one hand. "I have something for you."

I began to move toward the theater and Megan followed, her hand still in mine. We stepped into the lobby together, the glass door swinging shut and giving Megan an unexpected boost into the room.

"Some guy stopped by your shop today to drop these off. When he found out the store was closed, he asked if I could pass them along." She pulled a black canvas bag out from behind the candy counter and crossed to us. Now that I could see her without the distortion of the frosted lobby glass, I noticed she looked worn and tired and about as stressed as Megan had been five minutes before.

She handed the bag to me and I glanced inside, recognizing the five hardback books of Harry's I had brought to Clifford Thomas for autographing.

"Thanks," I said, looking up. "Thanks for doing that."

"Oh, no problem," she said with what looked like a forced smile. "Are you two on your way somewhere?"

The answer seemed obvious and I wasn't really sure how to respond without saying the verbal equivalent of "duh." But before I could begin to form an answer, we were interrupted by a voice from across the lobby.

"I'm not done talking to you," the woman barked as she moved toward us. She was tall with sharp features and not just big hair, but big *big* hair. Even though she was well covered by a puffy winter jacket and baggy sweatpants, I got the distinct sense that inside those clothes she was way too pale and skinny and sort of mean. Like a low-rent supermodel.

"Well, I'm done talking to you," Tracy said, not even bothering to turn and confront the angry woman.

"Fine," she snapped. "Just fine. We'll go up and look at his stuff on our own, don't need your permission."

Tracy still refused to turn around, but she amped up the volume in her response. "First, you do need my permission, and second, it you want to go through Tyler's effects, you'll have to take it up with the police or his estate or whatever."

The skinny woman froze in her tracks and turned back slowly, providing me with the time to get a look at her companion. He was thinner than she was, but in his case he seemed to come by it naturally.

He had a hawk nose, a scrawny goatee, and he wore the now standard hipster hat—is it a trilby? A fedora? Whatever it is, it was too small and made his head look overly large.

"They aren't *his* effects," she said, placing her hands defiantly on her nonexistent hips. "They're my effects. Mine to take. Mine to keep."

This statement was outrageous enough to make Tracy turn and look at the woman for the first time since we had stepped into the lobby.

"Really," she said, her voice still quavering with anger but now back down to a normal register. "And why is that?"

The woman eyed the three of us, and then turned her glare directly on Tracy.

"Because Tyler James is my husband."

This statement hung in the air for what seemed like a long time. Two other patrons, obviously recognizing the tone of the tableau as they headed into the lobby to buy a snack, quickly turned and headed back to the relative safety of the auditorium.

"Regardless of your alleged marital status," Tracy said, closing the distance between herself and the scary duo, "you are not entering that projection booth without a police order."

The twosome mirrored her actions, the man less confidently than his companion, so the three of them were now in a tight configuration in the middle of the lobby.

"We'll see about that," the alleged Mrs. Tyler James hissed.

Megan gave me a look and a head nod which could have meant either "let's get out of here" or "get in there and do something." I was hoping it was the latter, but when she tilted her head at the growing fracas I realized my options were down to one. Against my better judgment I stepped into the middle of the hostile trio.

"Okay, okay, let's just everybody calm down, take a breath and, well, calm down," I said, sensing immediately that my future as a professional negotiator was limited. "I'm sure we can sort this all out like adults."

"Mind your own business, clown." This was said by Mrs. James' surly companion and I was tempted to point out, with his tiny hat on his oversized head, he resembled a clown far more than I did. But instead I attempted to use humor to deflate the situation.

"Hey, hey," I said, using my "hey, we're all having a good time here" tone. "Watch it. Some of my best friends are clowns."

If nothing else, this got their attention and they both turned toward me as Tracy stepped behind me.

"Why is this any business of yours?" Mrs. Tyler James asked, and her companion nodded menacingly in support.

That's a good question, I thought. Really an excellent notion. Why was this any business of mine? Feeling the need to supply some justification for my presence in this conflagration, I finally stammered, "Well, I found Tyler's body."

This must have given me some small sense of authority, for the woman turned her full attention on me as Tracy faded behind me.

"He's got some of my stuff," she said. "He's got stuff at my place, I've got stuff at his place, and I want to get my stuff."

"I thought you said you were married to him?" I asked, more intrigued than I really had any right to be. "Why do you live in different places?"

This led to a deep sigh and a shake of her unruly hair. "It's a sad situation. We were separated on a temporary basis in order to work individually on some recurring issues in our relationship."

I gestured toward the lanky hipster to her left, who had been nodding in agreement at her pronouncement. "Who's this, your marriage counselor?"

She clucked her tongue and sighed heavily. "Gunnar is a dear, platonic friend who is helping me through this very stressful time," she said, using a phrase I suspect she had taken from countless celebrity tabloids. Gunnar dutifully nodded in concurrence.

"Really." I tried to make this sound like I was agreeing with her, but she must have heard the sarcasm buried deep beneath it.

"Hey, don't think Tyler didn't have his own share of tramps, morons and nitwits during our separation," she added defensively. Gunnar again nodded along and then stopped in mid-nod as the full weight of her statement landed. He had no time to really consider it, as the Widow James was just getting warmed up.

"As Tyler's legal, common-law wife, I have every right to reclaim items which might have been in his possession at the time of his demise, but which are in reality my property. The police wouldn't let me into his apartment," she continued, gesturing in Tracy's direction, "but I'll be damned if this tall drink of bathwater is going to prevent me from reclaiming my personal property from my late husband's place of employment."

She and Gunnar made a move toward the stairs to the booth, but I quickly sidestepped and put myself in their path.

"Look, nobody wants any trouble, least of all me," I said quickly. "But if you persist in this course of action, I have to warn you I will have no other option but to call the police."

"And if you don't get out of my way," Gunnar growled, "I will be forced to punch your lights out." He curled the fingers of his right hand into a fist and held it in the air, in some sort of pre-punch pose he might have seen in a movie.

"I would not recommend that," I said in what I hoped was a firm voice, free of any errant high-pitched cracking. "I have several very close friends in the police department and I can assure you I have them on speed dial." As if to prove my point, I pulled my phone out of my pocket and held it up in the air. Like that might scare them, it being a phone and all.

Oddly enough, it did. First Gunnar's eyes went wide and then Mrs. James' face began to pale as well. They began to back away from me, so I advanced on them, holding up the phone the way Professor van Helsing would hold up a crucifix to ward off Count Dracula.

"Let's just put this little incident behind us. You two hit the road or I hit the speed dial button—and it's number one on my speed dial—and you can tell the rest of your story downtown with the one and only Homicide Detective Fred Hutton."

This last threat must have done the trick, as the motley pair turned and burst through the lobby doors and out into the falling snow. They scurried across Chicago Avenue and disappeared into the night.

"With people like that," I said confidently, turning to Megan as I returned my trusty phone to its resting place in my coat pocket, "the threat of the police is always a strong motivating factor."

Megan smiled and nodded, and then looked from me to Tracy. I turned to look at her and realized that, during the course of my short exchange with the duo, she had ducked behind the candy counter. She had returned with a very solid and menacing baseball bat, which she now slung casually over her shoulder. I suspect her pose moments before had been far less relaxed and was likely the actual motivating force behind the couple's quick departure.

"And of course there's the baseball bat," I added. "Which is also a motivating factor." I looked to Megan to see if any shred of my masculinity remained.

"I thought I was number one on your speed dial?" she said, barely masking a look of hurt.

As the universe had predicted, it was going to be just that sort of day.

Chapter 15

Despite the short debacle over who, in fact, held the Number One position on my speed dial, the rest of my evening with Megan was surprisingly pleasant, with no bursts of jealousy on my part that had marred our other recent encounters. It helped that Quinton's name never came up.

The only interruption during the evening was the quick phone call I made to Deirdre to report our near-violent encounter at the movie theater.

The call confirmed Mrs. Tyler James' assertion that the police had denied her access to Tyler's apartment and I also learned they had rejected her request to claim his body from the morgue. Deirdre, being surprisingly chatty, went on to explain that Minnesota doesn't recognize common-law marriages, which put Mrs. James' dubious claims on even weaker footing.

After scrounging through Megan's remarkably sparse refrigerator and larder, I cobbled together a decent spaghetti sauce, pasta and salad. Both were exponentially improved by a bottle and a half of red wine. I noted that Megan's wine rack was clearly not suffering from the same lack of attention she paid to the pantry.

"You certainly were brave tonight," Megan said out of the blue during a short lull in the conversation while I opened the second bottle of wine. "I mean, facing down those two creeps. And you didn't even know Tracy had gone to get a baseball bat, did you?"

I shook my head and smiled smugly, as one does when one has demonstrated meritorious bravery.

"What choice did I have, really?" I said, refilling her glass and topping off mine. "I considered shirking, but how would that look? I mean, come on, I'm no shirker."

"You don't shirk," Megan agreed.

"And as a basketball player, Tracy has a lot more experience in scuffles and such. I couldn't be shown up by a mere girl."

"At over six feet, there is nothing mere about that girl," Megan said as she sipped. "Hey, did I mention how horrible customers were today?"

"You might have said something in passing," I said as I slid back into my chair. "But I never get tired of hearing about horrible New Age customers and their petty, self-righteous but environmentally-friendly needs."

That was all the push she needed. I sat back, sipped my wine and smiled as she recounted multiple examples of their innate horribleness.

The next morning I knocked lightly on Harry's door on the way up to my apartment, in order to join him in our daily breakfast ritual. However, when he didn't appear after repeated knocking, I hit the Number One on my speed dial, making a mental note to move Megan to that slot as soon as possible. Harry answered on the third ring and the tiredness in his voice gave me my answer before I even raised the question.

"Thanks, Eli," he said quietly, "but I'm beat. I think I'm going to sleep in for another hour. Are you okay to get breakfast on your own?"

I assured him I was. I started to head up to my apartment, but on the spur of the moment I decided to head over to the coffee shop on the other side of 48th Street. A change of locale for breakfast would do me good, I decided, and since I was already bundled up for the cold, it felt like the notion had been almost predestined.

Five minutes later I was sipping coffee and biting into a warm, flaky croissant with a chocolate center. I flipped open my iPad and was deeply engrossed in an article in *Genii* magazine about the pros and cons of the Erdnase bottom palm when my cell phone buzzed. I noted it was 9:01 and then answered the phone.

"You're at work early."

"The early bird has got nothing on me," said the far-too-chipper voice of my agent, Elaine. "I'm calling with a last minute gig for tonight. You interested? Available?"

I was both, but my primary reaction was one of tempered wariness. I hadn't heard from the elusive Mr. Lime in several days and this sort of last-minute gig scenario was his favorite gambit as a set-up for his patented creepy one-on-one meetings.

"Probably," I said noncommittally. "Is this a client you've worked with in the past or is this a one-off?"

"Oh, this is a meeting planner I've known for years. A bit flighty, not great with details, a bit of a lush and a complete clotheshorse, but a real sweetheart," she said in what could have been a perfect self-assessment if she had been so inclined. "Seems she got the call at o-dark thirty this morning from up on high that the one thing missing for her client's event tonight was some walk-around close-up magic. She called me. I called you. And here we are."

Here we were indeed, I thought. With the client properly vetted, I quickly decided to accept the offer, as my evening was open and—still stinging from Harry's recent criticism—I could always use the chance to polish my act to a level close to that of the almighty Quinton Moon.

"Sure," I said. "Text me the details and I'll make you proud."

"You always do. Now I've got to deal with the fallout from a recalcitrant and possibly inebriated piano player who got mad at a gig last night and played 'Piano Man' for two hours straight," she said with a laugh.

"What was his excuse?"

"He claimed once you get into the song, there's no way out," she explained with another laugh. "To be honest, he might have a point."

"We lead weird lives," I said.

"We do indeed," she replied, still laughing as the phone clicked.

"You know what Hunter S. Thompson said to do when the going gets weird?" The voice behind me was familiar and though I couldn't identify him on a conscious level, my unconscious reacted with a chill which ran the length and breadth of my body. I turned and looked up to see Mr. Lime. He gestured to the empty chair across from me and I nodded more out of habit than agreement.

I had never seen him ambulatory and was surprised at how tiny he actually was, noting he wasn't much taller standing than I was in a sitting position. He moved like a marionette being operated by a drunken puppeteer, as if each joint was being operated separately and badly. I had also never seen him in the sunlight, and the early morning glow bouncing off the snow outside made his skin look even more translucent, not unlike the visible man model we used in biology class in high school.

Recognizing, correctly, that I was at a loss for words, he continued his explanation as he lowered himself into his seat. "Mr. Thompson opined, 'When the going gets weird, the weird turn pro.' It's an odd expression, but once you hear it you'll be surprised at the number of applications to which it applies on a day-to-day basis."

I felt my brow began to furrow as I worked on forming a question, but he waved it away with his bony hand, which looked so thin I suspect it didn't even move the air as he passed it in front of me.

"Not to worry, Mr. Marks, I'm not following you. On the contrary, I was on my way to *see* you this morning. Harpo," he continued, gesturing toward the counter, "stopped into this lovely establishment to purchase some tea to help me stave off the chill and came back to the car with the happy news that you were already comfortably ensconced within."

I looked over at the queue which had formed at the counter and recognized Mr. Lime's silent henchman patiently waiting in line, just like anyone off the street. He saw I was looking at him and gave me a subtle tip of his nonexistent hat. I turned back to Mr. Lime, who now for the fourth time in my life was seated across from me, smiling his skull-like grin from ear to ear. Seeing him there, right out here in public, was wildly disconcerting, like seeing a mermaid sitting poolside at the YMCA...if that mermaid were a scary old psychopath.

"You were coming to the store?" I said. Saying the words aloud provided a chill all their own. "To the magic store?"

"Yes. I have never seen your establishment and figured by this time you've most likely had the chance to interview the four suspects I had suggested to the police. I'm looking forward to hearing your thoughts and am, admittedly, impatient by nature."

Again he smiled and again it was all I could do to keep from jumping up and running out of the coffee shop, screaming into the snowy morning.

It took effort, but I was able to suppress the desire, but at the same time I made a mental note that it would always provide a good hip pocket option.

"Did you have a chance to meet with them?" He leaned forward, his elbows resting on the table, and then intertwined his bony fingers and settled his chin upon them. The look would have been coquettish if he were a seventeen-year-old high school cheerleader, but the sheer ingenuousness of his pose simply made it all the more dark and frightening. "Did they prove thought-provoking?"

The question was presented innocently enough, but it was backed by such menace that—for a moment—I had a sudden fear for each of my interview subjects, sensing one or more could be in some form of homicidal peril.

"Each was thought-provoking in his or her own way," I began, not at all sure where I was headed. "I haven't spent much time in the past with extremely wealthy people."

Lime clucked his tongue and nodded. "Yes, money does..." He paused, thinking for a long moment. "It does funny things to people," he finally said, putting a spin on "funny" which made it sound anything but.

It looked like he had more to say on the topic, but Harpo arrived at this moment, bearing a cardboard cup of tea which he placed gingerly in front of Mr. Lime. The old man removed his elbows from the table and leaned back as Harpo reached past me for the sweetener options. He found two packets of actual sugar and opened them daintily, to ensure—I suspected—that no errant crystals found their way to the front of Mr. Lime's well-tailored black overcoat.

With the sugar safely deposited in the cup, Harpo produced a stir stick and gave the liquid what appeared to be the standard and regulated number of stirs. He tapped the wet stick on the side of the cup and then stepped away as silently as he had arrived.

Mr. Lime reached for the cup with both hands, looking up at me as he did. "Excuse me," he said, "but I have a bit of a chill."

"Me too," I agreed and we each raised our respective cups to our lips. He gurgled softly while sipping his tea. For my part, I couldn't take my eyes off his hands.

They were clasped tightly around the cardboard cup and I swear I could actually see the coffee shop logo through his rice paper skin.

He swallowed happily, set the cup down and licked his lips, his tongue darting in and out of his mouth like it was afraid of the sunlight. He smiled up at me and gestured with both hands.

"Proceed," he said. "I am very anxious to hear about your adventures."

Mr. Lime was remarkably quiet throughout my recap, nodding encouragingly and offering an occasional "Ah," or "Oh, yes, I see," but otherwise letting me recount the substance of the interviews, and my alleged perceptions, at my own halting pace.

I wrapped up my report and he looked at me for a long time without expression. Then suddenly, like a dead flower resurrecting back to life, his lips twisted into a smile which quickly spread across his lean and sallow face.

"Excellent," he said, his voice a hoarse whisper. "Simply excellent," he added, then picked up his tea and took a short sip.

"Thank you," I said from habit. I honestly wasn't sure which part or parts of my story were deserving of this praise.

"Let me ask you this," he said, setting down his cup and reaching for a paper napkin from the dispenser. It proved to be recalcitrant and so I pulled one out from the other side of the dispenser, just as Harpo appeared at the table. In his stubby, muscular hands he held a small pile of napkins, which he had produced seemingly out of thin air. Presented with these choices, Mr. Lime looked from one offering to the other, and then took the napkin I was holding. Before he left, Harpo turned and gave me a blank look, which I naturally read as cold and homicidal.

"Let me ask you this," Mr. Lime repeated once he had dabbed away the small amount of moisture from his lips, "and I'd like you to be completely honest."

"Certainly," I said.

"What does your gut tell you about each of these people and their relationship to the murder of Tyler James and the theft of *London After Midnight?*"

"I don't know about the murder," I began, "but each of them could, I think, have been the buyer of the stolen movie print."

"Expound," he said, once again resting his elbows on the table and his chin on his hands.

I sat back, considering the four suspects. "Okay, obviously each of them has enough money to make the purchase, which might have been as high as $750,000, if the $75,000 found in the projection booth was just a ten percent down payment."

"Agreed," he said with a sharp nod. "However, let us not forget that—on occasion—people take deep, sometimes homicidal pleasure from getting what they've paid for without actually paying for it. To 'spend' the money but still have the money, as it were."

"The miser's dream," I said.

"Exactly," he said, his smile getting even wider. "And speaking as a miser myself," he continued, "that dream never dies."

I wasn't quite sure what to do with this comment, so I turned my attention back to his original question.

"Clifford Thomas," I began, "likes kitschy, macabre things, if his Addams' Family house on Summit Avenue is any indication. He writes murder mysteries, and the plot of London After Midnight is, to some degree, a famous murder mystery. He admitted to buying items from Tyler in the past. And spending money like that, in what some might consider a foolish manner, could be his way at getting back at his more successful ex-wife," I added, "if you don't mind a little dime-store psychoanalysis."

"Not only do I not mind it, I encourage it," Mr. Lime said. "And what of our banker friend, the art collector Mr. Cavanaugh?"

"He takes great pleasure, perverse pleasure really, in possessing things he's not supposed to," I said, remembering his white-walled apartment in downtown St. Paul and the treasures hidden behind them. "It makes him feel like a bad boy, and I think owning something stolen by the Nazis and hidden by the Swiss—a one-of-a-kind treasure which everyone thought was long lost—would be right up his alley."

"An odd bird, that one," Mr. Lime said quietly, clearly not recognizing the irony of one odd bird calling out another. He looked back at me. "Think he is our secret buyer?"

I had already given this considerable thought, going back and forth on my opinion of his alleged guilt. I shook my head. "I don't think so," I said.

"Why not?"

"It's what he said. Chip Cavanaugh likes to look at his stolen treasures, hang them on the walls and hide them from the world for his own private viewing. I really don't think some old tin movie reels filled with disintegrating celluloid is the sort of thing he'd get excited about, let alone kill for."

"Good point. And what of the ice queen, Ms. Sherry Lisbon? Was she our mystery buyer?"

I took a sip of my now-cold coffee as I thought back on our meeting in her office at BuyMax. "She's a tough one to read," I said.

"Indeed."

"She doesn't strike me as a passionate movie memorabilia buyer," I continued. "In fact, I can't decide what her category would be, if any. She doesn't seem to care what she's buying, as long as she's able to take it away from someone else who wants to buy it."

"What does your dime-store psychoanalysis suggest to you about her?"

"That's she's a nut job," I said before I realized I was saying it out loud.

Mr. Lime chuckled at my assessment. "Yes, I think you've hit the nail squarely on the head with our friend Ms. Lisbon."

"But they're all nut jobs, really," I said. "I don't know if they were nut jobs before they got rich or if the money was the cause, but each of them struck me as strange in their own, unique, creepy and oddball way."

"I can say this about that: I started out dirt-poor and money hasn't changed me in the least." He stared at me, straight-faced, for a long moment, and then his face erupted into a huge smile. "Gotcha, didn't I?"

I had to admit he had. I could tell he was deeply pleased at his momentary ruse.

"And what of Randall Glendower?" he asked, getting back on topic. "Where does he fall on this spectrum?"

I couldn't help but smile thinking of the cheery, rotund comic-book storeowner, with his pet monkey, million-dollar website and fanatic's love of movies and movie memorabilia.

"He's the only one who admitted to bidding on buying *London After Midnight*. And he was outbid."

"Did he say by who?"

I shook my head. "I'm not even sure he knew."

"Yet one of our quartet has admitted to taking pleasure in outbidding people on the objects they love, just for the sheer enjoyment of taking it away from them."

I considered this. "Sherry Lisbon certainly could be the one who outbid him," I said. "But if she was the one who bought the movie from Tyler, she would hardly need to kill him to take possession of it."

"Yes, well, that brings us to the other side of our coin," Mr. Lime said, sitting back in his chair. "As you say, whoever bought the movie from Tyler would have no need to kill him for it. So we can assume, at least for argument's sake, our killer was not the final buyer. And yet, to date, no one admits to being the buyer. Or, for that matter, the seller. Which brings us back to square one."

He sighed deeply, to such a degree that his shrunken chest appeared to sink even farther into his tiny frame. Then his eyes once again brightened and he clapped his hands together with such force that several other patrons in the quiet coffee shop noticeably started at the sound.

"Enough of this," he said as his skeleton grin returned to his face. "Do me a trick and we'll call it a day."

I was still reeling from the sound of his hands clapping and it took me a moment to register what he was requesting. As soon as I did, I realized he had once again caught me unarmed, magic-wise. I recognized we were a short walk from a store which was packed wall-to-wall with magic tricks and classic illusions, but I wanted to leave that as a last resort. I had the feeling once Mr. Lime was invited into your home—like a vampire—things would progress quickly from bad to worse.

I scanned the room and then our table for inspiration, my gaze settling on the small container of various sweeteners that Harpo had selected from earlier.

In an effort to meet Harry's recent challenge—to give my current act some well-needed practice while adding to my admittedly limited repertoire—I had been reading up on possible tricks I could quickly slip into my close-up act. There was one with a sugar pack, called Very Sweet, by an inventive magician named David Gabbay which I had recently read about but had never attempted. As foolish as it was to try out a new trick without any practice, I recognized if I didn't do *something* I was likely to raise Mr. Lime's ire. And I certainly didn't want to experience what that might be like.

I pulled the sweetener container over, praying Harpo hadn't taken the last of the real sugar packets when he had sweetened Mr. Lime's tea. As luck would have it, there was one more remaining, stuck in amid the pink and yellow packets of artificial options.

"Like The Miser's Dream," I began, vamping like crazy while I ran the steps of the illusion through my mind, "everybody likes the idea of spending their money while still keeping it. It's basic human nature."

Mr. Lime nodded in silent agreement as I held up the sugar packet.

"Now let's say you want this sugar packet and it costs a quarter and all you have is a quarter and you'd rather not give up your last quarter but what are you going to do because you really want the sugar?" I was nearly out of breath as my run-on sentence finally found some desperately needed punctuation.

"Do you have a quarter?" I continued. Mr. Lime stared back at me as if I had suddenly begun speaking Mandarin. I repeated the question, in a shorter form. "A quarter?"

"Oh, dear," he said, looking—for the first time since I'd met him—perplexed and perhaps even a little lost. "I don't carry money. Haven't in years. A quarter, you say?"

He began to pat his pockets but we both knew how that was going to end.

To take him out of his misery, I quickly produced a coin from my pocket. "Not a problem," I said with a hollow laugh. "You can use mine."

I slid the coin across the table toward him.

He picked it up and examined it with great interest, like an archeologist who had discovered a relic from a lost civilization. While he scrutinized both sides of the rare treasure I'd given him, I reached into my coat pocket and pulled out my ever-present black Sharpie pen. I uncapped it and held it out for him.

"To make sure I don't switch the coin in the process of the trick, why don't you go ahead and put your initials on the coin."

Once again he gave me a blank, pained look. "Sign the coin?" he said in a whisper.

"Just your initials," I said, again pushing the pen toward him.

"Sorry to disappoint you, Mr. Marks," he said, regaining his voice. "But I don't sign things. Anything. Ever."

While I've certainly had audience members who were too drunk to sign their initials, this was a first for me. I glanced over at Harpo, who was seated straight-backed in a chair by the window, his hands folded neatly in his lap. He was staring at us unblinkingly. I had the feeling he had been doing this the entire time.

"And I'm guessing your pal Harpo doesn't go around signing things, either," I said, trying to put a jovial spin on my tone. Mr. Lime smiled ruefully as he gave his head a simple shake.

"How about I put my initials on it," I suggested, pulling back both the pen and the coin and trying to jumpstart the trick back to life. "I mean, if the magician puts his own initials on the coin, that does weaken the credibility of the trick somewhat, but we're all friends here, right?"

This last thought made Mr. Lime widen his smile, showing off his pointed and yellowed teeth. "Friends. That we are, Mr. Marks. That we are."

I fought the chill this statement sent throughout my body by refocusing my attention on the coin, the pen and my somewhat shaky initials. Then I capped the pen and picked up the coin.

"In order to obtain the sugar," I said, using the coin to gesture toward the packet on the table, "we are forced to give up the coin."

With that, I tossed the coin from one hand to the other, and then opened the hand to show the coin was gone.

I opened the other hand as well, which appeared to be equally empty.

This produced a delighted coo from Mr. Lime. I didn't take any time to bask in it but charged forward.

"We may have lost the coin, but now we possess the sugar," I said, picking the packet up from its place on the table. "But wouldn't it be a wonderful world if we could have both the sugar and..." I tore the top off the packet and handed it to Mr. Lime.

He took it gingerly with two fingers and, noting my gesture, turned the packet upside down. A flow of white crystals streamed onto the table top, along with the resounding clink of the quarter.

"....and the coin," Mr. Lime said, completing my sentence. His bony finger separated the grains of sugar on the table, revealing the signed coin within. He gently picked it up and looked closely at the initials, a look of wonder on his face.

"If you'd like," I said, brushing the pile of sugar into my hand, "you can keep the quarter as a souvenir."

"Oh, that would be wonderful," he said, not taking his eyes off the sticky, pen-stained coin. "Just wonderful."

I will say this about the odd Mr. Lime. He was undoubtedly a criminal. He was likely a murderer, perhaps on multiple occasions.

But, when things went right, he was also the best audience I'd ever had for magic.

I followed Mr. Lime and Harpo out to their car. It was parked boldly in a No Parking zone, yet bore no sign of a ticket. The old man clutched Harpo's arm as they navigated to the car's back door. I found myself extending an arm of my own to ensure the fragile marionette made it into the backseat unscathed. Once safely deposited, he looked up at me, squinting in the sunlight reflecting off the snow. As always, his pupils were deep black, even as his eyes narrowed in the bright light.

"Thank you, Mr. Marks, for your insights," he said. "And of course, for your magic. I'm afraid I've grown tired. We'll save our visit to your shop for another day."

"Looking forward to it," I lied.

"And you take care of yourself," he continued, as Harpo stood by patiently with one hand on the door handle, waiting to close the door and get on their way. "After your close call with the stolen car the other night, I would hate to lose you to a simple hit-and-run accident."

"You and me both."

"Yes," he agreed with an enigmatic smile. "Any other accidents I should know about?"

I was about to say no, but a thought occurred to me. "Actually, there was another accident."

He looked up at me with great interest, so I continued. "Tracy, the manager of the movie theater, fell off a ladder in front of the theater. Someone pushed it. No one saw who it was."

"And was this Tracy injured?"

"She cracked her head pretty badly, but she's okay," I said, remembering the frozen pool of blood on the sidewalk in front of the theater.

"That raises many questions for our consideration, but one in particular," he said, leaning back and settling into the leather seat. "What do you and this Tracy have in common?"

I thought the question sounded rhetorical and Harpo must have agreed, for he shut the door to the dark sedan and the car disappeared down 48th Street. But I didn't really notice, because I was considering what Tracy and I had in common. I had considered it before and had no trouble bringing it back to the surface.

It was this: We had both looked into the projection booth and witnessed the details, such as they were, of the Tyler James crime scene.

Chapter 16

"Surely your agent mentioned the costume."

"Not a word."

"We were very clear about the costume."

"This is the first I'm hearing about it."

It might have been cold outside, but there was also a definite chill in the green room backstage at that night's event. The client, a fashionably dressed woman with big hair and a tendency to whisper for emphasis, was not pleased with this turn of events. For the record, neither was I.

"It's in the contract. You signed the contract," she whispered.

"I have no doubt it's in the contract I signed. I thought it was a standard contract," I whispered right back.

"Costumes are always part of our standard contract."

"They are never part of mine."

She gave me a big, phony smile. "Why don't we just agree to disagree and you put on the costume." It sounded like a question until she got to the end of the sentence, and then it didn't.

You know the old adage about the customer always being right? I think that was made up by a customer.

My experience has taught me the customer is wrong about nine out of sixteen times.

The costume in question sat slumped sadly in the corner of the room. It consisted of a large rabbit, about six feet tall, holding a big black top hat in front of it. I wasn't being asked to be a big rabbit. I was being asked to be embraced by a big rabbit.

The idea was that once the performer climbed into the costume, the effect would be that of a giant bunny holding a top hat, with the magician sticking out of the hat. While the rabbit's legs would actually be my legs, the illusion that the rabbit was producing a magician out of his hat was a strong one. I knew this to be true, because ten minutes later I was fully encased in the costume and surveying my reflection in the mirror. There I was, a magician in a tux, protruding out of a large top hat held by an even larger rabbit.

This may be, I thought, the lowest point in my entire life.

A figure appeared in the mirror behind me and I was suddenly proven wrong. "Eli, excellent, I was afraid you wouldn't be available!" It was Quinton Moon, of course, because that was the only way this could get any worse.

"Oh, honey, you look adorable."

Wait. I was mistaken. Right behind Quinton was Megan, decked out in a spangled dress and wobbling toward me on new high heels.

I turned slowly, not for dramatic effect but because the costume didn't allow for quick movements in any direction. Quinton and Megan stood in the doorway, a stunning twosome ready for the red carpet.

And then there was me.

"You," I said through clenched teeth, trying to will the muscles in my face into a semblance of a smile. "I have you to thank for this, don't I?"

Quinton stepped into the room and clapped his hands excitedly. "Guilty as charged," he said. "I was talking to the client last night and I happened to mention my show often goes over much better if the audience has already had a wee taste of magic earlier in the evening. When she agreed, I immediately thought of you. And here you are."

"Yes," I said slowly. "Here I am."

"Eli that is such a cute costume." I checked Megan's face for any trace of irony or sarcasm, but came up empty. She sincerely thought I looked adorable. Knowing this, however, did nothing to help make me feel adorable.

"You're part of the act tonight?"

She nodded and giggled. "We've been rehearsing all afternoon," she said excitedly. "I'm not sure I can pull it off, but Quinton seems to think I'll do fine."

"You'll do fine," he repeated, moving a stray hair from in front of her face. "You look perfect and you'll be wonderful."

"You're doing Harbin's Zig Zag?" I asked, trying to sound as nonchalant as possible.

"Mostly," Quinton said. "I've also taken a tad from Paul Daniels' presentation, but not so much I feel guilty about it. Tweaked it here and there and made it my own. You know how it is."

His tone was very buddy-buddy, like two old pro magicians just chewing the fat. However, I'd never felt less like a magician, let alone the member of an exclusive fraternity.

"It's really fun," Megan said, clearly not sensing my mood. "It took some practice, but I think I finally got the hang of it."

"But now you'll know how it's done," I said plaintively. "You never want to know how magic tricks are done."

She waved this thought away with her hand. "Oh, Eli, you know me," she said, still smiling brightly. "I might know it now, but by tomorrow I will have completely forgotten how it works."

Despite my grim mood, I couldn't help but smile. I knew that would likely be the case.

Mercifully, it was time for me to mingle and amaze, so I excused myself and shuffled out of the room and into the hustle and bustle of the reception, which was already in full bloom.

One of the first things you have to get over, as a working strolling magician, is the problem of how you approach people out of the blue and ask them if they want to see some magic. Magicians are, not surprisingly, often somewhat introverted, and so going up to strangers is not an easy skill to master. Plus, you're butting into an existing social dynamic and immediately trying to turn it to be about you. You could be interrupting a regular conversation, a friendship-ending argument, or the beginnings of a marriage proposal.

I think I've gotten pretty good at it over the years, but that night I discovered almost immediately that if you really want to quickly break the ice with a group of strangers, you need to dress up in a bunny costume. This is certainly true in magic, but I suspect it might have applications in other social situations as well.

While in the costume, there was no need to introduce myself, apologize for interrupting or ask if anyone wanted to see some magic. When you see a six-foot rabbit coming at you holding an enormous black top hat with a magician sticking out of it, you pretty much know what the situation is. And if you don't, you want your questions answered, pronto.

The other thing which surprised me was how much fun I had doing it, and I don't think the costume played any part in this. The hours I had spent, at Harry's annoying suggestion, tearing my act apart and putting it back together had yielded some stunning results.

During the dismantling process, I had realized that two separate card tricks I did as part of the walk-around act could be combined, with very minor changes, into one trick which produces two effects—a climax, followed by an even bigger and more surprising climax. This new combination got a much larger, longer and heartier response than when it had been two separate tricks and it tickled me to do it again and again for the different groups as I shuffled my way around the reception area.

I had also made some scripting changes when I finally admitted to myself the reactions I was getting on two effects were not what I had intended. The audience was way ahead of me on my Card to Wallet routine and a prediction effect with a color-changing card wasn't coming off as a prediction effect, but instead appeared to the audience as just quick sleight of hand. But with some minor and not-so-minor changes to the set-up for each trick, I immediately started to get the right reaction to each illusion.

Not all the tweaks I made produced immediate or obvious results, but enough new and good things came out of the exercise that I promised myself to begin the dismantling process on my stage act as soon as possible. I even eliminated a really tough sleight of hand move from one trick, when I had realized I was only doing the move to impress other magicians. It might have been my imagination, but it felt like I got a better response to that trick than I had in the past, because my focus had shifted from being a slick "move monkey" to actually focusing on entertaining the audience.

I was working out how I might tell Harry of these small successes without admitting he had been right when they announced the featured entertainment was beginning and my audience began to stream out of the reception and into the show room. And somehow my high spirits chose that moment to exit as well, for the next seventy-five minutes were a special form of torture.

It was time for Quinton Moon's show to begin.

I missed the beginning of the stage show because I spent a frustrating ten minutes struggling to extricate myself from a bunny, and not the Hugh Hefner variety.

By the time I reached the back of the theater, sweaty and sore, the show was in full bloom.

I so wanted to hate it. And him. But the bastard charmed me— and the entire audience—at every turn.

When Megan and I had seen Quinton's chamber magic show at the St. Paul Hotel, I had been impressed at how intimate and personal he made the experience for a crowd of about fifty. Confronted with an audience that must have topped off at around four hundred, I assumed he wouldn't be able to replicate the feeling of a personal relationship with every member of the audience, but somehow he pulled it off. I don't know what he had done during the first ten minutes I missed, but by the time I got there he had won them over completely.

When I came in he was just beginning his version of Houdini's famous illusion where he walked through a brick wall. With the help of several audience members and some discreet stagehands, an impressive and solid-looking wall had been assembled on stage. Quinton recited his patter—which, of course, didn't sound like patter but instead sounded completely fresh and improvised—as the wall was completed, talking about how Harry Houdini had done this same illusion and done it so effectively that many people had come to believe he actually could do things like walk through walls.

The words "walking through walls" clicked in my head and I got a sudden image of the cops as they struggled to remove the bulky projection room door, behind which lay a very dead Tyler James. I hadn't considered this before, but the circumstances of his death did have the distinct feeling of a magic trick, where someone discovered a way to walk through a brick wall without the necessity of something as mundane as a working door. In the case of the trick Quinton was in the midst of performing, I knew how he was pulling it off. But the trick in the projection booth was still a mystery.

Quinton completed his walk through the brick wall to a thunderous and well-deserved ovation, and moved effortlessly into the next routine. But in his hands, nothing felt like a routine.

The show was a conversation which appeared to move spontaneously and randomly from topic to topic, the way real conversations do.

I knew most of the tricks he performed, but he gave each one a distinctive twist and made them all seem fresh and new. He even pulled out some old standards from every magician's birthday party repertoire and somehow made them seem completely dazzling and inventive.

Unlike some magicians, Quinton didn't make his focus fooling the crowd, creating puzzles and daring the audience to solve them. Instead—and I know how hokey this sounds, believe me—he created wonder and amazement on stage, not challenging the audience to figure out how the trick was done, but rather sharing in the moments of magic as he created them.

That's not to say everything went perfectly. He took some calculated risks and on two occasions I could see a routine was on the edge of failing. But he appeared to have an "out" for any situation, and from the audience's perspective every routine was flawless.

I was reminded of what my friend Nathan had whispered to me during Quinton's lecture at our store: "If I were a magician, I'd want to be Quinton Moon," he'd said, not taking his eyes off the presentation.

"But you *are* a magician," I had whispered back, also keeping an eye on the lecture.

"I mean, if I were a really good magician," Nathan had said and I knew exactly how he felt.

For the final illusion in his show, Quinton brought out the Zig Zag, which is a classic box trick. Some magicians hate box tricks, some love them. Box tricks come in all shapes and sizes and generally the effect is pretty straightforward: something goes into a box and is changed into something else. It might be a showgirl becoming a tiger or a showgirl turning into the magician or someone disappearing into a series of smaller and smaller boxes.

I never did box tricks much myself because they're a pain to haul around and assemble. Early on I'd learned to go with the tricks that are easy to transport, particularly if you're doing your own transporting. I know magicians who can do a ninety-minute stage show with only the contents of a bag that fits under the seat on an airplane and that's what I aspired to be.

I've spent my life listening to magicians argue over the pros and cons of box tricks, and as I watched Quinton set up the premise for his Zig Zag routine, I was reminded of something Johnny Thomson (AKA The Great Tomsoni) had said on the subject. It was during a visit to The Magic Castle when I was probably fifteen:

"When you are doing a box trick, you have to talk the box away."

That sentence had stuck with me for years and it wasn't until this very moment I really understood what he meant, because I was watching Quinton do exactly that. Even though the box was there on stage, big as life, the way Quinton presented the trick, the box was just one small element of the overall effect.

In the trick, someone—in this case, Megan—steps into a tight, vertical closet-like box. You can see the assistant's face through a hole at the top of the box, her hand through a hole in the center of the box, and her foot through a hole at the bottom.

The magician then shoves two wide, steel blades through the box, trisecting it into cubes, in essence dividing the assistant into three parts: the head, the torso, and the legs. Of course, all this happens behind the door to the box, but the blades look real enough and they appear to go all the way through the box, yet the assistant smiles the entire time.

Then it gets really weird.

The magician pushes on the center box, shoving it away from the top and the bottom boxes. With this move, the center box is now no longer under the top box or over the bottom box. It's *next* to those boxes but no longer part of them. And all the while the assistant smiles and waves her hand through the hole and wiggles her toes, even though the center section of her body has been pushed about two feet to the left.

Quinton talked the box away beautifully. In his version of the trick, it wasn't really about the box at all. It was about all of us and our lives today and how we were living them, with Megan standing in as the surrogate for the audience. He talked about the pressures of life, the need to be all things to all people, and how many of us effortlessly move from one role to another throughout the day, in essence splitting ourselves into various pieces to meet the needs of the people we care about.

This patter was made all the more engaging with Quinton's where-the-heck-is-he-from accent and the intimate way in which he spoke to the audience. For her part, Megan didn't have much to do, but she looked lovely with her smiling face peering through the small hole.

I had a sudden pang looking at her onstage in this magician's act. I understood I had never offered to put her in my act because she so adamantly didn't want to know how any of the illusions were accomplished. And, in my defense, she had never asked to be in the act. Then why would her appearing in Quinton's act hurt so much and feel like, well, a betrayal? If he had been a lesser magician would I be feeling the same conflicted feelings?

Quinton got to the portion of the routine where he pushes the center box away from the top and the bottom boxes. I knew Megan was doing the lion's share of the work, but to the audience it looked like Quinton was making a Herculean effort while Megan simply stood in the box and smiled.

Quinton stepped away, revealing that a third of Megan was two feet to her left, her hand still waving in the center box, while she smiled and wiggled her toes in the other two boxes. In most acts, this would produce applause, polite or otherwise, but Quinton did such a masterful job of talking the box away, the audience leapt to their feet as one, with some people going so far as to cheer and whistle.

The audience was still giving this standing ovation when I left the showroom. For all I know, they were still clapping by the time I got to the parking ramp.

The parking ramps in downtown St. Paul exist at two ends of a spectrum. A handful are state-of-the-art complexes that are shiny and new and bright and colorful. The rest, however, are drab, low-ceiling, cramped affairs, many of which appear—impossibly—to have been designed and built before automobiles had been invented or even imagined.

The addition of automated payment machines and subsequent elimination of booth attendants has increased the creepiness level by a factor of ten and I was feeling quite alone as I stepped into the elevator and pressed the button for my floor. The door began to slide closed and then suddenly jerked open, as someone must have hit the UP button on the wall outside.

That someone stepped into the elevator and I gasped. It was an involuntary and, in retrospect, completely appropriate reaction.

"I thought that might be you. Small world, isn't it?"

Sherry Lisbon reached past me to press her floor number. I stepped back to give her a wide berth, but she still seemed to be standing closer to me than entirely necessary. She was wearing a long, thick fur coat which looked anything but faux and she was made-up and coifed to the hilt. She turned to me and gave me a steady look, challenging me for a response.

"Yes, it is," I finally stammered. "Very small world."

"Were you working tonight?"

"Yes, yes I was. A corporate gig," I added, to fill the silence.

"So where's your bunny?" she asked, giving the elevator a cursory once-over.

"I was doing strolling close-up magic," I explained. "I left the bunny at home."

This was, of course, a flat-out lie, as I haven't worked with a rabbit in years. In fact, I had banned all animals from my act after the tragic intersection between a fugitive dove and a badly placed ceiling fan. It was for a children's birthday party and it was a performance for which I ultimately earned nothing but wisdom.

The elevator, which felt like it was running at a painful half speed, finally dinged, signaling the arrival at my floor. I moved forward in anticipation of my imminent release, willing the elevator with my mind to stop and the doors to open.

"Anyway," I said, beginning the end of our conversation, "it was fun running into you..."

The doors opened and just as I lurched toward my release, she placed what I assume could only have been an icy hand on my shoulder.

"Mr. Marks, do you mind walking me to my car?" she said quietly. "I find this parking ramp unsettling."

My immediate thought was that I was currently standing next to the most unsettling thing in a six-block radius, but chivalry won out and I reluctantly pressed the Close Door button.

"Sure," I said flatly. We rode in silence for what seemed like a long time, even though the light on the elevator panel indicated we were only traveling up one floor.

Upon arriving on her level, she marched ahead of me, her heels click-clicking on the concrete as we made our way through the murky ramp. It was colder here than in the elevator, the frigid air blowing in through honeycombed openings which covered the exterior wall and provided a limited view of downtown St. Paul.

"A paid gig, was it?" she asked over her shoulder, turning her head only the slightest degree back toward me.

"Yes," I said. "An insurance company, I believe. It might have been underwriters."

"Ah, well. I suppose they deserve entertainment as much as anyone."

"Yes, I suppose they do."

I don't really know cars, but I could tell immediately which one was likely to be hers. There were plenty of different makes and models parked where we were headed, but the one that caught my eye was low to the ground and sleek. It was a deep, rich red and it looked powerful and a little dangerous. She hit the button on her key fob and the car winked at us, silently congratulating me on being so astute.

"Let me ask you this," Sherry Lisbon said as she reached the driver's door. She turned and looked up at me. "This show you did tonight."

"Yes."

"Once you accept the job, is that it?"

"I'm not sure I know what you mean."

She put her hand on her hip and looked past me, up at the low ceiling. "I mean, what if someone calls with a better offer?"

I shrugged. "That's too bad," I said. "I already committed to the first show."

"What if they doubled the money?"

I shook my head.

"What if they tripled the offer? Or more."

I shook my head again. "It still wouldn't matter. I'm committed."

She looked at me for a long moment. "That you are, Mr. Marks. That you are."

Another long piercing stare from her. For a second I thought she was beginning to move toward me and I took a half step back, but it must have been a trick of the light. Instead, she pirouetted and popped the door, sliding smoothly into the low car and scooping her fur coat in along with her.

"Thanks for keeping me safe," she said and for a second it looked like she was just about to smile. Apparently she thought better of it, because before I could respond she snapped the door shut and started the car, backing it out swiftly. She gunned the engine and the sleek and undoubtedly expensive car disappeared down the aisle, taking the sharp turn at high speed with no indication of brake lights.

I could still hear the car long after I could no longer see it. I stood for several moments in the cold ramp and then moved to the exterior wall. I stood in front of one of the openings and looked out, enjoying the icy air on my face.

Up to my left I could see the top of the Cavanaugh Bank tower. Recognizing this landmark gave me a sudden idea and I looked to my right, trying to get my bearings. I walked along the wall, peeking out through the open-air gaps, until I had reached the far end of the ramp. I looked straight ahead and was not very surprised to see the ramp was attached, via skyway, to Chip Cavanaugh's condo building. In fact, if I hadn't found street parking, I would have likely parked in this very ramp when I visited him.

I tipped my head back and looked up, trying to determine which of the lights up there might be his, knowing the best I would be able to achieve was a rough estimation. I turned from my attempt and looked back at where Sherry Lisbon's car had been parked and then slowly pivoted and looked back at Chip Cavanaugh's building.

It's a small world, she had said. And I had agreed, wondering for a long moment just how small it might actually be.

Harry's apartment was dark when I arrived home, so I just continued up the steps to my apartment. I wasn't hungry, so of course I ate. And I was tired, so of course I flipped on the computer and surfed for a while.

I made my way to Randall Glendower's website, GeekintheKnow, and clicked through the Marketplace section to see what sorts of things his geeks were buying and selling at this time of night.

On a whim, I opened a message window in the WANT TO BUY section and typed a short message, using the terminology and acronyms which were common on the site: *ISO classic lost Lon Chaney silent masterpiece. Willing to pay $$$. Discretion assured.*

I looked at my message for a long moment and then clicked the SEND button. I waited a few minutes, somehow thinking I might get an instant response. When none was forthcoming, I climbed into bed and flipped on the TV, trying to fall asleep to the lulling sounds of the shills on Sherry Lisbon's BuyMax channel.

I was near unconsciousness when a resonant *ping* from my computer brought me back to the land of the living. Curiosity pulled me out of bed and I stumbled over to the computer, jamming my big toe in the process. Swearing silently, I clicked open the message window, surprised to see I had received a response from my request.

The message, from someone named ClassicSeller58 was short and to the point: *May have what you want, if London is what you need. Price negotiable. Will be in touch soon.*

I looked at the message and the name of the sender, searching for a clue to his or her identity, but nothing popped into my head. I waited to see if more information was coming, but after ten minutes I gave up and shut off the computer, to prevent subsequent pings interrupting my sleep. I made it back to bed safely, without further injury to my big toe.

Sleep finally came, amid dreams which mixed images of Megan in the Zig Zag box with Sherry Lisbon coming toward me in the parking ramp. In one iteration, her fur coat seemed to come to life, purring toward me like a giant, predatory cat.

This second fitful night's sleep came to a sudden and abrupt conclusion with the sound of my cell phone. The ringtone—The Rolling Stones' rendition of "It's All Over Now"—alerted me that it was from my ex-wife. I considered letting it go to voicemail but at the last second grabbed the phone from the nightstand.

"Good morning," I said with forced cheer. "How are you this fine morning?"

Not one for pleasantries, Deirdre got right to the point.

"Are you still in bed?"

"Maybe."

"You should probably get up, get dressed and come over here. One of the four suspects your friend Mr. Lime so kindly gave us was just found murdered."

CHAPTER 17

The warm, early morning light on Clifford Thomas' mansion on Summit Avenue did nothing to dispel the constant gloomy pall which seemed to hang over the house. The addition of several squad cars, unmarked police cars and the Crime Scene van didn't do much to lighten the mood either. Techs had created a path of sorts that civilians like me could use to get to the house without negatively impacting the crime scene, so I gingerly made my way along the narrow strip, cordoned off with yellow crime scene tape, finally arriving at the front door.

Deirdre was standing on the steps, either waiting for me or wishing she could grab a smoke or both. She'd given up the habit years before, but I knew when things got tense, her craving would kick in and she'd tried to assuage it with nicotine gum. Given the force with which she was chewing, she appeared to have taken on a full pack.

"They just took the body away," she said, turning and heading back into the house. "The crime scene itself is still fresh," she continued as I followed her, "but we can look around without tainting the chain of evidence."

The front hallway was as I remembered it from my previous visit, but instead of a smiling Clifford Thomas greeting me, the foyer was swarming with cops and techs and others whose functions weren't immediately apparent.

"What happened?" I asked, recognizing my understatement for what it was.

"Best as we can tell, Mr. Thomas had a visitor or visitors at some point last evening. There is no sign of forced entry, so we're assuming he knew the person or persons and let them in of his own volition."

I remembered my comment to him about his odd willingness to greet fans at the door and the offhanded way in which he had laughed it off.

"And then?"

"And then, at some point, while in the library," she said, gesturing to the large room where I'd met with the writer, "Mr. Thomas was attacked and stabbed. With a letter opener."

"Mr. Thomas in the library with the letter opener," I mumbled.

"What?"

"Nothing." I noticed the secret bookcase doorway was in its open position and I could see uniformed techs working within the room.

"That door was open?" I asked, gesturing to the bookcase.

"What door?" Deirdre said, giving me a look. "The front door?"

"No, that bookcase. It's a door. It slides open and closed, revealing the room behind it."

Deirdre moved toward the bookcase and gave it the once-over, peering behind it and then looking up at the recessed tracks in the ceiling. She gave a small grunt and then made a quick scribble in her notebook. "Don't know. It was open when we got here."

"Who found him?"

"Housekeeper. She comes in three times a week, prepares some meals for him to eat later and then does some light cleaning. She's been with him for years."

"Did she recognize the letter opener?"

Deirdre nodded. "She said it was his. It was always on the top of his desk."

"So you're thinking the visit was planned but the murder was an afterthought?"

"That's one theory."

"Anything else missing?"

"Yep. And that's where it gets a little weirder."

She walked past the bookcase and into Clifford Thomas' inner sanctum. The desk and the typewriter atop it had been dusted for fingerprints and a photographer was just finishing taking pictures of the desk and the objects on it, which consisted of a pencil, two pieces of mail and the typewriter. A key space on the desk was empty.

"They took the manuscript," I said quietly.

Deirdre turned sharply, stopping in her tracks so quickly I nearly collided with her.

"Yes. How did you know that?"

"Because when I was here, he made a show of taking a piece of paper out of the typewriter and adding it to the stack next to it. He said he always types his books and then someone else inputs them into a computer for editing."

"The housekeeper said the same thing. The current book is always next to the typewriter."

I shrugged. "When I was here a couple days ago, he said he was almost done with it. Maybe—"

She shook her head. "We called his typist. He'd told her to come over today to pick it up."

I gestured toward the desk and Deirdre nodded. I walked around the hulking oak bureau, looking at it from all angles, hoping this would spur some insight. None were coming.

"The typist said when he finished a manuscript, he always went through the same ritual. He'd add the title page, wrap it up in a ribbon and then go out for a drink. The Summit Club down the street said he came in last night around five thirty, had what he called a celebratory cocktail and went home. That was the last anyone saw of him until the housekeeper found him this morning."

"And that door was open?" I asked, gesturing to the sliding bookcase.

"She said she walked right in."

I looked at the desk again and noticed the small knob Clifford Thomas had pulled on when I visited. I gestured to Deirdre. Since she was the one wearing gloves and I wasn't, she slowly pulled the knob.

As before, the wooden surface slid out, but unlike the last time, I was now at an angle where I could really see the surface of the board. A piece of lined white paper, about four by seven inches, was taped to the board in a charmingly haphazard manner.

A list of handwritten titles filled the sheet, some written in pencil, some in pens with different ink, but all were in the same, unhurried hand. I recognized two recent Clifford Thomas titles—*Polar Vortex* and his latest bestseller, *The Endless Killing Frost*—but the rest of the titles were unknown to me. However the list was in keeping with the tone of all of his novels: *Blizzard Watch, Winter Storm Warning, A Snowball's Chance, The Milfoil Invasion, Frost Point* and the title I had inadvertently supplied to him, *Snow Blind*.

"What's this?" Deirdre asked, moving into my personal space to survey the list. I stepped aside.

"He added a title to this list when I was here," I explained. "It's his list of potential titles. I guess the title was always the last thing he added to the manuscript."

"The missing manuscript has one of these titles?"

"I would think so, unless it was already in his head and he never added it to the list. Two of the titles have already been used, so apparently he derived no pleasure from crossing each one off when he used it."

"Apparently," she said, but I could tell she didn't seem interested in where this conversation was heading. She signaled to one of the techs, who scurried over as if pulled in on a fishing line. "Make a note of these titles," Deirdre said, gesturing to the list. "And make sure the photographer gets a shot of it as well."

"I'm not sure that will be of much help," I said giving the list one final look.

"You never know," she said as she headed across the room.

I followed her, then stood in the archway to the secret room for a long moment.

I could hear Deirdre retracing her steps and coming up behind me.

"What?" she asked, clearly a little annoyed I was still standing there.

"I don't know," I said, giving the room and the sliding bookcase one last look. "I can't help but think—if there was going to be any mystery about how he died—Clifford Thomas would have preferred it be a locked room mystery."

"Don't worry," she said moving toward the front door, with me right behind her. "There's still plenty of mystery to go around. Fred is bringing in the other three suspects for some questioning about their whereabouts last night and their relationship with the late Clifford Thomas. Tag along and you can listen in."

I gave the secret room one last look and wondered, not for the first time, what sort of solution Clifford Thomas might have devised for this ever-evolving mystery, had he not just become its most recent victim.

It was fascinating to see how each of the three remaining suspects in the death of Tyler James reacted to the police request for them to come in for an informal interview about this most recent murder.

Both Chip Cavanaugh and Sherry Lisbon brought their lawyers, but the similarity between those two suspects ended right there.

Chip Cavanaugh seemed to delight in speaking at length after his lawyer had stated his client would not be answering a particular question. He came in grinning and presented variations on this smile—from wide to sardonic—throughout the course of the interview. Even watching through the one-way mirror—and with their backs to me—I could sense the annoyance of Homicide Detective Fred Hutton and Assistant District Attorney Deirdre Sutton-Hutton at his persistent snarky attitude.

"He's a real cutie pie, isn't he?" The voice came from behind me and I turned to see Homicide Detective Miles Wright, leaning in the doorway and watching the proceedings through the glass. "Fred and I did the initial interview with him. He was a shifty pain in the ass then, too."

I could imagine Chip Cavanaugh would have had great fun playing with these too-serious detectives. "Did you talk to him in his home or at work?"

"In his office," Wright said as he grabbed a chair and plopped into it. "What, is he a jerk at work and a nice guy at home?"

"He seems to be pretty insufferable regardless of the location," I said, wondering if either detective would've raised an eyebrow at the art collector's art-free living room, with its white on white walls.

"I hear that." We both sat back in silence as the questioning continued.

"You're saying you have no alibi last night, from roughly nine p.m. until eight a.m. this morning?" Homicide Detective Fred Hutton recited this question slowly, perhaps to forestall having to listen to a lengthy answer from Chip.

"Yes, Officer. I was alone in my apartment. All night. Alone but not lonely, if you take my meaning." Another big grin, as if we had somehow missed a very clever joke within his statement. "And so unless some person or persons unknown were aiming a high-powered telescope into my apartment from another skyscraper in downtown St. Paul, I'm afraid I will be unable to provide an alibi for my whereabouts last night during the hours in question."

Deirdre jumped in, I think in part to keep her husband from reaching across the table and throttling Cavanaugh. "Did you know Clifford Thomas?"

Chip's attorney, a heavyset man in a sharp but bulging three-piece suit, seemed to have given up and was sitting back patiently, collecting what I'm conjecturing was a hefty hourly fee. He pulled out his phone and glanced at it.

"We had met on several occasions, yes," Chip said.

"Do you remember the last time you saw him?"

"Oh, that would have been last night at around ten p.m., when I stood over his dead, lifeless body."

I couldn't see their faces, but the two interviewers' body language told me both had snapped to sudden attention.

"What?" Deirdre's voice almost cracked when she spoke.

"Oh, wait, my mistake," Chip said. "It was at the Christmas dinner at the Summit Club last month." His eyes darted to the others in the room and then he burst out laughing. "*Now* you're paying attention," he said, and burst into another round of giggling.

Deirdre breathed a deep and annoyed sigh and then continued. "Mr. Cavanaugh, I would request for the third and final time that you approach this interview with the seriousness it deserves."

"My client apologizes and is here to help in any way he can," Chip's attorney offered, taking his eyes off his phone long enough to rejoin the conversation. Chip nodded solemnly and the attorney set the phone aside.

"In our past interview, you said you had no interest in purchasing the copy of *London After Midnight* which Tyler James had offered for sale."

"Yes, thanks for remembering."

"Did you put in a bid? And did Mr. Thomas outbid you?"

Chip put up a hand in mock exhaustion. "One question at a time please, one at a time."

"Please answer the questions."

Chip sat back in his chair, a slight smile returning to his face. "No and no."

"Do you know for a fact that Mr. Thomas bid on the movie?"

"He said he did and I can't see why he would lie about it."

"Why are you just telling us this now?"

Chip shrugged, looking genuinely puzzled. "Because you asked."

"And why did you not share this information with the Homicide detectives when they first questioned you?"

"Because they didn't ask me. They asked me if I bid on it. And I said no. Because I didn't. It didn't interest me then and it interests me less now."

Deirdre and her husband exchanged a look.

"Mr. Cavanaugh, is there other information about the deaths of Tyler James and Clifford Thomas you possess and haven't shared with us?"

He gave her a long look and started to smirk, but apparently thought better of it. "I have told you everything I know on the topics."

"I hope for your sake, Mr. Cavanaugh, you are correct on that point."

That was essentially it for Chip Cavanaugh's interview. As the group exited the interview room, I spotted Sherry Lisbon, standing impatiently in the hall outside the room, flanked by two intense-looking women.

A small traffic jam formed as the two groups came head to head, but the first group went left and Sherry and her team went right and a pileup was avoided.

It might have been my imagination, but it really looked to me that both Chip Cavanaugh and Sherry Lisbon went out of their way not to look at or acknowledge each other as the two groups passed. I leaned forward in my chair to try to get a better look, but my view was blocked by the doorframe and Sherry's legal team as they moved into the room.

I remembered my odd encounter with her in the parking ramp the previous evening and considered what time it had taken place. I couldn't place it to the minute, but I reasoned that it was well before eight thirty p.m., as Quinton Moon's seventy-five-minute show had started promptly at seven p.m. and I had left just as it was concluding.

For what it was worth, that meant I couldn't be used as an alibi for Sherry Lisbon.

I took no small amount of relief in that fact.

"What was the name of the song you sang when we interviewed you?"

I had almost forgotten Detective Wright was in the room with me.

"What?"

"The song."

"What song?"

"When Fred and I were interviewing you about that whole psychic murder thing a couple years back—right there in that interview room—you sang a song into the recorder while we went out of the room."

The memory came back fast and I couldn't help but smile. "The song is called 'Mediocre Fred,'" I said.

"'Mediocre Fred,'" Wright repeated. "That's a funny name for a song."

"It's a funny song."

"You write it?"

His level of interest in this long-ago event really surprised me. "No, it's a Smother's Brothers song. I think Loren Paulsen wrote it."

"Oh, I always thought you wrote it."

"Nope. Wish I had." I didn't really wish I had, but I wouldn't have minded if I did.

"That thing really went viral. I mean, viral here at the station."

"That's what I heard."

Deirdre had read me the riot act about it after the fact. Apparently, all police interview recordings are transcribed and when the transcriptionist had gotten to that point in the interview, he or she found it so amusing they made a copy of the recording and emailed it to select employees. And those employees sent it to others and they sent it to others and before they knew it, the email server was overloaded, Homicide Detective Fred Hutton was made the fool, and there was hell to pay.

At the time my relationship with my ex-wife's new husband was, at best, strained. We've warmed to each other over the years, if only a little, and were I in the same situation today, I doubt I would sing the song while alone in the interview room.

Well, certainly not the entire song.

* * *

The tone of the second interview was different, but I doubt either Deirdre or Homicide Detective Fred Hutton would have characterized it as better.

Sherry Lisbon's two attorneys made the following abundantly and immediately clear: their client was here as a favor to the police, her time was both valuable and limited, and they should understand in advance that she was unlikely to have anything of substance to add to their ongoing investigation.

And, oh, did they mention her time was limited?

There were only four chairs in the room, so one of the attorneys—the junior one, I assumed—stood behind the other, while Sherry Lisbon sat back in her chair and languidly checked her makeup with a pocket mirror.

Deirdre's first three questions elicited the identical reply from the senior attorney.

"Our client, Ms. Lisbon, has already offered all the insight she has on that point." After this third response, the junior attorney produced a stack of papers and flipped to a particular page. She handed the sheet to her superior, who glanced at it, made three quick checkmarks on the sheet, and then pushed it across the table to the two interviewers.

"Those questions have been answered. As you can see in this transcript of her previous interview with the Homicide department," she added.

While I was by now well aware the police recorded and transcribed their interviews, this was the first instance I'd seen where the interview subject had done that as well.

Deirdre studied the transcript for a long moment, with Homicide Detective Fred Hutton looking over her shoulder. While they reviewed the paperwork, the two attorneys looked through their notes. For her part, Sherry Lisbon finished touching up her makeup, closed her purse and then stared across the room. It felt very much like she was staring right at me, although the gaze lacked any warmth or interest. I looked back at her, fascinated at how cold and blank a person's eyes could be.

"Boy, if I didn't know better," I said out of the corner of my mouth to Wright, "I would swear she was looking directly at me."

"Yeah, you get that sometimes," Wright said, with a patronizing tone in his voice I could have done without. "But as long as this room is dark, the nature of the physics of the mirror make it impossible—"

I cut him off. "But this room isn't dark," I said in a rushed whisper. "You left the door open."

Wright sat up suddenly in his chair. "Oh, crap. I hadn't planned on sitting down. Maybe I should shut that," he added as he scrambled across the room and eliminated the light source by slamming the door shut.

"Maybe you should," I agreed, turning back to the glass. Sherry Lisbon was still staring at the same point, her expression unchanged by the sudden shift in the lighting in our room.

She sighed dramatically and uncrossed her arms.

"Perhaps we can cut to the chase here," she said, her tone such that the other four people in the room immediately stopped what they were doing. She was turning on the CEO thing and it clearly worked for her.

"The issue, as I see it," she continued, "is one of motive. Insofar as I don't have one." She let this sink in for a moment, and then continued, as if to a child. "Alibis and timelines aside, it's quite simple. I had no motive to kill Tyler James and even less to kill Clifford Thomas."

"However—" Deirdre began, but Sherry cut her off without taking a breath.

"As I have explained ad infinitum, I had no dealings with Mr. James on his most recent investment opportunity and I certainly had no desire to buy the alleged movie from him or from Mr. Thomas."

"You can certainly sit here and say that, but how do we know that to be true?" Deirdre had switched to her courtroom voice, which I knew well, but I wasn't convinced it would hold up against the sheer force of Sherry Lisbon's will.

"If you're working from the premise that something went awry in the sale of the movie, you can remove me from the list of suspects for one simple reason: I can assure you, if I wanted to buy it, I would have bought it. And that would have been the end of it, with perhaps a few tears but no bloodshed."

"You're saying if you want it, you buy it and that's that?"

"Yes, dear. That's that." I could see Deirdre's shoulders tighten at the use of the word "dear."

"Do you buy everything you want?"

Sherry Lisbon gave Deidre her coldest smile. "Without exception."

She then stood up and headed toward the door. No one made any move to stop her.

CHAPTER 18

"For some reason I was hoping he would bring his monkey."

Miles Wright turned his head slowly and looked at me, his eyes becoming narrow slits. "Excuse me?"

I scrambled to explain my odd outburst. "This guy, Randall Glendower," I said, gesturing to the new occupant in the interrogation room. "He owns a monkey—a little Javan macaque monkey—and for some reason I hoped he would bring it in today."

Wright continued to stare at me. "To an interrogation?"

I shrugged. "A guy can dream."

I was saved from any further monkey talk by Randall, who moved suddenly, shifting our attention back to the interview room. He had been waiting patiently, sitting at the table and checking his phone for messages, but he suddenly jumped up and scurried over to the door. Extending his phone at arm's length, he took a quick selfie, standing and smiling in front of the lettering on the door, which read "Interrogation Room One."

He checked the photo, apparently pleased with the results, and returned to his seat just as Deirdre and Homicide Detective Fred Hutton came back into the room.

"Thanks for your patience, Mr. Glendower," Deirdre said. The tension that had been in her voice during the interview with Sherry Lisbon had vanished.

"No problem," Randall said, sounding far more chipper than a person being interrogated about a murder should sound. If he recognized this, he made no attempt to modify his good cheer.

"I'm sure you've heard about the recent passing of Clifford Thomas, and consequently we're revisiting some of the people we spoke to after Tyler James' murder."

"Makes sense to me," Randall said with a nod.

Deidre looked up from her notes. "And why would that be?"

This question seemed to throw him for a second. "Well, um," he said, now choosing his words with some care, "I figured Cliff was probably the one who won the bid for London After Midnight, and so his death would pretty clearly be tied to Tyler's in some way, right?" His sentence evolved from a statement to a question while he said it.

"Yes, we're proceeding on that assumption," Deirdre said, returning her attention to her notes. "Now, during your last interview, you admitted to having put in a bid on the movie, is that right?"

Randall, feeling on firmer footing here, nodded enthusiastically. "Yes, I must have been outbid. I never got the chance to ask Tyler about it," he added. "I mean, obviously."

Deirdre looked up and—even though I couldn't see it from my position behind the one-way mirror—I suspect she gave him a reassuring smile.

"And how did you feel about not winning the bid?" she asked, sounding offhand, although I knew she wasn't in the least.

Randall shrugged. "I didn't think I had much of a chance," he said. "I mean, there are people out there with far deeper pockets than mine. However, if I had known it was Cliff who was buying it, I wouldn't have been all that concerned."

"And why is that?"

"With Cliff, I knew the movie would get out there. People would be able to see it. Some collectors," he continued, lowering his voice, "I don't know, they're all about hoarding. About keeping it and hiding it, and they never let anyone see their stuff."

If he wasn't specifically describing Chip Cavanaugh, he certainly could have been. I leaned forward, straining to hear Randall through the small speaker.

"And neither you nor Clifford Thomas would have done that?"

"I can't speak for Cliff, but I doubt it. And if I had bought it, I certainly would have made sure it got out there. I mean, it's *London After Midnight* after all, right?" He waited for a response that matched his enthusiasm, but it wasn't coming.

"It's very rare," Deirdre finally offered.

"You bet your ass," Randall said with a big smile. "It's basically the Holy Grail of lost movies. I mean, they found the scene in *Frankenstein* where the monster drowns the little girl. They put *Touch of Evil* back together in the right order. But *London After Midnight*? I've been lusting after this movie since I was twelve years old and saw photos from it in *Famous Monsters of Filmland* magazine."

He paused and sighed deeply, truly emotional on this topic.

"I would have killed to see that movie," he finally said.

It took several seconds for it to really sink in, but Randall Glendower finally realized what he had just declared. He looked at Deirdre and then at her husband, his eyes searching their faces.

"I mean..." His voice trailed off.

His demeanor was suitably low-key during the rest of the interview and, on second thought, it was probably best that he had not brought his monkey.

For reasons I can't completely comprehend, after I left the police station I found myself heading toward St. Paul instead of back home. The whole situation with Clifford Thomas felt strangely unresolved, and several minutes later I found myself standing in front of his house on Summit Avenue, looking up at the ghoulish and cartoonish mansion.

Crime scene tape on the front door was the only remaining indicator that anything untoward had taken place in or around the residence. The creepy Santa leered down at me from the widow's walk and the decapitated snowmen on the front lawn were beginning to look a bit droopy in the semi-warm afternoon sun.

I knew I couldn't get into the house, and didn't know what I would do in there if I could, so instead I retraced our steps from the house down the block and across the street to The Summit Club. Clifford Thomas must have made this same round trip the night before, celebrating the completion of what was likely to be his next bestseller, never realizing that it would also be his last.

I stood in front of the exclusive club for several minutes, running my meeting with Clifford Thomas over in my mind. As I did, I absently turned and took in the view of downtown St. Paul below. The Cavanaugh Bank tower was the centerpiece of the vista, and I thought about Chip Cavanaugh and his offhanded joke about standing over Clifford Thomas' dead body the night before. It was a sick joke, perfectly in keeping with his dark sense of humor, but I couldn't help wonder if it held a deeper truth somewhere within. He admitted that he knew Clifford via their shared membership in the Summit Club. They were both ridiculously rich, and both oddball collectors of the rare and the obscure. Had they both been vying for ownership of *London After Midnight*?

No answers were forthcoming and as I turned my attention away from the scene below, one other building caught my eye: the St. Paul Hotel, nestled snugly across from Rice Park. That wacky Swiss, Quinton Moon, was probably somewhere within, charm oozing from every pore. I'm sure he would have made quick work of the handful of disparate clues I was struggling with, and probably would have cured cancer at the same time.

Annoyed at how quickly just the thought of him could overtake my normal faculties, I did the best to shake him from my mental processes as I headed toward the car and the short, unproductive drive home.

It had been unseasonably warm all day, resulting in lots of melted snow and running water trickling down Chicago Avenue as I pulled into a parking space that afternoon. As pleasant as the day had become, this sort of thaw in mid-January is always a double-edged sword. Wet streets and sidewalks at three p.m. can turn into icy nightmares by evening.

The movie theater didn't appear to be open yet, but I noticed Tracy had updated the marquee to another movie mash-up, yet one more that didn't derive from a suggestion of mine. Tonight's Parkway Double Play, *Saturday Night and Sunday Morning Fever*, looked to be a fun combo, but I still felt many of the options I'd presented had been punchier.

As I headed toward the magic store, I nearly convinced myself Quinton Moon had thought of it and called it into Tracy and that there was a vast title mash-up conspiracy going on behind my back. I was still swirling in this loop of self-doubt and paranoia as I went to open the door to the magic shop and found it was locked.

This didn't surprise me, as Harry and I have always had a very casual relationship with traditional business hours. I unlocked the shop, flipped on the lights and, in a very determined fashion, set about to begin the long-delayed and much-needed inventory process.

But first, I thought, I should check online to see if I'd gotten another response to the ad I placed on Randall's website. This was clearly a delaying tactic, but it had the ring of legitimacy to it and so I went with it.

A quick check via the store computer confirmed the only answer so far was the vague response from ClassicSeller58 I'd seen the night before. I surfed around the site, looking for further clues, but instead ended up falling down a rabbit hole of reasonable discussion topics which quickly escalated into flame wars.

Then I remembered a ring routine that Quinton had performed at his show the night before, during which he had acknowledged it was based on a Tommy Wonder classic. This led me to YouTube where I lost who knows how much time delighting in Mr. Wonder's various miracles.

I was roused from this video clip coma by the tinkle of the bell over the door and looked up, expecting to see Harry returning from some errand. But it wasn't Harry.

"You're the guy who found Tyler's body, right?"

It was Mrs. Tyler James, in all her big-haired glory. Standing behind her was her constant companion, still wearing the too-small hipster hat on his too-big hipster head. He peered around her, scanning the shop, his eyes going a little wide as they adjusted to the dim lighting which is our hallmark.

"We talked to you in the theater the other night," she continued, her tone suggesting it had been a trifle of a conversation which I could have easily forgotten. "About getting into the projection booth."

"I remember," I said slowly, scanning the shop to see what object might become a quick and handy weapon if the need were to arise. Unlike the theater next door, we didn't keep a baseball bat handy for occasions such as this. I noticed a can of fart spray on the gag gift shelf and considered it a likely first choice, as it had proven to be an effective impromptu defense in the past.

"I'm afraid I have no access to any part of the movie theater," I continued, but she waved my words away with her highly manicured hand.

"I know, I know. That *Bad News Bears* washout next door made it abundantly clear we're not getting into Tyler's booth." She spit the words out, and it was evident she was still harboring a lot of anger from her encounter with Tracy.

"She's actually more of *Hoosiers* washout," I corrected, and again she waved my words away.

"Whatever," she said, clearly already bored with the topic. "Here's the thing," she continued, her tone softening as she stepped toward the counter. "Tyler and me, we weren't always on the best of terms. My therapist said we were codependent, but I think in reality we were just a pair of drugged up hotheads who couldn't get along."

Her companion tugged at her sleeve. "Look," he said with a big smile. "This place is full of magic stuff."

She pushed his arm away. "It's a magic store, you dummy. What did you think you'd find in here? Tap shoes? Now shut your trap, Gunnar, I'm trying to talk here."

Gunnar lowered his eyes and slunk away, running his finger across the top of the counter as he moved toward a display of DVDs. A shamed five-year-old could not have executed a finer performance.

"As I was saying," Mrs. James continued, giving him one final look and a definitive roll of the eyes, "Tyler and me did have some good times, and I feel bad. About him being dead and all."

It struck me this was the first time since it happened that anyone had shown anything resembling grief about Tyler James' murder.

"Okay," I began, not sure I had anything to add to this conversation.

"I was just wondering," she continued, her voice softening, "if you two ever talked or anything. And if my name came up. Maybe ever," she added. Her brash exterior had faded away quickly, revealing a grieving woman just this side of crying, and doing her best to hold it back.

"I'm sorry," I said, shaking my head slowly. "I actually never met Tyler."

I was going to continue my explanation, but our conversation was interrupted by a sudden question from across the room.

"What's this?" Gunnar asked. He was pointing to a fabric strip with a string loop which Harry had left out on the counter after a demonstration.

"It's an invisible dove harness," I said absently, trying to keep my attention on the conversation with Mrs. James.

"But..." he said, scratching the small patch of beard that called his chin home. "But I can see it." He held up the fabric strip and had a sudden thought. "Oh, is it the dove that's invisible?"

"Sure, it's the dove that's invisible," I agreed, turning back to Mrs. James. Out of the corner of my eye I could see Gunnar scanning the room slowly, looking for any indication of the imperceptible bird.

"As I was saying," I continued, "Tyler and I actually never met. I'd seen him at work, through the window, but that was all."

Mrs. James sighed deeply, leaning on the counter as if in need of a little support.

"I see," she said quietly. "So you two never had a chance to shoot the breeze. About me. Or any of his online sales opportunities?" The last was casually tossed out as a throwaway thought, but there was a glimmer in her watery eyes which gave her away.

"No," I said sharply, recognizing I was being conned, and not too expertly at that. "We never spoke."

She took out a handkerchief from a voluminous handbag and dapped at her eyes dramatically, but I think we both understood the show was, essentially, over.

"That's too bad," she said, trying to deliver a sniffle and coming up short. "I think you two would have really hit it off."

"I'm sure we would have," I said, putting as much ice in my voice as I could. "Now, if there's nothing else, I need to get back to my inventory work." This was true, however "start" would have been a more accurate verb.

She gave me one more long look, then dropped the grieving widow act with the speed of a seasoned Las Vegas impressionist.

"Come on, Gunnar," she said, stuffing her unused handkerchief back into her purse and pulling out several sticks of gum. "We've got other fish to fry." The sticks of gum were unwrapped and deposited into her mouth with well-practiced speed.

She walked to the door and pulled it open, clearing her throat meaningfully. The sound produced a conditioned response from Gunnar, who dropped the magic wand he had been examining and made a beeline toward the door.

"Careful," he hissed, pushing her through the door and swinging it shut quickly as he gave the shop one last look. "You don't want to let the dove out!"

There was a quick slam of the door and they were gone.

*   *   *

I'd like to say the next two hours were productive, inventory-wise, but that would be far from the truth. I'm not even sure I can honestly say I made a dent in the process. But somehow, five o'clock came around and I closed up the shop in anticipation of a planned dinner with Megan. I was steeling myself for the inevitable recitation of her experience with Quinton Moon the night before, vowing to keep my jealousy in check.

I threw on my coat, shut off the lights and was locking the door and marveling at how warm it still was, even with the sun just about to dip below the horizon.

"Hey, stranger," said a familiar voice. "You coming or going?"

I looked up and broke into a wide smile. Harry was walking toward me, holding a small bag of what I assumed were groceries.

"I wasn't sure if our paths would cross today," he said, shifting the bag from one hand to the other.

"I've been in and out," I said.

"As have I," he said. "But I've been dying to talk to you. I didn't get to hear about your gig last night. How did it go?"

I realized a lot had happened in the last twenty-four hours, and so first I brought him up to speed on the untimely death of his favorite mystery author.

After getting over the initial shock, he too immediately commented on how Clifford Thomas would have preferred his murder have a locked room element to it, which in this instance was sadly lacking.

"The police think the two murders are connected?"

"They're operating under that assumption," I said.

"Hopefully that doesn't steer them down the wrong path. Remember what Dai Vernon so famously said," Harry added, pointing a finger at me for emphasis.

The problem was, the great Dai Vernon had said so many things Harry quoted, it was often difficult to land on which bon mot was the one he currently had in mind.

"Um, was it 'Confusion is not magic?'"

He shook his head. "No, of course not," he said, instantly annoyed. "Truer words were never spoken, but that's not what I'm referring to."

I took another shot. "'Don't make unimportant things important?'"

He gave me a pained look. "Of course not."

I racked my brain. "Um, 'If I could climax as many times as a Derek Dingle routine, I'd be a happy man?'"

"Oh, for goodness sake, you're not even trying," he said with irritation. "It was, 'The problem with magicians is they stop thinking too soon.'"

"I thought Al Baker said that."

This made him pause for a second, and then he waved it away. "Regardless of who said it," he snapped, "my point is, sometimes the police stop at the first right answer without looking a little further for a second, better, right answer."

I certainly couldn't argue with that, and even if I could, years of this sort of back and forth with Harry had taught me there was little point in trying.

"Be that as it may," he continued, his mood brightening, "how was your gig last night?"

I gave him a brief rundown of my successful evening, purposefully leaving out any mention of the shameful costume. I instead focused on how well some of the old routines had gone over, thanks to the new insight gained by taking them apart and putting them back together.

"Excellent," he said with a warm laugh. "There's nothing like putting some new life in the old act. It sounds like it was a good night for magicians all around last evening."

"How do you mean?"

"Oh, I heard through the grapevine Quinton Moon put on a rather dazzling display at a corporate event. Knocked their socks off, they say."

"Did he?" I said flatly, but Harry took no notice of my tone.

"He did indeed. Apparently the meeting planner said, in effect, that Quinton Moon 'walks on water and glows in the dark.' So sorry I missed the show," he added, as he put his key in the lock and unlocked the door I had just secured.

"Are you headed out?" he asked as he swung the door open.

I didn't have time to answer, though, because at that moment there was a sudden tremendous icy crash around my shoulders, and seconds later we were both lying flat on the sidewalk. I thought I heard some shouts and struggled to open my eyes. Then there was another cold, wet crash against my head and I blacked out.

CHAPTER 19

I must have been out for only a matter of seconds, but tracking time at that moment was not my first concern. I sat up quickly and instantly wished I hadn't. Black spots darted back and forth in front of my eyes, while wet snow and ice were slipping behind my collar and sliding down my back. Clearly a huge chunk of ice and snow had plummeted off the roof.

Despite the pain and confusion, the cold, wet sting of the snow produced a thought from out of the blue. This idea hit me as hard as the icy boulder which had plummeted off the roof, and then it instantly melted away, like the arctic trickle currently running down the back of my neck. I tried to remember the thought, which had seemed so bright and important for the brief second I had held it in my head. And now it was gone. I squinted up, not really knowing what I was looking for. And then I remembered Harry.

He was next to me, lying sprawled on the sidewalk, one side of his face pressed against the cold, wet ground. Scattered around him were chunks of ice and snow, the remnants of what had hit us before slamming us into the sidewalk.

My instinct was to roll him over, but I stopped myself, recognizing there could be some sort of spinal injury. I leaned in close and said his name, but got no response. However, he was breathing, which I took as a minimal good sign.

I looked up to see a small crowd had gathered and people were asking me questions, but my head was so scrambled I couldn't make sense of the words. I reflexively grabbed for my phone, but then the sound of an approaching siren told me someone in the crowd had already effectively handled that one detail for me.

I looked back down at Harry. His eyelids were fluttering just a bit, and I noticed his hat had been knocked off. For some unknown reason I felt the intense and overpowering need to find his hat and tried to stand up, but my knees gave out and I went down again.

I was conscious when the EMTs arrived, so as I saw them approach I gestured them toward Harry.

"I'll be okay, take care of him. I'll be okay."

I sensed I was at least minimally correct in my assessment. My third attempt to sit up was far more successful than my first, and the black spots which floated in front of my eyes were diminishing to gray specks as my cognitive powers, such as they were, began to return.

The idea which had burned so brightly after the snowy impact was still gone, but other than that my faculties seemed to be returning. Moments later I found myself sitting on the curb, a blanket wrapped around my shoulders, as the way-too-young EMT shined a light in first one eye and then the other.

"How's Harry?" I said, involuntarily squinting into the light.

"He's doing fine. We've got him immobilized and his vital signs look good."

"Is he conscious?"

A momentary hesitation on her part, and then her professional tone returned in full. "Not currently, but his vital signs look good. We're going to get him into the ambulance and then get one for you."

I shook my head and regretted it immediately. "I want to ride with Harry. I can sit up. I can sit up in back."

She gave me a long look. "You're not going to hurl in the back of my wagon, are you?"

I almost shook my head, then wisely thought better of it. "I promise to be hurl-free for the duration of the ride."

"Sounds like a plan. Let us get him situated first."

She got up and I turned and watched as they lifted Harry—strapped to a backboard—to the stretcher and then into the ambulance. The EMT assisted me to my feet and we were making the short walk from the curb to the ambulance when I heard a short scream. The crowd that had gathered turned in the direction of the sound and then parted.

A woman with blood running down her face had stumbled out of the theater and was staggering toward us.

It took me a moment to recognize it was Tracy.

The triage personnel in the ER determined Harry was their first priority, followed by Tracy, with me bringing up a distant third. So distant, in fact, that after a quick assessment, my treatment took place in the waiting room and consisted of two ibuprofen for my pain and a cold compress for the bump on my head. In their defense, we weren't the only emergency in the ER that evening, with people of all sizes, sicknesses, and injuries streaming in at a dizzying pace.

The doctor who looked me over asked me to stay for at least an hour, so he could give me another quick check before I took off. I told him I wasn't going anywhere without Harry and asked him when I could get in to see him. His answer as he walked away was authoritative and diplomatic and boiled down to the medical version of "when we say you can."

A vibration in my pocket reminded me that the room was plastered with signs instructing me to turn off my cell phone. I snuck a peek and saw it was a text from Megan.

What's going on? Heard there was an accident!

I shielded the phone from prying eyes and composed a short, non-hysterical text to the effect that Harry and I were in the ER and I would call when they let me out. I had barely hit send when a message came buzzing back at me.

On my way.

*   *   *

There is probably no more helpless feeling than sitting in the waiting room of the ER while someone you love is behind a locked door marked "Staff Only."

Staring at it intently seemed to have no perceptible effect, so I eventually gave up on that and spent the next twenty minutes going through a really old *Reader's Digest*. After not chuckling once at *Life in These United States*—which I'm sure was more a function of my mood than a reflection on the level of humor found in the anecdotes—I tried improving myself with the featured article, *I Am Joe's Pancreas*.

But after reading the sentence about how the pancreas contained features of two different glands—endocrine and exocrine—for the fifth time and still not understanding it, I shut the magazine and snuck another look at my phone.

"You know, I count five signs which explicitly state you're not supposed to be using your phone here in the ER."

I looked up to see Deirdre. "What are you gonna do, arrest me?"

"No, but I know people."

"What are you doing here?"

"When two ambulances and a squad car are called to the address of a recent murder, you'd be amazed at how quickly word gets around."

"Why a squad car?" And then I remembered Tracy's bleeding head. I'd been so dazed, I hadn't even stopped to consider why she had been bleeding. "What happened to Tracy?"

"Fred's talking to her right now. Seems she was jumped by someone in the theater. She said she saw the door to the roof had been opened and when she went to investigate, she got hit on the head."

"Someone was on the theater's roof?"

"Perhaps. Or they were using that as an access point to the roof next door."

I considered the implications of this. "So the ice and snow that fell on Harry and me, that might have been on purpose?"

Deirdre shrugged with classic non-commitment. "We're looking into it. What's the word on Harry?"

"They're not telling me, and the more they don't tell me, the more worried I get."

She pursed her lips, then patted my shoulder affectionately, which made me even more concerned. "Let me go rattle some cages and see what I can find out."

I started to get up, but her comforting hand shifted to a firm, commanding one, pushing me back down into my chair. "You stay here and talk to your friends. I'll get a full report."

"What friends?"

But she was gone. I watched Deirdre move through the crowded waiting room and then realized she hadn't been sarcastic. I did recognize faces in the crowd.

I recognized Megan, and behind her was Franny, both weaving their way through the huddled masses. I broke into a smile and then saw that right behind them was Quinton Moon. My smile faded and was instantly replaced with a fake one, which I hoped no one could tell from the real thing.

"Eli, what happened?" Megan pulled back the cold compress to check my head.

"How's Harry?" Franny looked from me to the reception desk and then back to me. "Are they stonewalling?"

"Deirdre's gone to get some answers. I have no idea. He was hit on the head, we both were, by some ice and snow that slid off the roof. He was unconscious. I don't know," I said. "They haven't told me. Deirdre's gone to find out." I recognized I had started to repeat myself.

Quinton stood awkwardly behind Megan and we nodded to each other.

"We were debriefing last night's performance," he said by way of explanation. "Megan was too worried to drive, and of course Franny doesn't drive, so, here we are."

We both nodded again. At that moment, the person in the chair next to me got up and Megan wasted no time sliding into the empty seat. She took my hand.

"What did they say?"

"Not much, really," I said, trying to remember any tidbit which might have relevance. Thankfully, Deirdre chose this moment to return with an actual report.

"Here's what they know," she said to me after a brief acknowledgment of the others. "It's a pretty severe concussion, with a scalp wound that produced a lot of blood, but they currently don't think there is any internal bleeding. He's still unconscious, but his vital signs are good and there is no indication of any spinal injury. They're going to take him down for a CAT scan and MRI. After that, they'll move him up to Intensive Care. You still look pale. Did you have dinner?"

I shook my head gingerly.

"You should eat something." She looked at the rest of the group. "Why don't you take him down to the cafeteria? It's going to be awhile before they know anything."

She started to head away, but I grabbed the hem of her jacket. "What about Tracy? What's going on with her?"

She looked back at me. "They bandaged her up and Fred is going to take her downtown and get a full statement. And Wright is bringing in Mrs. Tyler James and her, um, friend, to ask about her connection, if any, to this assault. And her earlier incident with the ladder."

"You mean when she was pushed off the ladder? You think this is connected?"

"We're looking into that. Anyway, the doctor said if you're feeling okay, you can go."

I put up a hand, but she cut me off. "I explained you'd want to stick around to see how Harry's doing." She looked at Megan. "Why don't you take him down to the cafeteria and get some food in him?"

"Yeah, let's do that," Megan said as she got up.

"I'll let you know what we find out from Mrs. James," Deirdre said, then turned and headed toward the front door. I stood up, with Megan holding my elbow, an unnecessary but welcome gesture.

"I'm staying here," Franny said with finality as she slid into my empty seat. "To keep an eye on Harry."

I recognized that tone and I knew it was pointless to argue with Franny when she got into that zone. "Can we bring you anything?" I asked.

"If they have hot chocolate with little marshmallows, I wouldn't turn it down," she said as she turned her attention toward the door marked "Staff Only." "But if they don't have tiny marshmallows, don't bother."

They did indeed offer hot chocolate with little marshmallows, so while I gathered some food for myself, Megan purchased a hot chocolate and headed back to the ER to deliver it to Franny while the drink was still relatively warm. This left me alone with Quinton and my tray of food. I had missed the dinner rush, when full meals were available, so I assembled an odd collection of items—a scoop of cottage cheese, a small bowl of peaches, a slice of pizza and a bowl of pudding—which made dietary mockery of the classic food pyramid.

We had our choice of tables so I picked one by the window, which afforded us a view of the downtown skyline and the beginnings of yet another new snowfall. Under other circumstances, it would have been a pretty sight.

"You picked an interesting time to come to Minnesota," I said to Quinton as I assembled my food selection in front of me.

"You mean it isn't always like this?"

"If you mean cold and snowy, then yes, it is always like this, except for two weeks in July, when it's insufferably humid. But if you mean the murders and the police and the concussions and the ambulances, no, not so much."

"It's a fascinating puzzle," he said, gesturing that I should go ahead and start eating.

"And it gets more fascinating all the time," I agreed, surprised at how hungry I actually was. "I spent the better part of the day listening to interviews with the three key suspects and I'm no closer to figuring this out than I was before."

"I thought there were four suspects?"

"There *were* four," I said. He gave me a look that indicated I should continue. I pretended to be slowed down by the presence of food in my mouth, but in reality I was weighing the pros and cons of actually asking for his help on this mystery. With the image of Harry sprawled out on the sidewalk burned into my brain, I decided that—at least for the time being—I would set my petty jealousies aside and add Quinton's brain power to the mix.

With that decision made, I filled him in on the facts surrounding the recent death of Clifford Thomas. My recap was interrupted several times by a table across the room—of what I am assuming were male nurses or orderlies—telling stories and laughing loudly at the recounted antics of past patients. It appeared that after hours, when foot traffic in the hospital was diminished, the cafeteria became a de facto break room.

"He didn't realize he'd been shot?" one of the nurses was saying.

"Didn't have a clue. He was just dropping off his brother when someone pointed out the bloodstain on his back and the drops of blood on the floor." This produced knowing laughter from the table across the room. I turned back to Quinton.

"All right, then," Quinton said, ticking the suspects off on his fingers, "you've got the big-hearted comic book store owner, the banker who collects and hides illegal art, and the executive who loves to swoop in and buy something out from under an unsuspecting buyer."

"And now one more late addition to the suspect list: the supposed wife of the first victim, Mrs. Tyler James and her constant companion, Gunnar." I gave Quinton the thumbnail version of my run-ins with Mrs. James and her friend Gunnar, including Tracy's handy and effective threat of a baseball bat in the theater lobby.

"Is that so?" he said. "It seems like this Mrs. James clearly thinks there is—or was—something of value in the projection booth."

"There was," I said as I finished off the peaches and moved on to the pizza. "There was an envelope with $75,000 in cash. And, at one point, a movie worth a whole lot more than that. She's just a little late to the party."

"Perhaps," he said, looking off into the distance. "But just because we're only seeing her now doesn't mean she hasn't been lurking and working in the background for some time."

I nodded. "Yes, I suppose that's true."

"And I would be willing to wager if you look at the statistics, wives kill husbands more than customers kill memorabilia dealers. As a general rule."

I nodded as I took a taste of the pudding, which had presented itself as vanilla but which turned out to be lemon.

I looked up and noticed a puzzled look on Quinton's face, which probably matched my own, but for different, non-culinary reasons.

"What's up?"

"Just had a notion. What kind of pet did you say the comic book store owner owns?"

"A monkey," I said. Laughter from a table across the room required me to speak up. "A Javan macaque monkey."

"I can tell you this much," one of the nurses said loudly, "I would want to get as far away from him as I could." This was followed by laughter and sounds of general agreement from the nurses, but something about the statement stuck in my head.

I looked over to see Quinton smiling at me. I glanced around, not sure what I had done to inspire it.

"I think I may have figured it out," Quinton said, leaning back in his chair.

"Figured what out?"

"The murders," Quinton said with a grin. "Well, the first one at least. But I'm assuming once we reveal the killer of the projectionist that will take us post haste to the killer of the mystery writer. In all likelihood, it's the same person."

As annoying as this proclamation was—and believe me, it was—I couldn't shake the statement the nurse had just made.

"I wanted to get as far away from him as I could," I repeated.

"What?" Quinton was leaning forward, but I was still following a train of thought, not sure where it would take me.

For some reason, the nurse's statement triggered a memory: I was standing in the back doorway of the theater, looking out at the snowy alleyway. In my mind, I turned away from the doorway and stepped forward, parting the curtains and looking up at the dimly lit holes in the far wall which defined the projection booth in the murky light. At that point, I was about as far away from the booth as I could be and still be in the theater, but that wasn't it. The words stuck with me: "I wanted to get as far away from him as I could."

And then, like dominoes tipping over, seemingly random images started to connect in my brain. Getting as far away from that guy as I could. The power and lack of permanence of an avalanche of ice and snow. One specific title from Clifford Thomas' list of potential book titles. Mrs. Tyler James' offhanded sports slur coupled with my stunning ignorance of athletics of any kind. Even conjoined movie titles, random as they were, suddenly all tied together in my head.

I pulled out my phone. "So you've solved the mystery?" I asked as I opened Google and did a quick search.

"I believe I have," he said. "Do you doubt me?"

I shook my head and for the first time in a long time it didn't hurt. "Not at all," I said as I scrolled quickly through an entry, confirming one key detail. "I might be on my way to figuring it out as well."

Before he could respond, we looked over to see Megan making her way through the cafeteria toward us, guiding Franny slowly toward our table.

Megan's face was impossible to read, as was Franny's, and the more I tried the more nervous I got. They finally arrived at our table and stood for a moment, both trembling. Franny's fingertips gripped the table's edge.

"It's Harry," Franny said, her voice cracking with emotion. "He just woke up." She took a deep breath and let it out slowly. "They say he's going to be okay."

"He's going to be just fine," Megan added.

With this important news safely delivered, Franny and Megan broke into huge smiles and I was quick to join them. The yells and whoops from our table startled the other people in the cafeteria, including the nurses, but none of them seemed annoyed at our emotional outburst. In fact, the table full of nurses even applauded.

CHAPTER 20

"This feels like a scene right out of one of Clifford Thomas' mystery novels."

I looked around the auditorium and had to agree with Nathan's assessment. "Yes, I think he would have felt right at home here."

"How did you get the police to agree to this?"

I shrugged. "They recognized that sometimes a little theater is the best way to generate a positive outcome."

"This isn't a little theater," Nathan said, looking out at the Parkway Theater's vast auditorium. "A little audience, sure, but not a little theater."

I could have taken the time to explain that my use of *theater* was differing from his, but thought better of it. Nathan was right on one point, though: There weren't many people in the first three rows of the Parkway Theater, but it was a veritable Who's Who of folks connected—directly and tangentially—with the deaths of Tyler James and Clifford Thomas.

Sherry Lisbon was in attendance, along with her two attorneys, while Chip Cavanaugh had come alone. Ms. Lisbon seemed to be in a sour mood about being summoned here, but Chip was, well, chipper. He had given me a friendly punch on the arm on his way in and then a quick wink before taking his seat. If he was putting on a fake front, he was doing a terrific job of it.

Mrs. Tyler James and her "friend" Gunnar had slunk in and slouched in seats near the middle, both looking annoyed at being called out of whatever rock they had been hiding under. Numerous times she turned and looked up at the projection booth, and then whispered conspiratorially with her hipster friend, who nodded in agreement at the injustices piled upon them.

For some reason, the word *louche* came to mind when I saw that pair. I made a mental note to look that word up when I had a moment.

However, my attention was pulled away from the two of them when I noticed Randall Glendower slowly trudging down the aisle. In one hand he held the handle of a large, draped square box. He stopped and looked around, trying to get his bearings. When he spotted me, his face lit up.

"Hey, Eli. They didn't tell me you'd be here."

We headed toward each other, meeting at about the halfway point of the long aisle.

"This is mostly my party," I said.

"That's cool," he said, then glanced around. "We can sit anywhere?" he asked, looking at the large empty theater and the relatively few people seated down front.

"Sure," I said. "But you might want to sit on the aisle, to make things easier."

"No problem," he said with a smile, not even bothering to question how any of this might be easy or hard. He headed toward the front of the theater still lugging his draped box and I turned back to see who we might still be missing.

Tracy, her head bandaged, stood in the doorway chatting with Deirdre.

I was pleased she had agreed to let us use the space, as it would have been difficult to pull this off in any other location. As they spoke, they parted to let some others pass and I winced when I saw it was Megan with Quinton. If there had been another way to transport him here I would have jumped on it, but we all had key roles to play and Megan was really the only option to provide the needed taxi service, short of calling an actual taxi, which I suddenly wondered why I hadn't done.

As they made their way down the aisle, I glanced back at Deirdre. I looked at my watch and then gave her a quick nod. I turned and headed toward the front of the theater.

"Good evening, everyone. I think we're about ready to get started," I said by way of introduction.

"Good, because I'm just about ready to leave," Sherry Lisbon growled from the front row. "I have yet to be offered an adequate explanation as to why I've been called here."

"All will be explained," I countered, treating her like I might treat an obstreperous heckler. "We're here this evening to take one last look into the mysterious murder of Tyler James. To get us kicked off, I've asked Homicide Detective Miles Wright to provide a short recap of what happened to Tyler James on the evening of his death."

Wright reluctantly stepped forward, looking like a grade-school kid forced to make an oral presentation before the class. He kept his head down and read from his notes in a flat, businesslike monotone.

"Somewhere between the hours of ten and twelve p.m., the victim was shot twice in the back in the projection booth at the Parkway Theater." He stopped and made an ineffectual gesture up toward the booth. But then several attendees turned and looked, so perhaps the move had more impact than I realized. When they turned back, Wright seemed flummoxed by their reaction. He ran his finger down the page and found his place in his notes again.

"The assailant fled, leaving the gun," he continued, "along with an envelope containing $75,000 in cash. In addition, two empty film canisters, bearing the label LAM, were found in the booth. Mr. James had secured and locked the projection booth from the inside before expiring."

He looked up to see if anyone was still listening, and then turned back to me, to see if he could be released from this torture. I nodded and he moved quickly to the rear of the auditorium, clearly relieved to be out of the spotlight.

"Thank you, Detective Wright, for that fine report."

Chip Cavanaugh began a slow clap, then looked around, feigning surprise that no one was joining him.

I gave him a long look.

He made two more claps and then put his hands in his lap, tossing me his best contrite smile.

"One of the many things which has bothered me, and others, about this sequence of events," I continued, "is if the killer left the gun, why did Tyler bother to lock the projection booth before he expired? Certainly the firearm would provide adequate protection if the killer returned, and picking up the small gun would be far easier than closing and locking the heavy metal door."

I scanned the small group assembled in front of me and then glanced up at the door at the top of the aisle, just in time to see Franny enter, holding Harry's elbow. They both moved slowly into the auditorium and took a seat in the very back row. Once settled, Harry tipped his hat to me and I returned my attention to the group.

"Quinton Moon—a world-renowned magician and performer— and I have discussed this at length. The conclusion we've reached is that the gun was not in the projection booth when Tyler locked the door, but was in fact placed there after the fact, to confuse the police as to where Tyler was shot and why. We differ on some of the details, but he has some thoughts he would like to share with us this evening." I gestured to Quinton and then stepped aside, handing the presentation off to him.

"Thank you, Eli," he said as he checked his hair and stepped forward. For a brief moment I thought he was going to ask the crowd for another round of applause for his opening act, but he immediately turned on his stage charm and took over.

"What we have here, my friends, is a puzzle," he said, his eyes twinkling, "and human beings love a puzzle. Just as nature abhors a vacuum, so too do we hate to let a question go unanswered. And the question that vexes me, on this occasion, is this: If the killer was in the projection booth with Tyler, why did our killer leave the gun and not take the money?"

"Leave the gun, take the cannoli." Chip Cavanaugh said this loudly and with a self-satisfied smirk. He looked around, clearly disappointed his bon mot, as bon as it may have been, had received no reaction from the group.

"Oh. *The Godfather*. Right," Randall Glendower said with a laugh, nodding at Chip. "Good one, man."

Chip winked in response and then both men turned back to Quinton, who was patiently waiting for the exchange to conclude.

"Yes, our killer left the gun and left the money," Quinton continued, playing with the words dramatically. "However, the mistake in looking at those two actions is to conclude they were born of the same circumstance. However, I believe they were two separate events which our killer hoped to solve with one single and—I think—remarkably clever solution."

Quinton started moving away from the edge of the stage and toward the aisle.

"Eli and I agree on many, many things," he said, flashing a smile in my direction, "and we do agree on this one key idea: Tyler James was not shot in the projection booth. He was shot elsewhere in the building but fled to the projection booth, either for his safety or to protect the money. Or both."

He began walking up the aisle, slowly and deliberately, keeping his gaze on the small audience the entire time. He turned and looked directly at Mrs. Tyler James.

"I don't believe he was shot in the projection booth," he repeated with emphasis. "I believe Tyler was in fact shot in the theater's lobby, where an after-hours clandestine meeting went terribly awry. The details may be fuzzy, but this much is clear: Tyler exited the lobby with two bullets in his back and one primary goal in mind: get to the projection booth and keep the killer from getting the $75,000."

Ever the showman, Quinton had positioned himself so virtually everyone in the audience was forced to turn and look over their shoulders to see him. And, amazingly, every single one of them did it, even Sherry Lisbon's two attorneys. The only exception was Sherry Lisbon herself, who I noticed was looking at me and not at Quinton. I turned my attention back to Quinton, hoping she would do the same but not wanting to check and see if she did.

"Tyler proceeded to his one place of safety, his beloved projection booth," Quinton continued. "There he locked the door and then collapsed and died on the floor."

Quinton let this pronouncement sink in for a moment as he slowly, oh so slowly, began to head back down the aisle toward the stage.

"So now our killer has two problems: The first is the money, which is out of reach behind a thick, well-secured steel door. And the other is the gun, which is on the wrong side of that same door. If the killer can get the gun into the booth and the money out, the motive for the killing will become fuzzy and the police will be led astray by focusing on a locked room mystery. What to do? What to do?" Quinton put a finger to his chin in a dramatic thinking pose.

"And then our killer landed on a solution which, effectively, solved both problems and left a puzzle for the police to solve. Which they—and everyone else—have been unable to do. Until today."

Quinton looked down. He was standing right next to Randall Glendower, who had kindly followed my instructions and had taken a seat on the aisle.

"Can I ask a favor?" Quinton asked in his calmest voice. "And in the same instant, speak a phrase that one can go one's entire life without having the pleasure of uttering?"

Randall, looking mesmerized, slowly nodded.

"Thank you," Quinton said, then added with a smile, "may I borrow your monkey?"

The next portion of Quinton's demonstration took a few moments to set up.

He headed up to the door of the projection booth, while everyone turned in their seats and watched. Detective Wright met him by the booth and opened the reinstalled door while Quinton turned to his audience below.

"To recap: We have a gun..." Quinton looked at Wright, who suddenly had the look of an actor in a play who has forgotten his lines. He patted his pockets and finally pulled out a tiny handgun.

"This is the same model of gun which was used to kill Tyler James," Quinton said in a booming voice as he held it up. The gun was so tiny, from our position in the front of the theater it virtually disappeared in his hand. He held it with the tips of his fingers and turned it until it finally caught the light, sending off a brief glimmer we could see from our seats.

"I should point out the firearm is unloaded and, for further safety, the firing pin has been removed," Wright added.

"Yes, but other than that, it is virtually the same as the gun which shot Tyler James, correct?"

Detective Wright nodded in agreement.

"All right, we have the recently fired gun on this side of the door," Quinton said as he reached into his breast pocket, "and an envelope with $75,000 in it on the other side of the door." He pulled a thick white envelope out and held it up for our approval and then handed it to Wright. The entire exchange was taking on the feel of a well-practiced stage routine.

"Detective Wright, would you agree the envelope you now hold in your hand is the approximate size and weight of the one found in the projection booth the night Tyler James was found murdered?"

Wright murmured something and Quinton immediately teased him. "I can't hear you, Detective."

"Yes it is," Wright said, now speaking louder than necessary.

"All right, the gun is on this side of the door, and the money and the dead body—" Quinton gestured to Wright, who again looked like an actor who's lost his place in the play. Wright held up the envelope one last time, then stepped into the projection booth and shut the door. "The money and the dead body are on the other side of a locked door." He waited a moment and then spoke again, this time louder. "Behind a locked door."

Even from the front of the theater we could hear the metallic *clunk* as the lock slid into place.

"Thank you." Quinton shook his head with a smile, which produced a laugh from the crowd. "We rehearsed and everything." He shrugged his shoulders in a "what are you gonna do?" gesture, then moved back into performance mode.

"All right, so I am the killer and I have two issues of high concern. I have the movie, but there is $75,000 on that side of the door," he said, with a nod toward the booth, "and I'm out here with the murder weapon. It looks like I am, as they say, *screwed*. Except in addition to the murder weapon, I also have a secret weapon."

He bent down out of sight for a moment. We could hear another, much smaller metallic clink, and when he stood up, Quinton was cradling what looked like a furry baby in his arms.

"Ladies and gentlemen, may I introduce you to my assistant: Jinx."

There was an involuntary coo from the ladies in the audience, with the exception of Sherry Lisbon.

"Cool—a monkey!" Chip Cavanaugh said, sounding truly excited by the sight.

"Not just a monkey, but a Javan macaque monkey. And this is the only thing small enough—and smart enough—to go through the small square hole in the front of the projection booth."

He gestured at the hole in the booth and we all looked from where he stood to the position of the hole. It was clearly out of the reach of a human, as it was in the center of an otherwise smooth wall with no obvious handholds in sight.

"I believe my furry friend here was able to successfully complete one-half of his mission that night, but the arrival of Eli Marks and the police forced him and his owner to depart sooner than anticipated."

All eyes turned toward Randall Glendower, who was watching the presentation with intense interest.

It slowly dawned on him he was the sudden center of attention and moments later he realized why.

"Hey," he said, suddenly standing, but then he noticed Homicide Detective Fred Hutton was moving toward him, so he took his seat again. Our attention was pulled away from him by Quinton's booming voice up by the projection booth.

"He was not able to get the money, but with Jinx's help, he was able to place the gun into the locked projection booth. Like this."

With that, he handed the small gun to Jinx and set the monkey on the edge of the seat in front of him. From where I stood, I watched as everyone in the audience—including Sherry Lisbon—turned their heads and visually traced the path the monkey was about to make: a simple jump up to a narrow ledge which ran the length of the wall by the door. Then a sharp turn, where the cables from the small hole in the wall that ran to the digital projector in the ceiling would provide swinging access to the larger, center hole. From there, it was through the hole and into the booth. An impossible trip for a human, but a simple romp for just about any small monkey.

Except, as it turned out, for Jinx.

He examined the gun, sniffed at it, gave the handle a lick and then tossed it on the floor. He turned and looked down at us and appeared to smile widely, showing a truly impressive set of white, wet teeth. Quinton picked up the gun and handed it back to Jinx, and then helped to get him started by placing him on the narrow ledge. Jinx didn't seem to care for the ledge, because he immediately jumped down, landing on Quinton's shoulder, and then he bonked Quinton in the head with the small gun.

Quinton patiently took the gun from Jinx's small, furry hand and placed the monkey back up on the ledge. He handed the gun to Jinx, who batted it away. Quinton offered it again, and again the monkey batted it away. On his third attempt, Jinx pushed the gun away, leaned down into Quinton's face and gave him the monkey equivalent of a raspberry.

"I've seen enough." The sentiment came from Sherry Lisbon, who stood up while declaring it, but I had the sense others in the small audience shared her feelings.

I held up a hand.

"If you would indulge me," I said. People who had started to get up took their seats again, either due to the force of my personality or the fact that Homicide Detective Fred Hutton was now standing beside me with his arms folded.

"I'd like to offer an alternate theory," I said. "But before I do, I'd like us to watch just a few minutes from that classic missing masterpiece, *London After Midnight*."

On cue, the lights in the auditorium went out and a white light filled the movie screen.

CHAPTER 21

The audience was remarkably patient and sat through a full thirty seconds of flickering white light before I sensed they were once again getting restless. I climbed up onto the stage and stepped into the beam of light.

"In my view, this is what remains of *London After Midnight*," I said, gesturing to the blank illuminated space behind me. "The film that was part of a sales exchange gone wrong was no more substantial than the light coming from that projector."

Detective Wright had finally become adept at picking up his cues and the projector light switched off just as the lights popped back on in the auditorium.

He peered down at me from the small square hole in the center of the back wall and gave me a quick thumbs up and a wide smile.

I nodded my approval at his timing and then continued.

"This investigation has focused on the various people who had the interest and resources to buy the movie if it existed," I said, scanning the small audience below me. "But no real time was spent looking at people who knew it didn't exist. And who also needed money.

"But I'm getting ahead of myself," I continued, carefully making my way off the stage and down the stairs. "It's safe to say the killer knew about Tyler and his black market dealings." I stepped off the last step and turned toward Mrs. Tyler James and Gunnar, both of whom turned away immediately. Just as in my act,

I seemed to have a sixth sense to find audience members who really had no interest in being part of the show.

"Mrs. James, you were aware of your husband's side business. Can you tell us how it worked?"

"How it worked?" she repeated, in a classic stalling action.

"Yes, if I had something to sell and wanted Tyler to handle the sale, how would I go about it?"

She rolled her eyes, sighed, and then spoke in a flat monotone which was designed to express her contempt at this process and, by extension, me.

"It was all done via email," she said, snapping her gum as she spoke. For all I knew, it was the same gum she had started chewing in my shop earlier in the week. "If you wanted to buy something, you'd email Tyler and he'd track it down. If you had something to sell, same thing. He'd look around for a buyer."

"And either way, he took a cut?" I asked.

"It wasn't a charity, if that's what you mean," she said.

"So it could be relatively anonymous," I added.

"Completely anonymous," she said.

"And how did the money change hands?"

She shrugged. "Sometimes there'd be a wire transfer, sometimes an actual money drop. It varied."

"Basically, anyone with access to Tyler's email could take part, as a buyer or a seller."

"Sure," she said, crossing her arms and settling back into her seat to physically demonstrate she'd said as much as she was going to.

"So," I said, turning my attention back to the full group, "if someone needed money, they could use Tyler's system to entice a buyer to hand over a large sum of cash for a treasured item."

"Like $750,000," Randall Glendower said suddenly.

I held up my hand. "Actually, I think in this case, all they were counting on was the deposit—$75,000. The killer knew the movie didn't really exist—or didn't care one way or the other—so they were only planning on taking the ruse as far as the deposit stage."

I looked over to see Quinton had taken a seat next to Megan. He was giving me a puzzled expression as he tried to see where I was headed with this theory.

"Let's assume the killer got in touch with Tyler, told him the print of *London After Midnight* was available to the highest bidder, and let Tyler go do his thing. After some negotiations, he found a buyer in Clifford Thomas."

"I knew it!" Randall Glendower nearly shouted as he started to get up, and then realized this probably wasn't the best place for an outburst of this type and settled back into his seat.

"Yes, you were outbid," I said to Randall, and he somehow found a way to both nod and shake his head at the same time. "Tyler may have had some help in jacking up the price by bringing in another, more competitive bidder," I said, turning to Sherry Lisbon.

One of her attorneys turned to her and started to whisper something, but Lisbon pushed her away.

"There's no way you can prove that," she snapped.

I shrugged. "No, I can't. I also can't prove Tyler took sympathy on Clifford when he recognized the writer's passion for the movie and let him win the auction, even though others would have gone higher, just for the fun of taking it away from him." I glanced back at Sherry Lisbon, but she was now staring straight ahead, clearly not interested in engaging further on this topic.

"Somehow or other," I continued, "Clifford Thomas won the auction and presented Tyler with a ten percent down payment on the purchase, which in this case was $75,000."

"In cash, no less." This observation came from Chip Cavanaugh, who had spent much of my presentation scrolling through messages on his phone.

"Yes, in cash," I agreed.

"That would indicate trust in the middleman," Chip continued, not taking his eyes off the phone. "Which would indicate Cliff had done a lot of business with Tyler." He looked up and seemed surprised all eyes were on him. "I'm just saying."

"Be that as it may," I said, trying to pull back the ownership of the presentation, "some sort of pre-arranged drop was made—Tyler left the money and picked up the film reels—but that's when things started to go wonky. Because when Tyler got the film reels back to the projection booth and opened the canisters, they were empty."

"But he would have known they were empty as soon as he picked up the canisters," Randall said, almost whining. "Film reels are heavy."

"Yes, which is why the killer had placed some free weights in the canisters. Tyler had a weight bench and some weights up in the booth," I said. "The night we found his body, I noticed he had a complete set, along with four other weights that weren't the same color as the full set. I think those were taking the place of the film reels in the canisters."

To prove my conjecture, I pointed up to the projection booth. Detective Wright was standing by the door. He held up a black twenty pound weight in one hand, and then held up another, lighter-colored weight in the other. Despite his serious expression, the demonstration had the distinct feel of a product reveal moment from a cheesy seventies game show.

"When he realized he'd been fooled, Tyler went to confront the seller."

"All right, wait, I thought the process was anonymous?" This, surprisingly, came from Quinton. Even he seemed a little unnerved he had suddenly spoken up, but then he pressed on. "I mean, isn't that the premise? That this was anonymous?"

"I believe it was," I said. "But I also believe somehow Tyler figured out who had put this alleged lost film on the black market. And when he went to confront that person, he didn't have to go far."

I scanned the room and everyone followed my eyes, nervously waiting to see where my gaze would land.

"It was a short walk," I continued. "Just down the hall to the theater manager's office."

CHAPTER 22

Tracy, seated on an aisle, looked first left then right, quickly assessing her situation.

To her left, one seat over, sat Deirdre. To her right, walking up the aisle, was Homicide Detective Fred Hutton.

She turned and saw Detective Wright headed toward her, coming down the aisle. With all avenues of escape apparently closed, she settled back into her seat and turned her thousand-watt smile on me.

"That's one theory," she said, turning and crossing her long legs into the aisle. "But it's a long shot."

"It is that," I said. "Want me to expand on it?"

She shrugged casually.

"I suspect there was a confrontation of some kind in your office," I continued, first to her and then looking out at the rest of the now rapt audience. "Perhaps Tyler demanded the money back and you gave it to him."

"And then you thought better of it and shot him in the back as he exited your office." This came from Detective Wright, who had taken a casual pose, perched on the armrest of the seat across from Tracy's on the aisle.

"It's a small caliber gun," I said, picking up the story. "The bullets didn't pass through Tyler, but he's smart enough to realize he's got internal bleeding and there's a crazy woman with a gun, so he races back up to the safety of the booth, tosses the envelope of money on the table and closes and locks the door from the inside."

Tracy looked up at me with a smile that could only be called inscrutable. I turned from her and headed back down the aisle, toward the stage.

"Now Tracy has a problem," I said, turning back to the now very attentive group. "She can't get into the booth to get the money, because the booth only locks from the inside. A privacy thing, for the projectionist who might be using the toilet. And the gun is not in the booth, so the police are going to look around to determine where the fatal shots were fired. She needs to steer them away from her office—to get them as far away from her as she could—because she's seen enough crime shows. She knows there is bound to be at least a little blood evidence somewhere in her office."

"We have a team in there right now, looking for just that," said Homicide Detective Fred Hutton.

His pose was the opposite of the relaxed one taken by his partner. He stood in the center of the aisle, his arms crossed, looking like a golem in an off-the-rack gray suit.

"She needs to put some distance between the method and the effect. What we call in the business a little time misdirection," I said. "Quinton, how would you define time misdirection?"

He didn't even have to give it a moment's thought. "Oh, that's a lovely ploy. I think it was Harry Lorraine who coined the phrase. You see, you make the audience think something happened here, but it actually happened—earlier or later—over there. Oritz called it temporal separation, because you're using time to separate the cause from the effect. Add in the spatial separation and you've got a very powerful method indeed. It's very common ploy, for example, in the bending of metal utensils—spoons and the like—however that's only the tip of the iceberg, as it were," he added.

"Yes, exactly. That's her problem—how to steer attention away from her office and radically change the question, from 'where was Tyler James shot?' and instead make the entire case about the question, 'How did the killer get out of a locked projection booth?' No small problem."

"What's a girl to do?"

I was surprised this came from Sherry Lisbon, who no longer seemed bored with the proceedings.

"If the girl in question is a former NCAA athlete who played ball semiprofessionally in Japan," I responded, "she's going to use her natural gifts to get the gun into the booth." I paused and looked at Tracy, who gave me nothing in return.

"But once again I'm getting ahead of myself," I said. "Let me back up." I took two steps backward and leaned against the stage, my little visual joke producing zero reactions. "You see, as it turns out, a quick Google check will tell you that this award-winning athlete had a bit of a gambling problem, and ended up being 'released' from her college prior to graduation."

"I got canned." Tracy said this without any sarcasm or rancor, just a straight-ahead fact of life.

"Your phraseology, not mine. But she was still a skillful player and there was money to be made playing in Japan, so off she went. Unfortunately, while there was money to be made, there were also bets to be placed. After a short stint playing some long odds, she was asked to leave that position as well. And then she made what was probably the only good choice she'd made in a long series of bad decisions..."

"Unless the courts made it for her," Deirdre added.

"That's always a possibility. Regardless, she came to Minnesota, land of ten thousand treatment centers."

"Gambling addiction," Chip Cavanaugh said, clicking his tongue and shaking his head sagely. "That's a tough one."

I waited to see where the punch line landed, but there seemed to be nothing else to his interruption, so I continued. "She went through treatment and when she was done, she got a job. Managing a movie theater." I looked to Tracy for confirmation. "Right?"

"In a general sort of way, sure," she said.

"Unfortunately, and I don't have specifics here, I think she must have suffered a relapse of some kind, because before she knew it she'd run up some big gambling debts with—I'm just speculating here—some people who didn't qualify as 'Minnesota Nice.'"

"Creeps," Tracy added. "Total creeps."

"So, she has a problem—a big gambling debt and no way to pay it off. Until Tyler tells her, in passing, about his side business."

Randall leaned forward, excited. "Yeah, yeah. So she gets the idea to try to sell a fake movie," he said, "with the plan to keep the deposit. She'll pay off her gambling debts and no one will be any the wiser. Because who's going to report being robbed while trying to buy a black market movie?"

Now it was Chip Cavanaugh's turn to lean forward. "But Tyler figured it out," he said, picking up the narrative from Randall. "He must have confronted her about it, and took back the money she so desperately needed."

"So she shot him," Randall added.

"I had no choice," Tracy said sharply and then her eyes went a little wide as she looked out at the assembled group. Like everyone else, she had gotten caught up in the narrative.

Sherry Lisbon shook her head disapprovingly. "Dear, no one in this room is buying that for one blessed second."

Randall Glendower slumped back in his seat, perplexed. He looked up at me. "That's all well and good, but how did she get the gun into the booth?"

"Clearly, she didn't use a monkey," Chip said, throwing a look in Quinton's direction.

I shook my head. "No. Sorry, Quinton. She didn't use a monkey. Instead, she used the skills she had been developing for years."

I headed up the aisle toward where Detective Wright was still perched on an armrest.

"Detective, what do your notes say about this back exit here by the screen?" I asked, motioning to the curtained exit at the foot of the aisle.

Wright pulled out his notebook and flipped through some pages, finally landing on the one he was looking for.

"'The suspect appears to have exited via the south rear exit,'" he read slowly, "'and stepped away from the building about two feet. Subject must have seen or heard something and returned to the building to seek an alternate form of egress.'"

"That's one way of looking at it," I said, holding out my hand to him. It took him a moment to figure out what I wanted, but a second later I was holding the small gun in my hand. "Another idea is she came down here, stepped out the back door, packed some snow around the gun until it was reasonably round, returned to the auditorium and threw it. Through that hole up there."

I mimed forming the snowball and making the throw with the small gun.

They all turned and looked at the square hole up in the back wall of the theater.

It suddenly seemed very far away.

"That's a tough throw for a basketball player," Chip Cavanaugh said sadly. "Even a really good basketball player."

"Yes, but you're making the same assumption I made about Tracy. Because of her height. And because of my woeful ignorance about sports in general."

"What's that?"

"That she played basketball." I turned to Tracy, who was staring straight ahead. "Tracy, what sport did you play in college and in Japan?"

She sat silently for a long moment, and then said quietly, "Softball."

"What position?"

Another long pause. "Catcher."

I turned away from her and back to Chip and the rest of the group, gesturing toward the small windows on the back wall.

"An impossible throw for a basketball player, probably. But a softball catcher can throw far, they can throw hard, and they can throw precisely." I took a seat on an armrest and glanced over at Tracy. "You see, I made the common mistake of thinking, just because she's tall, Tracy must have been a basketball player. Had I been paying attention, I would have noticed how often she used baseball terms in real life, but never basketball terms."

"I will give you all the money in *his* wallet right now if you can name one basketball term." This came from Deirdre, who was gesturing toward her husband while giving me a sly smile.

"I think we both know how that would end," I said.

"Badly," she said.

Homicide Detective Fred Hutton looked confused at the exchange but relieved the contents of his wallet were, for the moment, safe.

"As I was saying," I continued, "my mistake about Tracy's chosen sport was corrected in passing during a conversation with Mrs. Tyler James, thank you for that." I doffed an invisible hat to Mrs. James and she looked back, annoyed, clearly not remembering her referring to Tracy as the "*Bad News Bears* washout."

"That got me thinking. And I did a quick check on the internet, heeding some oft heard advice from my late aunt Alice," I said, holding up my phone. I looked over to where Harry was seated. He gave me a warm smile.

"My aunt Alice," I continued, "used to warn me all the time about my actions being set down somewhere in an unseen Permanent Record. She was a big fan of that concept, the Permanent Record. And that's a pretty fair definition of the internet. Tracy's gambling scandals—the college and Japanese versions—are well documented."

Randall Glendower had stood up and turned in his seat, squinting up at the projection booth. He pivoted back toward me. "She threw the snowball with the gun in it through that little hole?"

"Yes," I said, "using the strength and precision she had developed as a semi-pro softball catcher. The snowball hit the floor of the booth and the snow went flying, which explains the small puddles of water which were found once we got to the booth."

He considered this for a moment, and then turned. "But what about Clifford Thomas?"

"Yes, which brings me to my next point. That snowball also led to the death of Clifford Thomas." I looked to Tracy, but she returned my gaze with a stony expression, clearly having learned a lesson from her last outburst.

"The best I can figure," I continued, "is Clifford Thomas came by our magic shop to return some books he'd signed for my Uncle Harry. We weren't open so he left them next door—here at the theater. I'm guessing Tracy recognized him from the times he stopped by to talk to Tyler. Maybe he invited her to stop by his house some time. I'm not clear on the details, but I do know he wasn't shy about letting fans, particularly good-looking fans, into his house."

Randall Glendower nodded as I spoke and then cut in. "Then she went to his house, maybe to see if he'd figured out Tyler's murder—he was a mystery writer, after all. And he was the one who had put down the $75,000 deposit. Perhaps Tyler mentioned that when he confronted Tracy."

"Perhaps," I agreed, turning back to Tracy. "You're sitting with him in his library, behind that fancy moving bookcase. Then maybe he left the room for a minute, to get drinks or something, and your curiosity got the better of you. I think you took a peek at the manuscript of his new book on the desk and the title probably freaked you out."

"What was the title?" Randall was leaning forward, as was Chip Cavanaugh. Even Sherry Lisbon appeared to be sitting on the edge of her seat. Only Mrs. Tyler James and Gunnar seemed disengaged from the narrative, now that neither one appeared to be a suspect in either murder.

"I'm just speculating," I said, "but from the list of titles he kept in his desk, only one would have really caught your eye: *A Snowball's Chance*." I walked up the aisle and looked down at her. "Did you think he'd solved the crime and written it up as a novel?"

Tracy didn't meet my eye. "I didn't think. I just acted."

"That's right, you're impulsive," I said, remembering the kiss she had planted on me after driving her home from the hospital. "You picked up the letter opener, Clifford Thomas came back to the room, and that was that."

"That was that."

I turned and headed back to the front of the room, then stopped suddenly and turned around. "Oh, and you took the manuscript. Which wasn't about Tyler's murder, was it?"

Tracy shook her head. "No. It was about ice fishing and a murder using a frozen fish or something. I didn't finish it. Mysteries are stupid."

"Not to worry. I'm sure the prison library stocks many other interesting genres," I said as Detective Wright stepped forward with a pair of handcuffs.

CHAPTER 23

"You know what they say: A party's not a party until someone gets read their Miranda rights."

This wry observation came from none other than Sherry Lisbon. Even after I laughed, her two attorney companions still seemed unsure of the comedic intention of her proclamation. Then Sherry cracked what, for her, passed as a smile, and the two women instantly offered up their impressions of what a smiling attorney might look like.

This was just one of many odd conversations which filled the next half hour after Tracy was arrested and the rest of the attendees filed out of the auditorium, through the lobby and into the crisp cold evening. Deirdre stopped long enough to thank me for my help in arranging this.

"You were correct in your theory," she said. There was a grudging edge to her compliment.

"I got the broad strokes right, I suppose," I said. "Thanks for letting me stage it."

Deirdre shrugged. "Once you laid out the evidence, Homicide was in general agreement. We figured if Tracy was working with an accomplice, she would have copped to it when you confronted her. But it looks like she was working alone."

"That's the way it looks."

Deirdre glanced over at me, the slightest traces of a smile on her face. "Anyway, try to stay out of trouble. For at least a couple days."

I held the door for her and just as she exited, Chip Cavanaugh came up behind me and gave my back a playful slap.

"Thanks for throwing this shindig," he said with a wink. "And I hope I didn't tease you too much with my ad on Glendower's website," he added, winking again.

"That was you?"

He nodded, not even trying to suppress a smirk.

"Why?"

Chip shrugged. "Who knows? I clearly have too much time on my hands. And speaking of time," he said, glancing at his watch. "I better get moving. I tell you, this is the best party I've ever been at that involved handcuffs." He stopped and touched his chin thoughtfully. "No, strike that. Second best."

No one thought this joke was funnier than Chip, who was still laughing as he made his way out the door. From my vantage point in the lobby, I could see Sherry Lisbon was standing in front of the theater, perhaps waiting for her car to be brought around.

Chip scanned the area surreptitiously and then took a position next to her. From where I stood, it didn't appear they were speaking or relating in any fashion. They were just standing, quietly, side by side.

They stood there for a moment and then Chip reached over—slowly, very slowly—and took her hand. She batted it away without turning toward him. He waited several seconds and then made a second attempt. This time it was accepted, tentatively at first and then with more enthusiasm. They stood there for several moments, holding hands, as if it were a completely alien action for both of them. Then Sherry's ride—provided by her two attorneys—pulled up in front of the theater. Chip and Sherry immediately separated, like magnets being pushed apart, she getting in the car quickly while he turned and headed down the sidewalk in search of his own car.

I thought of my encounter with Sherry Lisbon in the downtown St. Paul parking ramp, the one connected to Chip Cavanaugh's condo building, and realized the two eccentric millionaires were conducting a courtship of sorts, in their own awkward, inimitable fashion. I smiled because the idea struck me as, well, sort of cute.

I was interrupted from this reverie by a grunt behind me. I turned to see that Mrs. Tyler James and her friend Gunnar were approaching me in an obligatory fashion, like I was the under-populated reception line at a one-person wedding. The pair stood there staring at me for a long moment, Mrs. James still masticating the life out of her gum.

"Thanks for coming by," I said finally.

"I didn't think we had a choice," she said in her typical sullen fashion.

"That's true. Sometimes when the police are involved in an invitation, the wording can suggest your options are limited."

"Whatever," was all she said as the pair slouched out.

I shook my head, thinking how proud Oscar Wilde would have been if he had exited an event with the same wit and élan.

"It's been quite a week, I'm going to turn in," Harry said as he buttoned up his coat, even though he'd only be outside for ten seconds on the walk from the theater to our door.

"And don't forget your hat," Franny added, tugging a bright red stocking cap over his already disheveled gray hair and pulling it tight around his ears. He readjusted it and she batted his hands away, putting it back the way she had it originally. He gave me a smile.

"Franny knitted me a hat," he said.

"I can see that," I said. "I can give Franny a ride home," I offered.

Harry shook his head. "That won't be necessary," was all he said.

He took her hand and they headed out the door and turned left. My curiosity got the best of me, so I pushed the lobby door open far enough to poke my head out. The two shuffled as far as the magic shop and then Harry pulled out his keys, opened the door and they disappeared inside.

I slowly stepped back into the lobby.

"Isn't it adorable?" Megan said. She and Quinton had come up behind me while I was spying on my uncle and the woman who was, apparently, his girlfriend.

"They're dating?" I said, not sure if that was even the right term to use for a couple whose combined age was pushing 150 years.

"They have been for weeks," Megan said with a laugh. "For a magician, you're not very observant. That's why Harry's been so tired, because Franny's been keeping him up late just about every night of the week."

Before I could even process this idea, Megan continued. "They've been taking line dancing lessons," she continued. "Apparently Harry's quite light on his feet," she added, turning to Quinton.

"That does not surprise me in the least," Quinton said, and then something across the lobby caught his attention. He raised his hand in a wave.

"I believe," he said, shouting across the room, "that something of an apology on my part is in order."

We turned to see Randall Glendower, in the midst of wrapping Jinx's cage with an extra blanket. He looked over at us and smiled a crooked, quizzical smile.

"Apology?" he said.

Quinton moved toward him and we followed.

"Yes," Quinton said. "I believe I unjustly maligned you and your monkey." He extended his hand to Randall. "No hard feelings, I trust?"

Randall struggled to his feet, using Quinton's extended hand for support as well as for its intended purpose as a sign of his apology.

"Oh, no, man, no problem," Randall said once he was upright. "It's not every day you get to be a murder suspect and your secret weapon is your monkey. In fact," he continued, looking off into space, "that would make for a really cool comic book series. *Man and Monkey*. I like that."

There was a short, sharp screech from inside the cage.

"Okay, how about *Monkey and Man*?" Randall offered. He took the complete lack of response from Jinx as his approval and began to zip up his large, furry parka in anticipation of the impending walk to his car. He picked up the cage and gave the lobby one last look.

"What happens to the theater now they are minus one manager?" he asked.

I had no idea, so I turned to Megan. "What does happen?" I repeated, then pivoted back to Randall to explain. "Megan is the landlord here. She owns the whole block."

"Wow," Randall said with genuine enthusiasm. "A land owner. Very impressive."

"Thanks," Megan said. "Well, the theater has been leased by an entertainment consortium out of Indianapolis for about the last ten years, so I figure they'll put out a call for a new manager."

Randall's eyes narrowed and lowered his voice. "When is their lease up?"

Megan lowered her voice to match his conspiratorial level. "Two and a half months."

"That's a fun fact," Randall said. "Very fun." He looked at his watch. "Do you have a minute to talk?"

"About leases? Sadly, yes. Always," Megan said.

He headed over to a corner of the lobby, in part to shield the monkey's cage from the blasts of cold air which pummeled us every time the lobby door opened and in part to shield the conversation from anyone who might be listening. Not that anyone was.

"I'm going to go talk to Mr. Glendower about the lease," Megan said. "Do you mind giving Quinton a ride back to his hotel?"

Before I could agree or disagree, she and Randall were already deep in conversation.

* * *

So, for the second time in the past ten days, I made the drive from Minneapolis to downtown St. Paul with Quinton Moon as my passenger.

"Here's what I don't understand," he said, turning to me once we were well on our way. "One of the homicide detectives, the taller one..."

"Homicide Detective Fred Hutton," I said.

"That's the one. He said Tracy would be charged in the deaths of Tyler James and Clifford Thomas. But he made no mention of the two attempts on your life and the one on Harry."

"That's because she didn't do them," I said.

"But Megan told me someone had attempted to run you down with a car?"

"Someone did, but as it turned out, it was just some guy stealing a car which had been left running. He probably didn't even realize he almost hit me."

"All right," he said, accepting that answer for the moment. "But what about the ice on the roof which was pushed down on you and Harry?"

I shrugged. "The police found no footprints on the roof and everything was melting that day. We get ice dams on the roof. And a bunch of it picked that moment to fall. Wrong place, wrong time."

Quinton nodded slowly as he considered this. "So we were all victims of a post hoc fallacy," he said.

I hadn't heard that phrase before. "Post hoc fallacy? How do you mean?"

"If event B happens after event A, then it must be connected to event A," he said. "You tap the box with the magic wand and then open the box to reveal a rabbit. The audience thinks the wand and the tapping somehow caused the rabbit to appear—they are always looking for causations, proximity, that sort of thing. Ah, well, the desperate human need to connect point A with point B. Where would we magicians be without it?"

I grunted in agreement, only vaguely understanding what he was talking about. We rode in silence, and then he spoke up again.

"But what about when Tracy was attacked?" he said. "When they pushed her off the ladder and then when she was attacked in the theater?"

"My best guess is both those events were courtesy of the goons she owes money to," I said. "Tracy just cleverly incorporated them into the overall murder scenario, which helped to deflect suspicion away from her."

"Ah, yes. Classic magic misdirection," Quinton said. "It's the same reason some of the best magic tricks work: Truth, truth, truth, half-truth, truth."

I looked over at him. "Quinton, you think about magic way more than I do," I said.

"Agreed. Some might say I think about magic too much," he replied.

"It seems to work for you."

Another pause in the conversation, and then Quinton turned to me again. "Eli, this may be an uncomfortable topic, but I can't help think our relationship has something of a toxic strain to it that, unless addressed, makes its long-term viability doubtful."

I processed the sentence as best I could and came back with the one word that expressed the totality of my comprehension. "What?"

"I believe our relationship—you and me—our potential friendship, has been poisoned by jealousy, and I so wish that weren't the case."

I was surprised at his perception, as I felt I had done a fairly good job of covering up my feelings the last two weeks. "Poisoned," I said, "is a strong word."

"I can think of no other word which fits the bill and I hold myself one hundred percent accountable."

I turned to look at him for a moment, but his expression offered no further information.

"How are you accountable?"

He laughed. "I certainly can't blame you for my all-consuming jealousy, can I?"

It took a moment for this to sink in. "No," I said slowly. "I suppose you can't."

I decided silence would be the best tool for ferreting out where this was headed, and moments later my patience was rewarded.

"Oh, I would so much like to have a relationship like the one you've forged with the divine Megan," he said softly.

"What's stopping you?" I asked, then quickly added, "I mean, with someone other than Megan?"

"Magic," he finally said, the word coming out like a sigh. "Here's what I know to be true: You can't spend eight hours a day, six days a week, throwing playing cards at high speed into watermelons and not expect it to have a detrimental impact on your adult relationships."

"I suppose so. But look at the result? You're a great—truly great—magician." It felt good to say this out loud, and even better, I was surprised to discover, to say it directly to Quinton.

"As are you, my friend, with—I suspect—far less of the attendant angst and gnashing of teeth."

"Oh, I wouldn't go that far," I began, but he cut me off.

"I watched you performing in that ludicrous Rabbit and Hat costume—sorry about that, by the way. I wasn't aware of the client's plan in that regard."

"It wasn't so bad," I said. "It proved to be an ideal icebreaker."

"You were magnificent," he said, punching the last word for full dramatic effect.

"I was just doing a little walk-around close-up magic," I said with a verbal shrug, but again he cut me off.

"No, not in the least. You were performing miracles," he said. "I watched your audience and they were swept away in the illusions. You've learned the one trick most magicians never master in a lifetime of performing, and you do it by second nature."

"What's that?" I was bowled over by his flow of compliments and more than willing to take one more.

"You never attempt to fool your audience, to one-up them, to outsmart them. Your goal is to create and share a true moment of magic and mystery with each and every one of them. It is the rare conjurer who has mastered that skill, my friend."

He let this sink in, which was helpful as I was having trouble processing what he was saying.

"You're no slouch yourself," I finally said.

"High praise indeed," he said.

I signaled to change lanes, heading toward the 10th Street exit into downtown St. Paul. I recognized the drive was more than half over and I still had one unanswered question.

"One thing I would like to know, if you don't mind," I began.

He spread his hands open in front of him. "I am all attention."

"Okay," I began, not sure how to navigate the delicate proposition of asking another magician how a trick is accomplished. "When you do The Miser's Dream..."

"Ah, yes, The Miser's Dream," he said. "A true gem. As Henry Hay so wisely put it, 'The Miser's Dream will repay you for everything you as a magician put into it.'"

"You've clearly put a lot into it," I said, still trying to navigate how to get to my question while simultaneously navigating the oddball street layout which is the heart and soul of downtown St. Paul. I could see the St. Paul Hotel in the distance, but the alternating one-way streets and sudden and unannounced direction-changing road construction was impeding my progress. I decided to put the time to good use.

"At the conclusion of the routine," I said, "when you pour all the coins out of the bucket and then pick them up, handful after handful, and pour them back into the bucket..."

"Yes," he said, a smile in his voice, clearly proud of where this question was headed.

"And then you turn the bucket over," I continued, remembering the shock and surprise which I—and everyone in the audience—had felt when the bucket was revealed to be empty. Truly and completely empty, with the exception of one single coin falling

out. I smiled at how that moment had thrilled me, and not in a
"Hey, I'm a magician and he fooled me" sort of way. It had truly
been, in the finest sense of the word, an illusion. A moment of pure
magic. I couldn't help but smile thinking about it.

"Yes," he said, gesturing for me to continue. "You wish to know
how that was accomplished?"

We had pulled into the circular driveway in front of the hotel
and one of the valets or bellmen was racing to the car. Quinton held
up a hand without even turning his head and the young man froze
in his tracks. Quinton looked at me, to confirm my question.

I shook my head.

"No. On second thought, I'd rather not know how it was done,"
I said. "I'm good."

CHAPTER 24

Amazingly, there was an open parking spot right in front of the magic shop.

I slid into the spot and then almost slid under the car when I stepped out, not realizing how icy the road had become.

"Very smooth," came a sultry voice from the sidewalk.

I used the door handle to maintain my balance and looked across the top of the car to see Megan, smiling at me from within a funky hat and scarf combination.

"Hey. How long have you been standing there?"

She gestured toward the theater. "I just finished up with Randall Glendower," she said, smiling happily. The marquee was dark now, displaying what I assumed would be the last of the Parkway Double Plays: *The Stuntman of La Mancha*.

"Is Randall going to lease the theater?"

"Better," she said as she stepped gingerly toward the car. "He's buying the theater and paying way more for it than any sensible person should."

"Will he still be scheduling Double Plays?" I asked, gesturing to the marquee.

"Better than that," she said, her smile getting even wider. "He's going to schedule both Double and Triple Plays. He's already got the first Triple Play figured out."

"Lay it on me."

She took a moment, looking up, assembling all the words in her head. "The first one will be *Close Brief Encounters of the Third*

Kind Hearts and Coronets," she finally recited, nearly running out of breath in the process.

"He's going to need a bigger marquee," I said, looking at the limited space the current one offered. "And how is it going to feel selling off parcels of the land your grandmother left you?" I remembered the trouble that had come when Megan's ex-husband had tried the same thing.

"It's one less headache for me to deal with," she said. "And don't worry, I'll still be your landlady. There's no change happening in that area."

"In that case," I said, slowly and carefully negotiating my way around the car and toward the curb, "does my landlady have any interest in coming up to my place for a spot of dinner and whatnot?"

"Yes to the dinner and double yes to the whatnot," she said, reaching out and taking my hand.

Together we helped steady each other as we moved slowly to the door of the magic shop.

I fumbled for my keys and in a matter of moments we were inside, where it was dark but warm.

"Shhhh," I whispered like a wayward teenager as we made our way stealthily up the stairs which led to my apartment on the third floor. I gestured toward the door to Harry's apartment on the second floor landing and Megan smiled and nodded, stepping even more quietly on the squeaky stairs. We had just passed his threshold when the door swung open with surprising speed, resulting in high-pitched yelps from both me and Megan—though I will argue hers was way higher.

"We thought we heard you two sneaking by," Harry said with a laugh. He was in his pajamas, over which he wore a black watch plaid bathrobe I had never seen before. He opened the door farther to reveal Franny, who sported an identical but smaller version of the same robe. Her long gray hair had been assembled into a quasi-bun on the top of her head, and she held two steaming teacups in her hands.

"Careful, this is hot," she said as she passed one to Harry.

"You two getting ready to turn in?" Harry asked.

"We're going to make dinner and then, sure," I said, not used to having these sorts of conversations with Harry and certainly not with Franny. I may have even blushed.

"We won't keep you," Harry said, blowing on his tea and sensing it was still too hot. "I just wanted to give you this, before I forgot."

He leaned back in the doorway and with his free hand reached up to where I knew he had a series of hooks. He pulled down a key and handed it to me.

"This is for you," he said, beaming. He turned to Franny and she returned the smile.

"What is it to?" I asked, turning the key over in my hand. It was old and scratched, but had a familiar look to it.

"It's the key to the shop," Harry said.

They both continued to smile big dopey smiles at me.

"Thanks," I said slowly. "But I already have a key to the shop."

Harry laughed and shook his head. "No, I'm not giving you a key to the shop. I'm *giving* you the shop. Chicago Magic. I'm giving it to you. As a wedding present."

This was a lot of information to take in over a short time, so I think I can be forgiven if it took me a moment for the last words to settle in.

"A wedding present?" I looked at Harry and then turned to Megan. "But we're not getting married. Are we?"

Megan seemed as puzzled by the declaration as I was. We both turned back to Harry.

"We're not getting married," I concluded. "I mean, not now. Not right now."

"Not soon," Megan said. "Or maybe," she added quickly.

"Or maybe, sure. We haven't really..."

"I mean, I'm not ruling it out..."

"By no means, but it's not really in the discussion phase yet..."

"That's right, there are phases, and we aren't—"

"Not you two, you baboons," he said, cutting us off sharply. "It's not a wedding present for your wedding. It's a present for *our* wedding."

Franny and Harry clasped their free hands together and then, like clockwork, each blew on their tea to see if it was properly cooled yet. They then leaned into each other and Harry gave her a kiss on the forehead. Franny returned the gesture with a loving touch on the end of his nose.

"Franny claims she predicted it months ago, but didn't want to bring it up," Harry explained.

"You can't do that. No psychic worth her salt would do that. You can't exert influence." She nodded at Megan, who nodded vigorously in return.

"Wow," I said, still processing. "This is quick."

"At our age, who has time for a long courtship?" Harry said. "When it's right, it's right."

"It's right," Franny said, nodding in agreement.

"So, the store is now yours and Franny and I are free to get out a bit. Do some traveling."

"You've traveled a lot already," I pointed out.

"No, I worked a lot and went to a lot of different places to do it. That's different."

"This time," Franny added, "it's strictly as a tourist."

"And what better way is there to travel," Harry said, putting an arm around Franny, "than with someone who can predict tomorrow's weather with one hundred percent accuracy?"

I was about to lean in and hug him, but then a thought occurred to me. I stepped back. "You're not just giving me the store to get out of doing inventory, are you?"

He smiled up at me, his eyes twinkling. "Not as far as you know, Eli."

EPILOGUE

I am beginning to think I am, truly, the least observant magician in the world.

I have no idea how long the car followed me as I ambled down Chicago Avenue, because I was deep in thought about a new way to conclude an ace assembly trick I was tearing apart and rebuilding. The new approach would include a ballsy top change, but I was worried it was a sleight for the sake of a sleight and it wouldn't really increase the impact of the effect.

I stopped for a moment to picture the effect in my mind, and noticed out of the corner of my eye a black shape was hovering in my peripheral. I turned and recognized the dark sedan immediately, my heart taking a sudden and involuntary leap straight down into the very pit of my stomach.

The front passenger window, which was tinted to near blackness, descended and I leaned down to peer into the front seat. Harpo sat straight-backed behind the steering wheel. He turned his head stiffly, and gave me his traditional deadeye stare. With the least possible amount of physical exertion, he jerked his thumb toward the backseat and a moment later I heard the snick of the door unlocking.

The backseat was, mercifully, empty. I slid into the seat and pulled the door shut. At the same instant, the car began to move forward. Whatever was going to happen had already started and I was—literally—just along for the ride.

*   *   *

During my last experience in this car, Mr. Lime had made it abundantly clear that if the idea was to harm me—and he assured me it wasn't—then it would have already happened. I took a very small amount of solace in this memory and watched out the window as we made our way east, across town, in the general direction of the Mississippi River.

About ten minutes later, we pulled up in front of a nondescript one-story building on Minnehaha Avenue. A small sign above the door read "Trylon," but before I could consider the implications of that, my door jerked open and Harpo was ushering me out of the car and into the building.

The front part of the space was dark, but Harpo moved through it confidently to a lit area in the back. He rounded a corner and by the time I caught up to him, he was standing behind a small candy counter, filling a popcorn box from the popcorn machine. He pushed the box into my hand and then came out from behind the counter, going around me to open a door into an even darker room. With popcorn in hand I stepped through the door and felt a small rush of air as Harpo shut the door behind me.

I had been in the Trylon once before and had often thought about coming back. It's what's called a micro-cinema, which means it's like a regular movie theater in miniature form. In this case, the room held about fifty theater seats, all which appeared, in the dim light, to be empty. And then I saw Mr. Lime, nearly swallowed up in a seat in the dead center of the theater. He held up his popcorn box in lieu of a wave.

"Mandrake, welcome. Have a seat."

There was no time to respond, because the next second the lights flicked out, plunging the room into true darkness. The only light came from a hole in the back wall, through which I could see Harpo leering down at us. I could just see a portion of his face, and then he turned away. A moment later, I heard a projector start up and the screen was filled with light.

I groped for a seat and by the time I looked up I could see a very old, black and white version of the MGM logo, with the lion roaring soundlessly. It faded out and a moment later a title faded up, filling the screen.

The title onscreen read *London After Midnight.*

There we sat, the two of us, in utter silence as the movie unspooled quietly before us onscreen. The opening titles were in English, but all the dialogue title cards throughout the movie were in German, one of the multitude of languages I don't speak. I recognized a word here and there and was able to pick up the gist of the story, but I'm sure many of the subtleties were lost on me, as subtleties usually are.

Several times, when nothing of particular interest was happening onscreen (which, to be frank, was often), I would sneak a peek over at Mr. Lime. He sat rapt, looking up at the screen, his mouth hanging open just the slightest bit. Occasionally he would pick at his popcorn, seeming to eat it one small piece at a time, never taking his eyes off the screen. The light flickered off his face, making him look paler and more semi-translucent than ever.

The story, such as it was, finally came to an end, but he continued his vigilant observation right through the final credits. The screen then went black and a moment later the lights in the tiny auditorium popped on to full brightness. We both squinted, adjusting to the light, as we turned to each other.

"You had a print of *London After Midnight* all along," I said, jumping right to the obvious.

"Yes," he said, smiling widely, showing off two rows of sharp, yellow teeth. "I've had one for years. In fact, I was convinced, with good reason, that I did in fact own the only extant copy."

"So when you heard someone had a copy to sell, it piqued your interest."

He nodded. "Piqued. Yes. A good word." He gestured toward the empty screen. "What did you think?"

I considered the question, wondering how diplomatic I actually needed to be. "Well," I began, "It's an interesting artifact..."

"No," he said, waving a bony finger at me. "What did you really think?"

I shrugged. "I don't know. It's kind of dull."

He nodded and chuckled. "Yes, it's no one's best work. If we didn't know it was lost, I doubt anyone would miss it."

"It certainly caused quite a stir, at least for a couple weeks, around here."

He turned in his seat and set one arm on the armrest. I turned to mirror his position and for a fleeting moment, I felt like slimmed down Ebert to his skeletal Siskel.

"I think it was the idea of the movie, more than its physical manifestation, that was so appealing," he said. "I can speak from personal experience: there is an undeniable thrill in possessing something which no one else can have."

"I can see that," I conceded. "Randall Glendower said, if he had been able to buy it, his plan was to donate it to the National Film Registry."

"Very magnanimous of him," Lime said. "I have a similar plan in place, when—and if—I should shuffle off this mortal coil."

From where I sat, it looked like that could happen at any second. Or might have happened already in the recent past.

"I thought you might enjoy seeing what all the fuss was about."

"Thank you for that."

He looked up at the screen for a long moment. "Yes," he finally said. "With the exception of the makeup design, it really is no one's best work. If it weren't missing, it would hardly be remembered." He turned and looked at me, giving me his most penetrating stare. "But isn't that always the way—the moment you can't have something, it becomes oh so desirable. I suspect there's a valuable life lesson in there somewhere, although I must admit I would be at a loss to articulate it."

"Perhaps you just did."

"Perhaps I did." He pivoted in his seat and waved up at the projection booth. "I'll have Harpo give you a ride home. I just need him to start another feature for me before he goes."

"Another lost masterpiece?" I asked as I stood up, my legs grateful for the stretch.

"Do you really want to know?" he said, his smile morphing into a playful leer.

"No, probably not."

"As you wish."

I stepped out into the lobby and a moment later Harpo stepped down from the projection booth, heading toward the front door without a word. I could hear music playing behind me and I turned toward the sound. I looked at the door which led into the auditorium and—for a brief moment that seemed to go on forever—I almost reached for the door handle to peek back in and see what was being projected onscreen.

But my better angels prevailed, and several seconds later I was once again in the backseat of the dark sedan. It was snowing, once more, and we were just on this side of dusk.

The ride home was, as one might expect, a quiet one.

John Gaspard

In real life, John's not a magician, but he has directed six low-budget features that cost very little and made even less – that's no small trick. He's also written multiple books on the subject of low-budget filmmaking. Ironically, they've made more than the films. His blog, "Fast, Cheap Movie Thoughts" has been named "One of the 50 Best Blogs for Moviemakers" and "One of The 100 Best Blogs For Film and Theater Students." He's also written for TV and the stage. John lives in Minnesota and shares his home with his lovely wife, several dogs, a few cats and a handful of pet allergies.

In Case You Missed the 2ND Book in the Series

THE BULLET CATCH

John Gaspard

An Eli Marks Mystery (#2)

Newly-single magician Eli Marks reluctantly attends his high school reunion against his better judgment, only to become entangled in two deadly encounters with his former classmates. The first is the fatal mugging of an old crush's husband, followed by the suspicious deaths of the victim's business associates.

At the same time, Eli also comes to the aid of a classmate-turned-movie-star who fears that attempting The Bullet Catch in an up-coming movie may be his last performance. As the bodies begin to pile up, Eli comes to the realization that juggling these murderous situations—while saving his own neck—may be the greatest trick he's ever performed.

Available at booksellers nationwide and online

Visit www.henerypress.com for details

Henery Press Mystery Books

And finally, before you go...
Here are a few other mysteries
you might enjoy:

ARTIFACT

Gigi Pandian

A Jaya Jones Treasure Hunt Mystery (#1)

Historian Jaya Jones discovers the secrets of a lost Indian treasure may be hidden in a Scottish legend from the days of the British Raj. But she's not the only one on the trail...

From San Francisco to London to the Highlands of Scotland, Jaya must evade a shadowy stalker as she follows hints from the hastily scrawled note of her dead lover to a remote archaeological dig. Helping her decipher the cryptic clues are her magician best friend, a devastatingly handsome art historian with something to hide, and a charming archaeologist running for his life.

Available at booksellers nationwide and online

Visit www.henerypress.com for details

MACDEATH

Cindy Brown

An Ivy Meadows Mystery (#1)

Like every actor, Ivy Meadows knows that *Macbeth* is cursed. But she's finally scored her big break, cast as an acrobatic witch in a circus-themed production of *Macbeth* in Phoenix, Arizona. And though it may not be Broadway, nothing can dampen her enthusiasm—not her flying cauldron, too-tight leotard, or carrot-wielding dictator of a director.

But when one of the cast dies on opening night, Ivy is sure the seeming accident is "murder most foul" and that she's the perfect person to solve the crime (after all, she does work part-time in her uncle's detective agency). Undeterred by a poisoned Big Gulp, the threat of being blackballed, and the suddenly too-real curse, Ivy pursues the truth at the risk of her hard-won career—and her life.

Available at booksellers nationwide and online

Visit www.henerypress.com for details

ON THE ROAD WITH DEL & LOUISE

Art Taylor

A Novel in Short Stories

Del's a small time crook with a moral conscience—robbing convenience stores only for tuition and academic expenses. Brash and sassy Louise goes from being a holdup victim to Del's lover and accomplice. All they want is a fresh start, an honest life, and a chance to build a family together, but fate conspires to put ever-steeper challenges in their path—and escalating temptations, too.

A real estate scam in recession-blighted Southern California. A wine heist in Napa Valley. A Vegas wedding chapel holdup. A kidnapping in an oil-rich North Dakota boomtown. Can Del and Louise stay on the right side of the law? On one another's good side? And when they head back to Louise's hometown in North Carolina, what new trouble will prove the biggest: Louise's nagging mama or a hidden adversary seemingly intent on tearing the couple apart? Or could those be one and the same?

From screwball comedy to domestic drama, and from caper tale to traditional whodunit, these six stories offer suspense with a side of romance—and a little something for all tastes.

Available at booksellers nationwide and online

Visit www.henerypress.com for details

COUNTERFEIT CONSPIRACIES

Ritter Ames

A Bodies of Art Mystery (#1)

Laurel Beacham may have been born with a silver spoon in her mouth, but she has long since lost it digging herself out of trouble. Her father gambled and womanized his way through the family fortune before skiing off an Alp, leaving her with more tarnish than trust fund. Quick wits and connections have gained her a reputation as one of the world's premier art recovery experts. The police may catch the thief, but she reclaims the missing masterpieces.

The latest assignment, however, may be her undoing. Using every ounce of luck and larceny she possesses, Laurel must locate a priceless art icon and rescue a co-worker (and ex-lover) from a master criminal, all the while matching wits with a charming new nemesis. Unfortunately, he seems to know where the bodies are buried—and she prefers hers isn't next.

Available at booksellers nationwide and online

Visit www.henerypress.com for details

CPSIA information can be obtained at www.ICGtesting.com
Printed in the USA
LVOW07s1004011115

460620LV00018B/661/P